THE DEMON INSIDE

Deputy Harold Crawford took the call, the code—261—striking sparks of recognition from his days with the LAPD. He had seen such things before, but not in years, and never in the Run. The scene shook him more than he liked to admit. He could feel the girl's haunted eyes upon him as he took her statement in the county ER, and he felt a small shiver of excitement, shot through with shame. It reminded him too much of a certain moonlit warehouse, that nasty little rush. . . .

As a witness, the girl was useless. She remembered only two things that might prove useful: the knife the perpetrator had held to her throat as he did it—a six-inch switchblade with a pearl inlay—and something he said, the only words he had spoken.

"He asked me to help him," the girl said. "There was a demon inside him."

THE FALLEN

Dale Bailey

A SIGNET BOOK

SIGNET
Published by New American Library, a division of
Penguin Putnam Inc., 375 Hudson Street,
New York, New York 10014, U.S.A.
Penguin Books Ltd, 80 Strand,
London WC2R 0RL, England
Penguin Books Australia Ltd, Ringwood,
Victoria, Australia
Penguin Books Canada Ltd, 10 Alcorn Avenue,
Toronto, Ontario, Canada M4V 3B2
Penguin Books (N.Z.) Ltd, 182–190 Wairau Road,
Auckland 10, New Zealand

Penguin Books Ltd, Registered Offices:
Harmondsworth, Middlesex, England

First published by Signet, an imprint of New American Library,
a division of Penguin Putnam Inc.

 REGISTERED TRADEMARK—MARCA REGISTRADA

ISBN 0-7394-3005-X

Printed in the United States of America

For my parents,
Frederick and Lavonne Bailey

ACKNOWLEDGMENTS

No aspiring novelist could wish for more generous and able assistance than that I received in the process of writing *The Fallen*. James Patrick Kelly, Barry Malzberg, Kris Rusch, and Batya Yasgur all read and commented on various drafts of this book, as did my agent, Matt Bialer, and my editor, Laura Anne Gilman. My thanks go to Sherrie Bohrman, who helped answer my medical questions; Glen Litman, who shared anecdotes from his years as a mechanic in the coal mines of West Virginia and Ohio; Larry Grimes and Frank Gorman, who responded to various theological inquires; Don Cox, my dissertation advisor, who gave me time to complete the first draft; and Jack Slay, who was always available to talk. I am especially indebted to my parents and my wife, the lovely and talented Jean Singley Bailey, both for their careful reading and for providing support and encouragement in ways too numerous to mention.

There were giants in the earth in those days.

—Genesis 6:4

Prelude
Sauls Run
1973

Pain.

Far down under the mountains, the thing shifted in its age-long slumber. Sensations arced along nerves mired in centuries of numbness. Neurons fired. The thing stirred, half aware for the first time in millennia. It sensed its icy subterranean prison; men encamped on the skirts of the mountain, their lives as ephemeral as the lives of insects, and just about as meaningless; and something else, something fatally awry in the complex labyrinth of its own biology. Pain.

The thing thrashed restlessly. Stone crumbled. A blind, burrowing creature raced terrified into the dark.

How long it had lain here, the thing could not guess; it did not count time as men count time. How it had come to be there, it could not say. It remembered almost nothing, knew almost nothing. Just sleep, the long reaches of a sleep that bordered death, and now—in its slow drift toward awareness—its pain.

Below, at the edge of the sleeping town, a doe trotted across the narrow ribbon of pavement called Plug Hollow Road, its hooves ticking in the stillness. It paused and cocked its head at a square green sign:

SAULS RUN
A GOOD PLACE TO RAISE YOUR CHILDREN!

The doe's nostrils wrinkled as it sampled the air. A moment later it bounded into the underbrush, white tail flashing. The car it had sensed as a rumor of steel and thunder purred out of the curve and braked, slowing as it entered the town.

The man within took a deep breath, feeling calmer. At twenty-four years old, he weighed two hundred eleven pounds, most of it muscle, and stood six-four in his stocking feet. His name—the name he'd been born with—was Delbert Grubb, but his driver's license and Social Security card read Harold Crawford. As far as Crawford was concerned, Del Grubb, formerly a beat cop for the LAPD, had died in a South Central alley almost a year ago. Crawford could still recollect the tide of rage that had welled up inside him when the perp started lipping off. He could remember the muzzle flash of his revolver in the darkness, the way it had felt to pull the trigger. Something oily and excited had rolled through him as he stood there listening to the guy moan.

"Jesus," Crawford's partner had said, and then he called for the meat wagon.

The guy—LeMarius Oxford—had died in transit. Sixteen years old and unarmed—that was the way the papers played it. Crawford figured it might fall out that way. Two years as a cop had shown him how the system could turn on a man; they had also taught him that the wheels of justice grind slowly. He put the time to good use. He spent the next nine months calling in favors on the street. It hadn't been cheap and it hadn't been easy, but by the time Crawford left L.A. a week before he came to trial, Del Grubb had effectively ceased to exist. Crawford felt he could live with a new identity easier than he could live behind bars. The California penal system wasn't known for its kindness to ex-cops.

He'd been driving east for four days by the time he wheeled the car onto a curving road that led north toward the center of town. To his right, a lake lay like a black mirror to the stars; above it, atop an outthrust promontory of rock, an enormous house stood sentinel above the silent streets. Sauls Run looked scrubbed in the pale luminescence of the streetlights. Nothing moved other than his car. To Harold Crawford, fresh from the mean streets of L.A., the town looked almost magically peaceful, a good place to lie low for a day or two, to catch his breath and think about what came next.

It was too late to try to find a hotel, so he pulled the car into a municipal lot bordering a park and shut off the engine. He lay back, aware suddenly of how peaceful his mind had become. Once again, he thought about what had happened in that alley, that tide of rage. It hadn't been the first time. There had been the time in junior high school, the kid he'd almost beaten to death, and thank God for the sealed records of the juvenile courts or he never would have made it into the police academy. And there had been the girl. Hardly a day passed that Crawford didn't think about the girl.

Crawford didn't know how to explain it, but the tide of rage and desire had always been there, an oily undertow hungry to suck him down. For a time, Crawford believed that the death of LeMarius Oxford had sated that hunger. Now he knew better. He had felt that black tide surge through him twice on the cross-country drive—once when a platinum-blond truck-stop waitress shortchanged him outside Vegas, and again when an eighteen-wheeler crept over on him east of Nashville, forcing him to the shoulder of the highway.

Both times, he had swallowed hard and held on till the tide went out. Del Grubb was dead, he had told himself; he had to build a life for Harold Crawford.

Crawford took a deep breath. He studied the street, the green and rolling park, the hills rising in forested ranks around him. Everything looked serene and perfect, the Hollywood idea of a small town. For the first time Harold Crawford's internal waters were still. He closed his eyes and slept the sleep of the innocent.

A mile and a half away, in a white ivy-trellised house atop Widow's Ridge, Lily Sleep drifted heavy-lidded in the nether state between wakefulness and dreams. She listened to the sonorous respiration of her husband, half aware of a stream whispering to itself beyond the open window. She felt a trickle of warmth between her thighs, a reminder of the lovemaking just past.

Not for the first time, she allowed herself to wonder about the man she had taken into her life some eight years past. The Reverend Quincy Sleep. She let the words roll through her mind, recalling how amusing she had found him when they had first met back in Georgia in 1965, right when the Beatles and the sixties—generation of free dope and free love—had just gotten rolling. What a throwback Quincy Sleep had been, heavy muscled and close shaven and almost painfully earnest, puzzling through the mysteries of theology even as other men his age had been dying in Vietnam. And yet sweet somehow, so sweet that he had charmed her.

She could never square the sheer physical ardor of their relationship with her husband's ascetic discipline. But Quincy Sleep was a man full of contradictions. Shy and soft-spoken in private, he commanded your attention at the pulpit. He allowed himself two fingers of Evan Williams every night in the book-lined study where he wrote his sermons, but she couldn't remember ever having seen him drunk. He read C. S. Lewis and Einstein, and somehow reconciled his faith and modern science. He didn't seem to mind that Lily had about as much interest in either one as in the Watergate situation that was lately all she ever seemed to see on television.

Lily had been reluctant to follow him to Sauls Run. Now she couldn't imagine living in another place. The Run, as she had learned to call it, really *was* a good place to raise children. Just lately Lily couldn't seem to think about much else. Henry, their first child, had been a difficult delivery, and Lily had subsequently decided not to have more children, despite Quincy's wishes to the contrary. But Henry had grown into a sweet, quiet boy of five—too quiet, Lily sometimes thought—and she wondered if a little brother or sister might help to bring him out. She laughed to think that she had arrived at such a place in life; the radical girl she remembered from college, glutted on Simone de Beauvoir and Betty Friedan, seemed to have gotten lost along the way somewhere, and it turned out that Lily didn't much miss her.

Three months ago she had stopped taking the pill, though she hadn't told Quincy. She wanted to surprise him when she knew for sure. Maybe tonight, she thought, and as she drifted off, she imagined a tiny cluster of cells growing and dividing within her womb.

Sheer curtains billowed like ghosts into the bedroom. Lily Sleep lost herself in dreams.

In Holland House, atop its tongue of rock, Zachary Holland stood by the fanlight windows of the darkened third-floor library and looked out across the black expanse of Stoney Gap Lake at the Run. He watched a lone pair of headlights crawl down High Street and turn into the municipal lot by the park. His head throbbed, as though someone had driven a nail through his temple just above his right eye. He could hear Willa a floor below, cooing at their five-year-old son, Perry, like some kind of goddamned bird. Perry was crying again—Perry was always crying—and Zachary might have wondered if the kid was even really a Holland, if maybe Willa hadn't been getting a little on the side, except Willa wouldn't dare. Besides, Perry *looked* like a Holland. He had that narrow patrician face, the black eyes and hair, the hint of decadent sensuality about the overripe lips. The kid would grow up to be a goddamned lady-killer if he weren't such a sniveling cunt.

"You just can't shut that child up, can you?"

Zachary Holland turned to face the other thorn in his side, *his* father, Jeremiah Holland. The old man leaned heavily on his cane, stout and healthy at ninety, looking maybe seventy and no doubt planning to live until he was a hundred and three. Family lore had it that Titus Holland, who laid the first stone of Holland House half a hundred years before Sauls Run became the county seat in 1923, had lived to one hundred twenty. People had a way of living a long time in the Run, but Zachary privately held that Jeremiah's longevity was absurdly prolonged. At fifty-seven years old, Zachary should have been running the town, not playing crown prince to his father.

He swallowed the urge to lash out. "He's afraid of the dark. It's natural."

"He's five years old."

Zachary shrugged.

"You didn't let Willa baby him that way, boy might grow up to be something."

"What do you think I ought to do?"

"You're the man in the family."

"Seems to me you never took that attitude with Mother."

Jeremiah Holland laughed. "Seems to me I never had to."

Downstairs, Perry let fly with an especially stentorian bellow. Zachary could feel it, like a hammer at his temple, driving the spike of his headache to the core of his brain. He stared out into the night, his hands clenching into white-knuckled fists. It was all he could do some nights not to go downstairs and smack the kid and Willa, too, smack them both until they just shut the fuck up. He had never quite allowed himself to do it. Something—he couldn't say quite what—always prevented him, but he could feel the impulse trembling at the ends of his fingers. His nerves tingled with it.

"I'm going to bed," Jeremiah said behind him. "Maybe if that kid ever shuts up, I can get some sleep."

Zachary stood by the window for a long time after his father left, gazing beyond the ghostly reflection of his face into the night beyond. *I hope he never shuts up*, he thought. *I hope he fucking kills you.*

Far down in its mountain prison, the thing drifted into deeper sleep. The blind, burrowing rodent crept closer, its velvet nostrils wrinkling, its whiskers brushing the sides of its tunnel as it descended.

And then another wave of agony rolled over the creature. It thrashed and cried aloud, a forlorn whirlwind of anguish. The blind rodent paused, trembling. Too late, it turned to flee, its narrow tunnel collapsing in a landslide of rubble.

Somewhere in the labyrinthine network of coal mines, a prop snapped like an old man's bone. The mountain groaned. Dust and sand sifted down around the broken prop, and for a moment the tunnel hovered at the brink of collapse.

Below, in Sauls Run, Harold Crawford stirred in his sleep, dreaming suddenly of the girl he had tried to forget, his cock rigid as an iron pipe.

Atop Widow's Ridge, a tiny bundle of cells buried deep in Lily Sleep's body divided frenziedly for half a minute before lapsing once again into dormancy.

And in Holland House, Zachary Holland threw open the bedroom door of his five-year-old son, Perry, and wrested the boy from his wife's arms. The slap sounded like a gunshot in the quiet room. The stricken child's eyes widened. He swallowed, a scream dying in his throat. The silence was a soothing balm to Zachary Holland's soul.

Upstairs, old Jeremiah Holland cried out as a blood vessel burst inside his brain and Zachary Holland came into his inheritance at last.

Homecoming
The Present

Chapter 1

Dream labyrinths. Nightmare corridors of sleep.

Henry Sleep fled through darkness, a pulse drumming at his temples. A cramp stitched his side. Breath burned in his lungs. When he paused, his heart hammered at his ribs.

He turned back the way he had come, straining his eyes against the omnipresent black, the old terror on him now—the terror of pursuit and loss, the hollow ache at his core. He lifted the flashlight: darkness, bifurcated by a column of watery radiance. A thousand sparkling dust motes glimmered within it.

He stood very still, hardly daring to move.

His heart beat leadenly. He could hear nothing else, no human voice or footfall, not the stir of pursuit in the fallen reaches of the labyrinth.

That was worse somehow, that silence. Silence could mean anything. Silence could mean pursuit was far away, lost in the twisting corridors. Silence could mean that it was closer than he dared imagine, lurking in the dark. Waiting.

Henry drew a slow breath, angling the light into the dark. Walls. Walls of sweating gray stone, rough-hewn and seamed with black; a floor of fallen slate, stitched with rusting track; dank stone above him, reinforced with heavy crossbeams, thick as railroad ties. Dry as year-old kindling, they buckled under the tremendous pressure of rock. Looking at them, he had a sense of the terrific depth of the place, a mile below the daylit surface of the planet, an abyss of night and silence, with only those ancient rotting crossbeams to protect him.

It's a dream, he told himself. *The* dream.

The thought calmed him.

Yet the labyrinth had the gritty feel of a real place, a place he knew. And the fear—the fear felt that way too.

He began to climb again, slower now, time plastic, twisting away into a blur of branching passages, that sense of something lost, the terror of pursuit closing on him like a starved rat, gnawing, retreating, lunging at him again. A deep subterranean chill enclosed him. Still he climbed. At the black mouth of every opening, he paused to search the dark interior.

Sounds haunted him. The faraway drip of water, the trickle of dirt and dust, shifting in some hidden place. The groan of crossbeams, bowing beneath their mighty weight of earth.

And something else, almost imperceptible.

He paused, flashed the light into the corridor behind him.

Walking again, faster now, he could hear his heart and breath, blood booming at his temples. But the other sound had grown clearer, too: a distant rustle of pursuit. He pressed on, probing every tunnel with the light, searching—

—my fault, my fault—

—searching.

And still the sound of his pursuer drew closer. Still it gained on him.

He broke into a run, black passages hurtling by him, the search forgotten. The light leaped before him in fitful glimpses of damp stone, the debris-strewn floor. He turned a corner, the flashlight shattering the darkness before him and—

—stopped, breath catching in his throat.

A man stood before him.

A man he knew. Iron hair swept back from a stern face. Searching, thoughtful eyes.

Henry stumbled away, gasping. "Dad?"

Quincy Sleep stepped forward, dressed not in clerical

garb but as Henry more often thought of him—in washed-out jeans and leather shoes, the sleeves of his flannel shirt rolled back to reveal the forearms of a man muscled like a logger. He made no sound, and when he reached out to touch Henry's face, Henry felt nothing, or almost nothing—an icy caress from another place, like the chill from a door into February, standing ajar in a distant room.

"Dad?"

"It's time, Henry," the apparition said. "Come home."

And then it was gone.

The silence swelled, burst into a clatter of pursuit. Henry cried aloud. He could hear the thing close behind him, just beyond the last turning of the corridor. He chased the light through glimpses: now the stony ceiling, now the track-scarred floor, now the walls, looming, steep.

And he ran.

He never saw the thing that tripped him—a rock maybe, or a spur of the narrow-gauge track. But suddenly he was flying through the dark, the tiny ember of the flashlight flipping away to shatter somewhere, extinguished. And then the floor rose up to hurl itself against him.

The air burst out of him in a stunned exhalation. For a moment he could think of nothing but the agony of breathing. And then he remembered where he was, the labyrinth of dream.

He heard something close behind him now.

The thunder of onrushing wings.

Henry woke to darkness. For a moment the pulse of those tremendous wings seemed to linger in the air. He sat up, mopping his forehead with the sheet. The efficiency loomed up around him, shadowy and spare, devoid of personality. The rump-sprung sofa, the appliances, the black-and-white television—these had been supplied by the landlord. The books alone were his. Now, staring at them—in stacks on the table by the sofa, on the desk, on the floor by the bed—Henry thought briefly of the impending spring semester, scant days away. At any other moment, he would have felt its weight—grading, conferencing, preparing, the whole weary grind. Now the pressure had faded.

Now he was thinking about the dream.

For a time—how long? a year? more?—he had known peace. The dream had haunted him as a boy—icy terror, zero at the bone, one, two, three nights a week, from the sodden summer when his mother died until he finally fled Sauls Run, eighteen then, longing for peace. The dream had faded. He had gone back to the Run only once in the years since, the summer he had finished his master's. The dream had been waiting for him, and again he had fled—fled the dream, fled the father he had grown to despise, fled Emily Wood and the town, loving them both and relinquishing them both. He came south, to Ransom College.

Slowly, blessedly, the dream had abated yet again, once a week, once a month, at last nothing.

Yet here it was, and strangely altered, too, a new element. He saw the apparition again, felt that icy caress.

It's time. Come home.

Henry switched on the lamp with shaking fingers. He glanced at the clock as he pulled on jeans, a discarded T-shirt. 5:47. There would be no more sleep tonight.

In the kitchen, he sipped instant coffee. You can never escape the past, he thought, staring blindly at a table scarred by dozens of short-term renters. It reaches out for you, if only in your dreams. There was so much he could not remember. Just shadows, just glimpses, just dreams.

At nine thirty, the telephone rang. Henry recognized the voice at the other end: Asa Cade, his father's oldest friend.

"Henry? Is that you?"

"Yes, Asa, it's me," he said. "Is there something wrong at home?"

Asa Cade sighed. Henry heard the *snick* of a cigarette lighter, a labored inhalation, and these sounds, so familiar, sparked an image in his imagination: Asa in shirt-sleeves and suspenders, bony fingers cupped below his craggy face in the posture of a longtime smoker, the half-rim glasses he affected tilted precariously at the end of his nose. Henry had seen it a hundred times.

"Hell, son," Asa said, "I'm just an old country doctor. I don't know how to go about these things."

"What is it?"

Asa exhaled, and when he spoke again, he sounded bone weary. He sounded old. "It's a terrible thing."

Henry did not speak. He felt abruptly as if the earth itself had ground to a halt, the world still beyond mere stillness, as if everything everywhere had simultaneously paused. For a single irrational moment he felt sure that if he were to stand and walk to the window, he would gaze out at a world mute and frozen: cars arrested head-long in their plunge through winter-blighted streets, windblown trash forever harried in a single changeless eddy, birds suspended midflight.

And then he found his voice. "Dad?"

"Yeah," Asa said. "Yeah. I stopped by for coffee this morning, same as always. He was in the study. Jesus, Henry, he— I don't know how to say this. He killed himself. With a gun."

Henry rocked back in the chair. He closed his eyes.

"Was there a note?"

"They haven't found one, not yet."

"Why? You have any idea why?"

"Who the hell knows, son. I was hoping you could tell me." Asa cleared his throat. "I'm sorry. I know you had your differences." He hesitated. "You will be coming home, won't you?"

"Of course I will," Henry said. "Give me a day, I have a few things to wrap up."

But for a long time he could not bring himself to move. So he would have to go back. He would have to face Sauls Run, he would have to face Emily, he would have to face the dreams. And his life here? A cheap apartment and rental furniture, a teaching schedule he had already grown to hate? Well, it would wait. And if it wouldn't, there were always other jobs. He had some money, enough to see him through the spring. After that, he could improvise.

He sipped at his coffee again, but it had gone cold. It was time to go. He had a lot to do. He showered and dressed and stood before the mirror to shave, and that was when he saw the enflamed spot on his left cheek. Unbidden, his hand came up to caress it. Like a burn, the imprints of the dead man's fingers.

Chapter 2

And so, at twenty-nine years old, a narrow-framed man with the delicate features of a mother he barely remembered, Henry Sleep came home. He came on a frost-heaved ribbon of state road that twisted northwest through chinks in the barren January hills, and as the Appalachians drew up around him, as mute and hostile as a convocation of petrified giants, he felt the old midnight terror sweep over him, an icy tide shot through with currents of fresh anxiety, the bone-stark chill of his father's death—

Suicide, he corrected himself. His father's suicide.

He intended to face the thing squarely, if he could, just as he intended to face the rest of it—the house, the dreams, even Emily, if it came to that.

At twilight, he guided his '83 Volaré—bald tires and a chassis more bondo and primer than original metal—into a scenic overlook high above the Run. He studied the folded ridges for a long time, gradually letting his gaze slip past the long-abandoned mines of Holland Coal—their rusty tipples towering like dinosaur skeletons among the trees—to Crook's Hollow, a tangle of cramped streets north of the incorporated limits of the town. Just looking at the clapboard houses reminded him of Emily—dark-eyed, small-boned Emily—and that made him feel a bit like a dinosaur himself, fragile as a museum piece strung together from shards of a half-remembered past. A flicker of emotion—guilt? regret?—forced his gaze away, to the town itself, twilight-jeweled in its narrow cleft of hills.

He took a deep breath, clenched the wheel, thumbed the heater up a notch. Nothing had changed. Nothing at all. Not the black mirror of Stoney Gap Lake, not Holland House and not the courthouse, grandiose relics of another age, staring solemnly at one another from their perches at the opposite ends of High Street. From this distance, even High Street itself looked the same, a stretch of Depression-era brick and glass culminating in the Stone Bridge, arcing high above Cinder Bottom, the old rail yards. Widow's Ridge stood beyond, a purple smudge behind the courthouse. He tried to pick out the house where he had grown up, but it was too far away, lost in sun and shadow, in time.

He could remember it well enough, though: a good house, burdened with memory, the hard years after his mother's death. And now this new emptiness, the vacuum of another death. His father's death.

Henry winced and closed his eyes.

He opened them again just as the last blazing crescent of sun slipped past the far ridge. For a single spectacular moment, coppery light flooded the sky, kindling everything it touched. Each molecule of air seemed to erupt, each singular tree to burn so fiercely that he might have mistaken them for women, hair aflame against the purple sky. He watched as the conflagration consumed the ridge—as flames leaped from tree to naked tree and finally to the town itself, solitary within the steep-walled valley.

Then everything was plunged into dark.

When Henry reached up to put the car into gear, his hands were shaking.

Fifteen minutes later, he pulled up before his father's church. It stood at the intersection of Front and Holland, a thick, graceless brick building with a massively earthbound steeple. An illuminated brick sign read:

FIRST CHRISTIAN CHURCH
REV. QUINCY SLEEP

On the white placard below, plastic black letters proclaimed:

FELLOWSHIP SUPPER SATURDAY JANUARY 21—
EVERYBODY WELCOME!!!

The surrounding streets wound away into darkness, relieved here and there by the bright windows of houses.

Wind gnawed at him as he crossed the street and tugged on the heavy oaken doors of the front entrance. Locked. He wondered what else he had expected. Turning, he walked down the sidewalk by the chapel, a long shrub-lined building with tall stained-glass windows, pictures from the Gospels, three crosses black against a setting sun, Lazarus stumbling blindly from his tomb. Even now, it all came back to him: shattered rainbows of sunlight lancing through those windows, somehow miraculous after the endless weeks of rain and flood; the smell of oiled sandalwood and flowers; his mother, still and pale and dead in her casket before the altar.

His father had quoted the Twenty-third Psalm, had proclaimed that Lily Sleep had gone to a better place, a shining, peaceful realm. Henry, twelve then, alone in a pew with Asa and Cindy Cade, wondered if his father really believed that. He desperately wanted to believe it himself, but the sickroom stink of urine and bed sores still polluted his nostrils.

No God could allow such pain. Certainly not the one his father had believed in.

Afterward, Henry and his father rode to the cemetery in the privacy of the funeral home limousine. In the backseat, behind the protective panel of smoked glass that separated their compartment from the driver, Henry's father reached out and clasped his hand.

"We can't see it, Henry," he had said, "but your mother's death is part of a larger design—it contributes to some higher purpose. You have to believe that it's part of God's plan."

Henry, angry suddenly, had tugged his hand away. "God can go to hell for all I care."

Now, as he remembered, these words struck Henry as cruel and unnecessary. But where another man might have struck him, Quincy Sleep had merely sighed. Neither of them had said a thing, not then, not ever, but the words had been there all the years since, poisonous as an unlanced boil.

Henry paused now to gaze the length of the sanctuary. The steeple reared dumb against the night. The sky was gray, the moon just climbing into view. Briefly, he remembered the optical illusion he had seen at twilight— the whole town burning, burning—but then he blinked his eyes, and that was gone, too.

He turned away. It was time to go home.

Full dark had closed in by the time Henry parked the Volaré on Widow's Ridge, a hundred yards south of the driveway. He got out and stood wearily, gazing through a patch of barren woods at the house—white, ivy-trellised, smaller than he remembered; like the Run itself, or his father's church, reduced somehow, however large it loomed in memory.

The years had a way of doing that to you.

It wasn't supposed to end like this.

Henry closed his eyes, watching for maybe the fiftieth time that day the grim little movie his mind had spliced together after Asa Cade hung up the phone: the ice-blue barrel of the revolver between his father's lips, his knuckle blanching around the trigger, the white-hot bludgeon of the bullet.

And for the fiftieth time, he tried to believe it.

But he could not—could not square the image with the man he remembered, remote and taciturn, but strong. Like old wood or weathered stone, asking no quarter of the world, expecting none.

Henry glanced up the winding street. The Richardson place, elaborate and well lit, loomed beyond the modest profile of his own boyhood home, its windows dark among the trees. Here and there other houses glimmered from spacious lots, spinning out gray wreaths of smoke.

Henry turned to open the door of the Volaré.

At the same moment, the light in his father's study came on.

Henry stood there, breath suspended in his lungs while he ticked off explanations in his mind. Option one was clear enough: Asa Cade had dropped in to feed Aquinas, the rangy black tom who had strayed in during Henry's last summer in the Run. So was option two: the police had returned to wrap up some loose end. Candidate number three took him by surprise.

He's back, a sly voice whispered inside his head, and almost before he had the chance to ask himself the obvious question—

—*Who?*—

—the voice answered him:

The man who murdered your father.

Henry paused to consider this final thought, realizing suddenly that the possibility—

—*murder*—

—had been there all along, the jagged rock just under the opaque surface of his conscious thoughts.

The second voice, the sensible one, started up, saying, *Don't be absurd*—

But Henry was already moving.

He left the car and ducked into the woods, raising an arm to ward off unseen branches. A car swept by, headlights shattering the murk like prison searchlights. It disappeared beyond the curve, trailing a dopplered wake of country music, as he emerged at the edge of the lawn.

He surveyed the long, tree-screened yard, the street beyond. The driveway—empty—circled back on itself, throwing a spur toward a basement garage. Suddenly, he felt vaguely embarrassed—

—*Told you,* the sensible voice hissed—

—like an overgrown child playing army in the lawn. Yet the light had come on, hadn't it?

He hesitated a moment, then crossed the moonlit lawn and mounted the steps of the covered porch that ran the length of the house. A cold blade slid along his spine.

Beyond the screen, the door stood slightly ajar.

Henry released the latch and opened the screen. He pushed the door all the way open and stepped inside, easing the screen into its frame with an almost imperceptible click.

He stood in a small foyer, dark except for a wedge of light below the study door at the far end of the hall. Hoping his eyes would adjust, he delayed momentarily, but the light at the end of the corridor seemed only to enhance the darkness elsewhere. He envisioned the space in memory: the foyer with a coat-tree in the corner to his left and a narrow, mail-cluttered table of knick-knacks to his right. Beyond that, the house opened in three directions, the living room to his right, the dining room to his left, the stairs just ahead, parallel to the hall.

He stepped forward and peered into the living room, hardly daring to breathe, but saw only blackness, broken by the pale intervals of windows, the gray unblinking eye of the television screen. He sensed, rather than saw, the heavy masses of furniture along the walls.

And something else. In there, in the dark.

Movement.

His hands knotted. He forced himself to swallow. The entire house contracted into the concentrated range of his perceptions. Blackness. A musty odor, dry heat and something else, something ripe and unpleasant. And once again that sense of movement in the living room, an almost physical intuition, a subtle disturbance in the air.

No.

He was imagining things. He had to be.

The darkness swarmed with luminous motes, counterfeit perceptions. He glanced down the hall at the thin wedge of brightness, razor-edged against the shadows. He drew a long breath, listening as the two voices argued inside his mind. The sensible voice won out.

Asa, he thought. It has to be Asa.

"Hey, who's there? Asa?"

So there. It was done.

Henry stepped forward more confidently, nothing to lose now, probing for the Persian runner that extended the length of the hall. Something crunched underfoot, and he felt a sick weight swing loose inside him. In the same instant, the study light snapped off. A glittering arc of broken glass sprang into view, jeweled by the moonlight filtering through the open door. He glanced sharply over his shoulder, at the narrow vertical windows set to either side of the door. The lower pane on the left-hand side had been punched out.

Christ.

Henry turned back toward the porch.

Too late, he sensed movement again. Close. He took a panicky step, felt something swift and silent under foot—

—*Aquinas*—

—and stumbled. He threw out his hands to catch his balance and lurched forward, his palm skating across the foyer table as he went down. Something fell with a crash.

Aquinas yowled, coiling through Henry's twisted legs. Henry caught a single glimpse of the startled tom—glowing yellow eyes, a glimmering white breast in a field of sable fur—and then he was gone, his claws beating a faint tattoo against the hardwood as he raced upstairs.

The study door banged open as Henry heaved himself to his feet. Disoriented, he turned, fumbling for the door handle. A dark figure loomed up, shambling, tall. He caught a snatch of labored breathing and then a bomb went off against his skull. He stumbled, reeling.

"Wait," he grunted, but somehow he was falling again.

His fingers closed on something—a sheaf of papers?—but the intruder tore them away.

The screen door slammed. Silence filled the house.

Chapter 3

"Terrible thing, him being a preacher and all."

The sheriff took off his hat and nodded solemnly into the study, and Henry was struck once again by how little he had changed, how little everything had changed. Fifteen minutes ago, climbing out of his police cruiser, the sheriff had introduced himself—"It's Harold Crawford, Mr. Sleep. Remember me?"—but he needn't have bothered. Henry had remembered him all right, had remembered his sleepy way of moving, had remembered his bulk—less like a bodybuilder now, more like a prizefighter gone to seed. He had remembered the sheriff's eyes, too, there in the dim radiance of the porch light— eyes so lightly blue as to be almost without hue. Eyes the color of rain.

"So you're the boss, now?" Henry had said, opening the door.

"That's right. Ever since old Dean Blaylock retired and moved to Florida. That was what? Ten years ago, now, I guess. Doesn't time fly, though?" The big man stepped inside, extending his hand. "Doc Cade tells me you're a professor. Down North Carolina way. That right?"

"Something like that. Asa's a tad generous, maybe."

"I recollect you when you were a boy. How old were you when your mom died, son? Eleven?"

"Twelve."

They were silent a moment, remembering.

"Thing about this job," Crawford said, "you never for-

get the tough ones." He hunkered down to study the
glittering spray of glass on the hardwood floor, and then
he glanced up at the broken windowpane. "The world
don't let up, does it?" He shook his head. "First your
daddy and then something like this. I mean who does
something like this? It's just a hell of a thing."

Now, surveying the study and tapping his hat against
one fleshy thigh, he said it again: "It's just a hell of a
thing. I'm awful sorry, Mr. Sleep."

"So am I." Henry paused in the doorway. The faint
odor he'd noticed in the hall—like apples at the edge of
rot—was worse in here, stronger. The room was lined
with books on three sides, the desk facing the windows
on the far wall. He stepped inside, glancing over a row of
Victorian novels—Dickens, Trollope, Collins. He could
catalog the shelves from memory: science, history, theology, a map to his father's mind. Neither of them said
anything for a moment. In the silence, Henry could hear
two deputies talking quietly in the foyer. He turned to
face the sheriff.

"You must have a file or something. I'd like to see
that."

"I'd like to. I really would. But an open case like
this—"

"I'm family. I thought—"

"I wish I could."

They stared at one another for a moment. Something
flickered in the policeman's eyes.

"Departmental policy, Mr. Sleep. I'm real sorry."

"Would you mind telling me about it?"

"You sure you want to do that?"

"I think I have to."

The sheriff nodded as if that was about what he had
expected. "I was off duty, but they called me in. They
do that with anything out of the ordinary. We don't get
many—" He hesitated. "Well, I can count the suspicious
deaths I've seen in the last twenty years on one hand."

"So you'd call this suspicious."

"Well, there was a gun, wasn't there?"

Henry slipped his hand in his pocket, touched the slip

of paper he had wrenched away from the stranger. After calling the sheriff, he had stood in the bright foyer and unfolded it with trembling fingers. A scrap from a yellow legal pad, nothing more. Now he nearly brought it out, but something—

—those eyes—

—prevented him from doing so.

"I wouldn't call it suspicious, exactly," Crawford was saying. "Folks said he'd seemed distracted lately—"

"Who?"

Crawford glanced at him. "Doc Cade for one. That lady works down the church for another."

"Penny Kohler."

"You've named her exactly." He tucked his hat under one arm and ran his fingers through dark hair, sprinkled liberally with gray. "He must have been sitting at the desk when he did it. We found him on the floor here, the chair overturned under him."

Henry stepped forward, and now he could see it, a faint brownish discoloration on the carpet. God, he thought. He caught another whiff of that faint apple-rotten odor, and now he thought he might be sick.

"Deep breaths," Crawford said. "You'll be all right in a minute."

Henry leaned over, his hands on his knees, breathing as Crawford had told him. After a moment, the faintly metallic taste in his mouth retreated a little.

"This is no good," Crawford said. "What do you say we grab a cup of coffee and talk in the kitchen?"

"Doc Cade paid to have the carpet cleaned," Crawford said. "Didn't want you to have to come home to it. But the truth is, cleaning won't ever get it out. What you need to do is, you need to get someone out here and just rip it out, lay new carpet in that room."

Henry didn't answer. He sat at the table, his face cradled in his hands, listening as Crawford busied himself with the coffee.

"Five minutes, we'll have a fresh pot," Crawford said. "You'll feel better."

Henry sensed his weight settling across the table. He looked up and Crawford met his eyes.

"You all right?"

"Fine."

They sat quietly, listening to the coffee perk. Crawford took a notebook and pencil from his breast pocket. He licked the end of the pencil.

"You mind if we go over a few things? Just routine."

Henry shrugged.

"Now, the last time you talked to your dad, that was how long ago?"

"It's been a while."

Crawford said nothing.

"Almost three years, I guess."

"You recall the date?"

"The day I moved. I guess I could figure it out."

"Three years is a long time. You have a falling out?"

"Not exactly. Things have been tough ever since . . ."

"Since when?"

So this was how it was to be, Henry thought. Everywhere the past looming up to haunt him. *Ever since Mom died,* he had meant to say, but what came out was, "It was about three years ago."

The coffee stopped perking. Henry stood.

"You live in Ransom, North Carolina, right?"

Henry poured coffee. "Sugar or cream?"

"Just black."

Henry placed a steaming mug in front of Crawford and leaned against the counter, holding the other mug of coffee, savoring its warmth, its rich aroma. "Yeah. Ransom."

"And that's what, four hours from here?"

"Five and a half."

"Now, the last time you and your dad talked, how would you characterize that conversation?"

"Your standard stuff. I was leaving, he told me to be careful, something like that."

"You argue?"

"Not then. We had been, I guess."

The sheriff nodded. "That happen a lot?"

"We didn't talk enough for it to happen a lot."

Crawford paused, as if debating whether the point was worth pursuing. Then: "Yesterday, Doc called about—"

"I don't see how this is helping."

Crawford said nothing.

"Talking about my relationship with my dad—how does that help us find the person who broke in here?"

"I have two men working on that right now, Mr. Sleep. I'm just trying to get the lay of the land."

"The person who broke in here, you think he had anything to do with my dad's death?"

"It doesn't seem likely."

"Why not?"

Crawford picked up the mug of coffee, put it down, and said, "What is it you teach down there at Ransom College?"

"English. Composition mainly. A few lit courses."

"You have much occasion to run investigations in that line of work, son?"

"No."

"Then why don't you cooperate and let me do my job?"

Henry crossed the room and sat down.

Crawford's voice was gentle when he spoke again. "I didn't mean to be abrupt, Mr. Sleep. Let me explain, if I can. Your father had seemed edgy lately, distraught— the people he was close to, they all agree to that—"

"But—"

"There's more. We're getting some preliminary lab work back now. The angle of . . ." He paused, searching. "The angle of entry—I'm sorry, there's just no other way to say it—it was consistent with a self-inflicted wound. Plus, your dad had powder residue on his fingers. That means he fired the weapon that killed him. He bought the gun legally over in Charleston just after the new year. It was licensed and the dealer's records check out."

"But there wasn't a note."

"Sometimes there isn't."

"What about tonight?"

Crawford shrugged, lifted his hands. "I'd like to know that myself."

"Then why do you need to know about my relationship with my father?"

"Way you go about this, Mr. Sleep, is you ask people questions. Most of them come to nothing, but once in a while you turn something up. And it's not always the obvious questions that do it. So why don't you help me out here?"

Henry sighed.

"So Dr. Cade, he called you yesterday morning at what time?"

"It would have been nine or so."

"So you left first thing this morning?"

"I had some things to take care of at the college. Classes haven't started yet." Henry hesitated. "I told them I wanted to take the spring off."

Crawford sipped his coffee, studying Henry over the rim of his mug. "You planning to stay in the area?"

"I wanted to keep my options open."

"So you left today at what time?"

"Around noon. I drove straight through. You know the rest."

"Which is what I don't understand, Mr. Sleep."

Henry waited.

"Why didn't you come directly to the house? Why did you park in the street out there?"

"I needed a minute to get myself together."

"That's an explanation, but I can't help having another thought."

"What's that?"

"You sure you weren't suspicious right from the start for some reason?"

"What are you suggesting?"

Crawford licked his pencil again, doodled in the margin of his notebook. "You sure you hadn't talked to your father in the last week or two? Maybe he mentioned something that made you a little uneasy?"

"Like what, Sheriff?"

Crawford shrugged. "How about Asa Cade?"

"He told me what had happened. He said he found him here yesterday morning, that he called you."

"Nothing else?" Crawford fixed him with those washed-out eyes of his. Once again, Henry caught a distant flicker of something else in those eyes—as if this was the question the sheriff had been driving at all along. "Did Doc mention anything that might have caused you to be concerned, to take extra precautions?"

"No. He didn't say anything else."

Crawford made a note, nodding. Just then the deputies appeared in the doorway—the first one, Ricks, a tall man, nearly as tall as Crawford, but spare and hard looking, with a nose that had been broken once or twice; the second one, Mears, slower, running to fat, with sad eyes and a hangdog expression.

"We're about finished up here, Sheriff," Ricks said.

Crawford stood, flipping the notebook closed. "Fine."

Henry followed them to the front door. They paused in the foyer. Mears nodded at one of the elongated windows beside the door. A cardboard square had been affixed in place of the broken pane of glass.

"You'll want to get that taken care of."

Henry nodded.

Crawford clapped his hat back on his head. "We'll be in touch if we turn something up, but something like this—" He shrugged. "You never know."

They went out onto the porch. A wind had come up, sharp as a flensing knife, and a few stray flurries of snow whipped through the bright cone beneath the porch light. The three cops, burly in their slick jackets, were halfway down the walk when Crawford turned, his face cast half in shadow.

"We'll be in touch," he said again. "In the meantime, if something comes back to you—something your father might have said, or Asa Cade—you let us know."

Crawford and his deputies had been gone more than two hours by the time the phone call came. In the interval, Henry had carried his bags in from the Volaré: two

trips up the narrow stairs with the faded runner. Two
trips, almost everything he owned, and as he lowered his
bags to the floor, he felt time slip around him once
again—here in the room where he had slept as a boy,
bathed in the spectral radiance of a high thin moon.

Henry snapped on the light.

Taken together, the furnishings—a high school pen-
nant, book shelves lined with Marvel comics and spine-
broken paperbacks, a Darth Vader bank—suggested a
kid of maybe twelve, as if the room had gotten mired in
the summer his mother had died, unchanged by the six
additional years he had slept here before leaving home
for good. Like a time capsule, a monument to the boy
he had been.

The thought shivered him. It reminded him of another
room on this hall, another monument, a door he hadn't
opened in seventeen years. Henry shook his head. Too
much history, too many ghosts. He wasn't ready to face
them yet.

Downstairs, he found a six-pack in the refrigerator.
He was in the study, looking through his father's desk
and working on his third beer, when the telephone rang.

After a moment, his father's calm tenor filled the
room, the same rich tones Henry had heard him use to
deliver a life's measure of sermons.

*You've reached the home of Quincy Sleep. I can't take
your call right now, but if you'll leave your name and
number, I'll get back to you as soon as I can.*

Then the tone.

Henry stared at the answering machine. A ravaged
masculine voice came out of the tinny speaker.

"I'm trying to reach Mr. Henry Sleep," the voice said.
"My name is Benjamin Strange. I'm calling from the
newspaper down here in town, the *Observer*. You don't
know me and I know you're busy now—I'm sorry about
your dad, Mr. Sleep—but if you get this message I hope
you'll take a minute and call me here at the paper." He
added the number, and said, "I'm not trying to hassle
you, Mr. Sleep. Reporters sometimes do that at a time

like this, but I think you'll be glad you called." He
paused, as if he were trying to decide whether to add
something else; then he hung up.

Henry stared at the machine, remembering the long
months after his mother had died, the whispers, the con-
stant stares, bright with suspicion. So that was how it
was going to be. He should have known it. Already he
could feel the eyes of the townspeople boring into him,
the weight of the unspoken question in every mind:
What happened? What happened to your father's faith?

He thought of Harold Crawford—*Terrible thing, him
being a preacher and all*—and his two deputies mooning
about the house, their eyes filled with the same question,
and he felt a little wave of bitterness crest within him.

A reporter. A fucking small-town gossip. He stabbed
a button with one finger, erasing the message, but it was
too late: rusty gears had been set to turning. Memory
beckoned.

Seventeen years, he thought. Seventeen years.

He should never have come back.

That long-ago summer was too close here, too real,
too palpable beyond the parchment-thin tissue of years.
Standing there in the study where his father had died,
Henry could smell it, taste it—he could almost touch it:
the stench of the sickroom as his mother's face shrank to
fit the death mask underneath; the damp heat of Harold
Crawford's car; most of all, the rain.

The endless unforgiving rain.

Chapter 4

Storms battered Sauls Run the year Henry turned twelve. Blizzards rolled out of the mountains in February, surrendering the high country to battalions of black thunderheads as the season turned. Gully-washers, old-timers called them. Thunder-gushers. Streams swelled toward high-water marks, and Stoney Gap Lake lapped ominously against the pilings of the town dock.

Upstairs in the house on Widow's Ridge, Henry and his father mounted a deathwatch.

At Christmas, Lily Sleep drank eggnog by the fireplace. By May, she was bedridden, her face a wizened mask of morphine and anguish.

The sky cleared for a week that month. Henry sat in his mother's sickroom and watched miraculous shafts of spring sunlight lance through high clean windows unchanged by their passage. It was an ideal he could aspire to: transparency, a life unscathed by events passing through it. He rocked in his chair and stared at his mother sleeping her drugged sleep across the room. He thought:

I am made of glass.

"No way," said Perry Holland, "you first."

Henry Sleep fixed the other boy with a cool gaze and smiled, a broad, empty smile designed to show Perry that he feared nothing. And indeed, he didn't. There was nothing inside him, not fear or anger or even sorrow, just bright, glittering emptiness, like glass. Like someone had pried open his mouth and poured gallons of molten glass down his throat and it had clotted there inside him. A blister of perspiration slid out of the hair at his temple.

Perry turned away.

Henry glanced at the railroad tracks that wound through the hills below. The tin roofs of Crook's Hollow glinted among the trees down there, giving way to the broad thoroughfares of the Run at the valley floor. Perry's house—Holland House itself—brooded over the eastern end of High Street. A tiny car trundled over the Stone Bridge toward the courthouse. Otherwise the July streets lay silent, steaming in the muggy prologue to another storm.

"Forget it," Perry said. "Let's go back. If my dad knew, he'd kill us."

"How's he going to know?"

Henry rattled the fence and a chain-link harmonic rolled away from them. At his feet, the rusty mesh had buckled, leaving a crawl space in the damp grass.

That morning over breakfast his father had said, in that strange, toneless way he had of speaking lately: "You need to stay close by today, Henry, hear?"

"Why?"

His father stared at him. "Your mother," he said, as if that explained everything.

"What about her?"

"Just stick around. That's the end of it."

Henry had dropped the matter, but he couldn't stand the thought of another day cooped up inside. Rain, rain, go away, he thought. The sun was out. He could feel its lure.

When his father trudged upstairs to tend to Henry's mother, Henry stole outside and retrieved his bike. At the top of Widow's Ridge, he slung his leg across the seat and shot down the shady tunnel of Christian's Fork toward town. And he didn't feel a shred of guilt. He didn't feel anything at all.

He ran into Perry on High Street. They knocked around aimlessly for a while—playing pinball at the Grand Hotel until they ran out of quarters, skipping stones over Mill Creek—and then, in the manner of boys with nothing much to do, they had somehow decided to mount an expedition to the old Holland mines. The plan required a measure of ingenuity to put into action. It was midafternoon by the time they sneaked back into Henry's house for a flashlight. Thunderheads were massing over the ridges to the west.

"I don't know," Perry had said. "It looks like rain."

And Henry had said, "Are you scared?"

Now, standing high above the town, their bikes hidden in the brush below, he said it once again: "What's the matter, Perry, you scared?"

"No."

"Then come on."

Just like that he wormed his way under the fence: on the far side, the world he had known all his life, thronged with damp greenery, storm brewing in the air; over here a moonscape of mud and steel, a rolling escarpment littered with husks of discarded machinery. Rutted roads snaked away from a brick machine shop emblazoned with Holland Coal's fading logo. Slag heaps lay in the shadow of disused coke ovens. Spurs of railroad track wound upward, visible in flashes between the arms of the mountain. The mines lay higher, rusty tipples glimmering among the trees, their mouths blasted into rubble.

Henry took a deep breath.

The breeze had turned a shade cooler. Thunder boomed through the skies.

Henry turned his back on Perry and trudged off. A moment later, he heard the mesh sing as Perry started under the fence.

"I can't believe I'm doing this. If my dad finds out—"

"Your dad won't find out. And what if he does? It's not like you're trespassing." Henry spat into the mud. "How come they ever closed all this down anyway?"

"Maybe there wasn't any coal left. I don't know."

"You don't know? What do you mean you don't know? You practically *own* the place."

Henry winged a flat chunk of slate off the tin roof of

the machine shop. Hollow reverberations banged back
to them, a kettle drum in an echo chamber, blending
seamlessly into a distant rumor of thunder. The gray sky
lowered over them.

Ten minutes later, they found themselves following a
railroad spur into a narrow hollow, the larger vista of
the coalfields going, going, gone. The shadow of a tipple
fell across them, metal creaking eerily in the breeze.
When the thunder started up again—a low, continuous
throb that seemed to last forever—Henry paused to look
up. A mine loomed in the mountainside above him, a
blasted tumble of debris crumbling to an apron of
muddy shale and weeds. Tracks arced away into the moraine. Henry felt his heart quicken.

"Check it out."

"I don't think this is such a good idea," Perry said at
his shoulder.

"Go home, then."

He kept walking. A pregnant drop of rain slapped
his cheek. Another splashed in a weedy gap between
the ties.

"Henry."

"I'm not going back."

"It's raining."

"You won't melt," Henry said. And then he winced:
that was a thing his mother used to say.

Glass, he thought. I am made of glass. He had an
image of himself made all of glass—how everything
would pass right through him.

He clambered across a rusting, flat-topped railcar with
a steering wheel at either end—a mantrip, the miners
called it—and dropped to the ground on the far side.
He glanced back at Perry, crouched atop the mantrip,
backlit against a boiling sky. Wind whipped by, hurling
spikes of electricity at the high ridges. A barrage of rain-
drops spattered at his feet.

"We're gonna get soaked."

"No, we're not," Henry said.

He studied the wall of rubble. It looked impenetrable,
a massive rockslide sloping down from the cliff face

above. Here and there, disconsolate clumps of witch-grass poked from between the rocks. One or two tenacious saplings had sprung up in narrow crevices, leaves hissing in the wind.

"Come on, Henry!"

"Shut up, Perry. You can go crying home to your Dad if that's the way you're going to be."

Henry heard Perry scramble to the ground behind him as he hunkered down to examine an aperture between two massive chunks of rock—a narrow gap, three feet high and two wide. Big enough to skin through if you wanted to get out of the rain. Switching on the flashlight, he peered into the dark.

"Henry. Are you crazy? It's dangerous in there. There could be pits. The air might be bad."

Henry glanced at the sky as the first scattered blades of rain knifed down at him. Storm-pregnant clouds, swollen guts veined by twisting spokes of electric blue, hung so close he could almost touch them. Thunder blasted out of the sky in a deafening cannonade.

"We'll just crawl inside. Just to get out of the rain."

And then the heavens opened.

Rain. Rain like nothing Henry had ever seen before—like Noah might have known on the first of his long forty days. Rain cascaded from the fretful sky. Rain carved runnels in the mud, undercutting the railroad tracks at his feet. Rain pounded the corroded surface of the mantrip. Lightning rent the dark curtain of sky. The scene danced around them, leaping close in bright, discordant flashes and drawing away in quick, ephemeral dark. Thunder shook the mountain in deafening peals.

"Shit," Perry said, his black hair greased against his skull. "Shit!"

Henry started to duck inside the wormhole, but Perry's hand closed on his shoulder, jarring the flashlight out of his hand. He spun, that mocking phrase—

—what's the matter, Perry, you scared—

—jumping to his lips, and just then an enormous stroke of lightning carved the sky. Thunder boomed simultaneously, rattling pebbles through the moraine. His

father had taught Henry to calculate the distance of
lightning by the interval between the flash and the concussion. No interval meant no margin of safety. Especially when you stood in a graveyard of twisted metal.
Even as this conclusion leaped unbidden into Henry's
mind, another bolt of lightning slammed from the forbidding sky. Its lambent zigzag ripped away the dark and
smashed with a vast hollow bang into the tipple below.
The entire superstructure blazed electric blue, and the
stink of ozone sizzled in the air.

Perry Holland's face went bloodless.

Wordless communication flashed between the boys.
Henry dove to the earth, scrabbling for the flashlight.
His shoulder bounced against the rail, and a white-hot
burst of pain fired along his nerves. Simultaneously,
Perry lunged for the aperture between the rocks. As
Henry came up with the flashlight, his shoulder
throbbing, he saw the bottoms of the other boy's sneak-
ers disappearing into the dark. Henry scrambled after
him as another galvanizing streak blasted the mantrip at
his back. The world went flashbulb white around him,
and every hair on his body stood simultaneously on end.

In, deeper and deeper, he thrust himself, chasing the
soles of Perry's tennis shoes, half glimpsed in the watery
radiance of the flashlight, and then—

Then what?

Nothing. Memory failed him.

Seventeen years later, Henry had only a fragmentary
recollection: dust motes spinning in the shaft of the
flashlight beam, a sense of the wormhole opening out
before him into a larger space, nothing else.

A lacuna of darkness.

Just the labyrinth. Just dreams.

Then rain, more rain. He could remember that, that
and the sky a bruised welter, fat-bellied clouds gravid
with lightning, trees bending horizontal before a gale-
force wind, the banshee shriek of the tipple as he fled.

His clothes clung to him, his jeans, socks, underwear,

everything soaked and leaden. Geysers of mud spewed
out at his heels. He stumbled and fell, scrambling to his
feet with coal grime and mud clinging to his clothes. He
scraped filth from his face, unplugged his nostrils, bolted
off again as exhaustion sent a bright stitch—

—*glass, I am glass*—

—through his left side.

A rusty shard of chain link snagged his shirt as he
wormed under the fence, and then he was through,
prone in the wet grass, sobbing.

A hand fell against his shoulder.

He twisted, digging at the swampy earth, looked up
into Perry Holland's wild, affrighted face. "Son of a
bitch," Perry hissed. Perry's fist blurred toward him,
rocking him backward as he scrambled to his feet. Henry
fell back into the muck, without resistance—

—*why*—

—actually welcoming the blows, as if the pain might
burn something out of him, punish something that
needed punishing. Perry was on top of him, pinning his
arms down with bony knees. Perry hit him in the face.
Again.

"Don't you ever," Perry gasped. "Don't you ever—"

Hail started to pelt down, big chunks of glittery ice,
bruising. In the flashing intervals between the thunder,
Henry could hear them sing against the tin roof of the
machine shop.

"C'mon," Perry said, hauling him to his feet.

They went on together, through the woods and into
the brush by the tracks, where they had stashed their
bikes. Henry knew that something was over between
them, a friendship he had struck up in kindergarten finished. But he didn't care; he was glass.

By the time they reached Crook's Hollow, the old
company houses rising ghostly out of the mist, the hail
had tapered off. But the rain kept coming, steady and
intent, like it meant to stay awhile. It could not be much
past five, but the sky had gone the color of twilight.
Streetlights began to blink on. The ditches churned with
foul, swift-moving water. Mill Creek, which paralleled

the tracks from here to Cinder Bottom, lapped at its banks. Quick little rivulets began to pool in the broken streets.

"Listen," Henry said. "Perry . . ."

But Perry lowered his head and pushed his bike along without a word.

Lightning struck somewhere close by, a sharp sizzle of ozone and a crack as though the earth itself had split open. The streetlights flickered and went dark.

Henry flung a leg over his bike and started to push off.

Just then a sheriff's car topped the knoll ahead, its panic lights turning the water-glossed streets to rivers of blood. Henry could not say why, but even before the car pulled diagonally across the street, blocking their way, a black seed of foreboding had lodged in his breast, like a fragment of ancient grain encased in a museum paperweight.

He scooted off his waterlogged seat and waited there, the bike leaning between his legs, his knuckles curled white about the rubber handgrips.

Rain slammed out of the sky. Rain bounced and hissed against the pavement. Rain enclosed him like a curtain of crystal beads. That dark seed of premonition quickened in Henry's heart.

I am made of glass, he told himself. Glass.

And he squeezed his eyes closed and tried to picture it to himself: a black prism of a boy, the light of the revolving flashers whirling in his depths, glancing back in bloody reflections or passing through him, but never, never touching him.

He heard the heavy door swing open, heard the radio inside buzzing with chatter, smelled the steaming, tropical interior of the car push out at him through the downpour.

He opened his eyes.

A deputy got out of the car, a broad-shouldered, solid-looking man of perhaps twenty-five, with light blue eyes. Light and rain polished his rustling slicker. Water poured off the brim of his hat.

Henry felt that seed of terrible knowing tremble in his

chest. It pulsed outward, straining to be born, spinning tenuous roots through his breast, hairline fractures skating through his glassy heart.

I'm sorry, God, he thought in desperation.

I'm sorry, he prayed. I'll be better. I'll be good. Just don't, don't—

"Is that Henry Sleep?" the deputy asked.

A terrible keening sound was in the air. Henry wanted to lift his hands to hold it in, but he could not imagine what it might be, or why he thought it was coming out of him. And then that dark knowing—that seed of premonition—blossomed within him like a black, black rose. Sharp slivers of pain exploded through him, but he had to puzzle over the terrible sound a moment longer before he recognized it at last as the clatter of all the glass in the world—all of it, shattering at once.

Henry remembered.

He remembered the deputy's broad face as he said, "You need to come with me now, son," not even seeming to notice the streaks of coal dust and mud ground into Henry's clothes. He remembered drawing close to the man, as if mere proximity to another living being— to an adult and his dimly apprehended power in the world—might shield him from the knowledge that every line of the deputy's body confirmed: his shoulders bowed with news, and his wide eyes, and his blunt fingers curling with anxiety. He even remembered the deputy's name, Harold Crawford. Oh yes.

"Is that you, Perry Holland?" Crawford said.

Perry nodded, silent on his bike.

"You go straight home, Perry. I don't have time to deal with you. Get home, before you drown."

"Yes, sir."

"Perry," Henry said.

The other boy paused.

"I'm sorry."

Perry didn't speak. They stared at each other for a moment, and then Crawford flapped his hands.

"Get going now," he said, and straightaway Perry was

gone. Henry watched his figure dwindle in the rain, and then he looked up at Harold Crawford, those big hands clenching and unclenching at his thighs.

The rain pummeled them. It poured off Crawford's hat and drenched his slicker and still he stood there, a faraway stare in his eyes.

"Where you been, son? Your dad's been worried sick."

But the way he said it, you could tell he didn't expect a reply. Henry just waited. He would have given all the wealth in the world to wait like that forever, the rain ticking off the pavement around them, the black knowing inside him unconfirmed.

"Come on, son," Crawford said. He lifted the bike into the trunk, and Henry would remember this as well: the black maw of the trunk, its light glimmering against the metal box of a first-aid kit, the burnished snout of a shotgun.

He remembered the ride home: the ribbons of steam curling from the rain-spattered hood, the dank odor of wet clothing, even the sour stink of perspiration that Crawford gave off. When he lifted one hand to scrape away the fog that grimed his window, all he could see was rain—rain slamming against the pavement in sheets, rain choking the gutters and streaming away to pool in fields and front yards.

Why doesn't he tell me? Henry thought. Why doesn't he say something?

But Crawford said nothing, even when he turned off the courthouse square onto Christian's Fork, climbing toward Widow's Ridge.

Never would Henry forget his dread as the car surged doggedly up the rain-washed road. Never would he forget his first vision of the house, every light ablaze as they rounded the curve. At last he could hold it back no longer; he had to give it voice. "It's my mom, isn't it?"

The car plowed relentlessly on.

Harold Crawford bit his lip. "I'm sorry, son," he said. "I'm so sorry."

Sauls Run
1978

Chapter 5

Sunk fathoms-deep in sleep, the thing curled close in its high mountain fastness.

Four thousand million years and longer, it languished in the planet's rocky mantle, imprisoned in a gulag of solitude. Earth's surface raged, rent by volcanism. Vast plumes of ammonia, nitrogen, and methane glowed against the abyss of space. Tectonic plates clashed, thrusting mountains into the first faint wisps of atmosphere. Water condensed from the steaming air and gathered slowly into streams, rivers, seas.

When the first progenitor of humanity slithered from ocean's womb, the thing did not stir. When pterodactyls spread leathery wings to the Mesozoic sun, it lay unknowing in its oubliette. By the time the last Neanderthal died, what power had been left to it—not much, as it measured power—had already begun to wane.

Even it grew old.

In the end, even it felt pain.

For a single instant—weeks as men count time—its power flickered.

Those were hard weeks in the Run.

It was about that time that Emily Wood, ten years old, first heard death rattling around inside her mother's lungs. Her father—Boone—had passed six months back, crushed by a kettle bottom in a Copperhead mine. Ever since, Emily had lain awake nights, wondering why she couldn't bring his face to mind. Days, she hung close about her mother's skirts—too close, her mother chided her—determined not to let the world steal her away as well.

So she was right there when it happened—right there on the cellar steps, watching her mother wrestle a basket of damp Holland laundry to the line. One minute, her mother was running on about old Mrs. Holland wanting more bleach in her whites. The next, she lurched into Emily like a High Street drunk on a three-day binge. Emily stumbled on the splintered risers as two loads of freshly laundered sheets—ten dollars of work—went tumbling over the rail to the damp concrete below. *Mama,* she started to say, but the sounds her mother was making—rending airless gasps, like a woman drowning— froze her voice inside her throat. Deep in her bones, at an almost cellular level, Emily knew that sound, knew it the way you know the voice of an old friend on the telephone in the dead of night.

Death.

Just calling ahead to say he'd be along. Sooner or later, he'd be along.

A long terrible moment later, Emily got her words thawed out. "Mama?" she said. "Mama? You all right?"

"I'm fine, honey," her mother whispered. "I'm just fine."

But in her heart, Emily knew it was a lie.

It was the start of something. She knew it somehow, she did not know how.

Earl Kimball had a demon inside him. His mother had told him that when he was seven years old, and in thirty-five years he had never forgotten it. He had never entirely believed it either.

He believed it now.

He stared blankly at the television—*The Price Is Right*, daytime television at its best—and wrestled the demon inside him. He could feel the demon winning. When he finished his beer, it was the demon that made him call out, "Hey, Bobbi Jean. C'mere a minute, will ya?"

She banged around at the other end of the trailer for

a minute before she came into the living room. She slouched lean and coltish in the door, looking five years older than twelve, and brushed dark hair from her fine-boned, resentful face. Earl felt the demon stir inside him.

"What do you want, Earl?"

"Fetch me a beer, will you?"

"Something wrong with your legs?"

"Hell, I'm tired, girl. Now don't just stand there."

"You're not my daddy," she said. "Get your own beer."

She stared at him long enough to let him know what she really thought, and then she turned away. The demon watched her flounce down the hall, her shorts tight across the seat. *How about a little respect, Earl?* it whispered.

Cursing, Earl got his own beer. Standing at the sink, he finished it in one swallow and popped the tab on another.

Just then music erupted down the hall, drowning out the television. Disco. Earl hated that shit.

"Hey, turn that down," he hollered.

The bass line throbbed in his bones. Earl closed his eyes and watched Bobbi Jean prance down the hall, her ass flexing inside her shorts. What was it she had said? *You're not my daddy.*

It's not like it would be a sin, the demon told him.

"Hey, turn that down! I can't hear the fucking TV!"

If anything, she cranked it up a notch.

R-E-S-P-E-C-T, the demon sang inside his head.

Earl drained his beer, dropped the can into the sink, and lumbered into the hall. He shouldered her door aside and paused there, letting his shadow loom over her. She was on the bed, flipping through a magazine, and when she looked up, he saw a light go on down inside her eyes.

She reached over to silence the music. Her shirt stretched taut across her breasts.

"You ain't supposed to be in here."

"Maybe you forget who makes the rules around here."

"Mama'll be home soon." Her voice caught, false bravado cracking. Earl thought about that light he'd seen in her eyes. Fear maybe. Or respect. The two weren't that far apart.

He felt a stirring in his loins. Thirty-five years of denial, thirty-five years of holding the demon in check.

"You and me, we're going to have a little talk," he told her, but the words sounded funny. They sounded like the demon he heard inside his head. They sounded like his own true voice.

Earl Kimball stepped into the room. He shut the door behind him.

The demon capered and grinned.

Eight months into his marriage, Boyd Samford found out for sure that his wife was cheating on him. He had suspected it for months—since she turned cold in the sack—but it had been easy to make excuses: nothing like a shotgun wedding and a screaming newborn to cool the libido. But when the baby started sleeping through the night and Marie still didn't have any interest, Boyd knew something was up. Long as he had known Marie Richards she had loved nothing better than a little backseat boogie.

Confirmation came when Boyd left work a couple hours early one day, sick to his stomach. He felt even sicker when he pulled up in front of the house. The car had been parked right there in his driveway for God and all the neighbors to gawk at: Sam MacLean's Camaro.

His stomach cramping, he drove to the McDonald's on Cedar Grove and High and emptied his bowels in the men's room. With every twist in his guts he could envision them, Sam and Marie tangling together. He gritted his teeth and hammered on the stall with his fist. It wasn't supposed to work out like this, not for him. Nineteen years old, a wife and kid, a dead-end job stocking shelves down the market. Now this.

When he got back to the house fifteen minutes later, Sam's Camaro was gone. Marie looked up when he came through the door. "Boyd?" she said. "You okay?"

And it was like he wasn't even in the room, like he was watching it all happen on a flickering video feed with a ten-second delay, a NASA broadcast ten million miles from the world he had known: his hand coming up and smacking her across the face, his weight bearing her to the floor. Marie was screaming, and then the baby was screaming, too, but none of that mattered, not now.

"I know," he whispered. "I *know*, you bitch."

Her sweats tore away, her hot stink enveloped him. He wedged a knee between her legs, and then—

—no, no—

—he was inside her, with one thick hand mashing her lips, while he whispered in her ear, "Since you're passing it around, honey, I'll take a little for myself." Nothing had ever felt so fine.

Those were hard weeks in the Run.

In Holland House, brooding like a feudal castle high above the town, Zach Holland marked his son up pretty good, the first time he had laid hands on the boy since Perry was five years old. In six short weeks, eight apartments came open in the Ridgeview Assisted Living Community as retirees began to pop off like Fourth of July fireworks—an epidemic of heart attacks, strokes, and aneurysms. More than once, Frank Bukowski, owner of the Tipple Supper Club up in Crook's Hollow, settled brawls with a dusty Louisville Slugger that had languished unused behind the bar for years. And up on Widow's Ridge, Lily Sleep couldn't rest. She felt an aching in her bones.

All over Sauls Run, that was a hard summer.

That was the summer Harold Crawford got a dog.

He found the dog, a bony mongrel the color of mud, on the verge of the county road that wound by his farm. Five years had passed by then. Crawford had begun to settle in, to feel safe in the Run, at home for the first time in—how long? His whole life, he supposed.

It hadn't always been so easy. Mountain folk were wary of outsiders, and during his first days in town, everything about Crawford—his accent, his manners, even the way he carried himself—marked him as a stranger. That was okay, though. He didn't intend to stick around. The plan had always been to find a city in the south, some place warm and populous—Atlanta maybe, or Jacksonville—some place that wouldn't freeze his Southern California blood, some place where he could lose himself in the crowd. That was still the plan. But sleep came easy that first night in the Run, and so he stuck around another night, and then another, and somehow time slipped away from him—a seductive procession of dreamless nights. The dark tide that had always threatened to drag him under receded. For the first time in his life, Harold Crawford was at peace.

He took a room in a cheap motel on the outskirts of town, spent a month tramping the steeply wooded hills, working the toxins out of his system, letting the clean, sharp air scrub everything away—L.A. and LeMarius Oxford and the girl he had tried so hard to forget, everything. By the time he started running short of cash, he felt renewed. He packed up his car and drove south, heady with optimism. Then, eight hours down I-77, some asshole in a Firebird cut him off in traffic, and Crawford had found himself pursuing, swept up by a rising breaker of fury. Ten minutes later, with the speedometer needle hovering just over ninety, he forced himself to pull over. He sat on the shoulder, gripping the wheel white-knuckled while he waited for the tide to go out.

So he would have to stay in Sauls Run—that was all. He would have to stay. Better to put his new identity to the test—better to risk everything—than surrender the peace he'd worked so hard to attain. Back in the Run, Crawford applied for work in the sheriff's department. Dean Blaylock called him in for an interview two tense weeks later; another week after that, Crawford found himself back in uniform, back on the streets.

He leased an apartment overlooking High Street and spent his off-hours hunkered in the living room, waiting for the knock at the door that would mean the whole elaborate tissue of lies had begun to come apart. The knock never came, and slowly, slowly, Harold Crawford began to relax. A year passed, then another and another. He opened an account at One Valley Savings on Oak Street and began putting away a little money each month. Maybe it was over. Maybe it was over at last.

Crawford found himself rising steadily through the ranks of Dean Blaylock's department. He turned out to be a gifted mimic, and soon he had developed a way of speaking, of carrying himself, that made him indistinguishable from men who had grown up in the mountains. When asked about his past, he alluded vaguely to the Midwest, a love affair gone sour. And while he risked no friends beyond his circle of professional acquaintances, he felt increasingly at home.

By this time, the savings account at One Valley had grown considerably. One day after work, he called a real estate agent, and together they spent the next few weeks looking over available properties. Anxious for a little privacy after four years in an apartment, Crawford settled on a run-down clapboard farmhouse in the middle of twenty-six acres of scrub. A fixer-upper, the agent called it. Crawford called it home, and set about making the repairs enthusiastically, scrubbing the place room by room, replacing Sheetrock weak with dry rot, sanding and painting, though he did little more than sleep in the house. He spent most of his time on the road in his county car. He certainly didn't have the time for a pet.

But something—he couldn't say what—made him stop when he saw that bony mutt crumpled by the roadside. It staggered up at his approach, whimpering. At first he thought a car might have gotten it. Its fly-swarmed hind leg told another story: It had come up short in a fight. The dog whimpered again when he hunkered down beside it.

Getting soft, Harold Crawford, he told himself, and so wholly had he obliterated his past that there wasn't even the faintest echo of his real name in the thought.

Crouching, he stroked the dog's shank. It rolled its head and gazed up at him from one watery eye. "Well, shit," he said. He found a blanket in the trunk of his

car, wrapped the dog carefully, and moved it to the front
seat. Then he headed back to the house.

It was only a dog, he told himself.

How much harm could it do?

He had left the dog in a bed of old straw in the barn.
When he got back from work, it thumped its tail in
greeting. He fed it from a bag of dry Alpo, then cleaned
up the leg. He held the dog gently and cooed at it as he
boiled away the grit with hydrogen peroxide. The cooing
seemed to help some.

When the dog had settled down, he bandaged the raw
flesh. Then he fished his knife out of his trousers. A
door came ajar in his memory when the long blade
flicked from the haft—the first time in years that had
happened. Maybe it was the barn that did it—the vast,
looming barn that reminded him of the empty warehouse where the girl had died. Or maybe it was the
knife, gleaming in the falling sun from the loft. For a
moment Harold Crawford paused, feeling the old tidal
pull, that slick undertow of rage, and then he did what
he had to do: He slammed the door shut before he got
a good look at what stood in the darkness behind it. The
past was past, he told himself. You are a good man. Let
it lie.

Yet his fingers shook as he worked them through the
dog's coat, pausing now and again to cut out a burr or
knot. By the time he finished the job, stars buttoned
down the black scrap of sky in the loft door. He sat in
the dark for a while and cradled the dog's head, breathing the damp and doggy odor of the barn and listening
to the night music, the peepers and crickets and tiny tree
frogs with the big voices as his thick hands moved in the
mutt's rough fur.

That night he dreamed that he walked along a strand
frosted with the sheen of a crescent moon—a horned
moon, his father would have called it. The black water
heaved at his shoulder, luring and restless and immemo-

rial. He could feel it singing through his body, that old tidal pulse of blood and desire.

But he stayed the course.

Something awaited him at the limits of his vision, a black heap heaving gently in the swells, just where the water met the shore. Harold Crawford felt a surge of hope. He couldn't identify the black heap, not yet, but he knew what it was the way you know things in dreams: an opportunity. A chance to make things right.

The dog improved. The next day it hobbled out to meet him at the barn door as he clumped up in his heavy boots. The day after that, it waited for him at the edge of the porch, frisking at his heels, favoring the bad leg. Crawford had never had a pet. He wasn't sure how to talk to it. "Hey, boy," he said, and by default that became the dog's name.

Boy sat on the porch with him in the evenings when Crawford allowed himself a solitary beer. One beer at nine thirty to ease him off to sleep, then eight hours in the sack. He woke at the same time every day, shaved whether or not he had to work, kept his few possessions—his weapons, his uniform—in relentless order. Order and ritual and iron resolve: Such were the raw materials he used to dam off the past, to wall away the man who had left the City of Angels in his rearview mirror.

At ten o'clock every night, he took Boy to the barn.

At ten fifteen he brushed his teeth.

At ten thirty he was in bed.

By midnight he was walking down the broken beach of his dreams, resisting the lure of the dark water and straining to make out the black form bobbing in the distant tide.

Boy woke him.

In another life, he had stood in a cop's house in L.A. and watched him drop three goldfish into a tank of piranha. Deliberately starved for days, the piranha swarmed the goldfish—a flurry of arrow-swift motion. Blood clouded the water. Crawford—

—Grubb, your name is Grubb—

—had stumbled back a step, stunned by the force of his own excitement.

Now, waking headachy and exhausted with the dog barking at the moonlit sky, barking and barking until Crawford wanted to scream—now the moment came forcibly back to him: the roiling water, the bright silver darts of the piranha, most of all the hunger. That was what it was, wasn't it? Hunger.

Yes, and he'd known what he was going to do even as he lifted the window sash and leaned out into the humid night. "Hush now!" he shouted to the dog. "God-damn it, I said hush!" But it was all an act, this little display of annoyance, the habitual deceit of a man always on the run—from the law, from the past, from himself. He'd known what he was going to do from the moment he'd seen the dog whimpering by the roadside, hadn't he? That was why he'd stopped in the first place. He'd known even then how it was all going to end.

He reached for his pants, hanging over the bedpost.

Outside, the night was warm, the yard silvered by the ethereal radiance of a full moon, reminding him for a moment of the broken beach in his dreams. Then Boy appeared in the door to the barn, moonstruck, barking, barking, barking.

"Hush up," Crawford said. And louder: "Hush now!"

The dog darted past him and spun in the yard, its muzzle lifted to the sky, baying. Howling.

"Boy!" Crawford shouted.

The dog darted at him, squatted playfully on its haunches. Barked. Barked and barked and barked.

Fucking dog thought it was some kind of game.

"Come here, now," Crawford said.

Boy circled him, nipped at his trouser legs, and dashed away to hunker down with his muzzle low to the earth, his tail a joyous blur. Crawford feinted at him, spun, got a handful of air, and went down. He could feel the impact all along his spine. He felt the old familiar tide tug at him. Calmer inside, ice, he smiled. His voice changed, friendly, cajoling: "Come on, Boy! Here, Boy!"

The dog hurled itself into his lap, a yammering bundle, tongue bathing his face. Crawford gripped the squirming creature by the loose flesh at its neck. With the other hand he fumbled in his pocket.

High in its mountain fastness, the thing coiled in agony.

A door banged open in Harold Crawford's mind: the girl writhing underneath him, the blade glittering in the vast moon-splashed warehouse as he knotted his hand in her hair, wrenched her head back, and felt an orgasm smash through him.

Yes, he thought. Oh yes.

A dam crumbled inside him, a black and buoyant tide.

He held the dog close against his side with one hand and lifted the other to the sky.

Abruptly, the dog went still, its glazed eye fixed on something in the moonlight. Something shiny.

The knife.

In its dungeon under the mountain, the thing cried out as the wave of pain at last receded. Its life force flickered, flickered, and caught. It subsided once again into dreamless sleep.

Below, moonlight fell on the Run.

It fell on the vacant expanse of High Street and the Stone Bridge arching over Cinder Bottom. It fell alike on the grim folk who had been miners once and upon the man who had been their master, in his high house. It fell on them all, wise men and grave men and doomed men who aspired to be better than they had been or had any hope of being.

In a winding hollow east of town, it fell through a high window to burnish Harold Crawford's grinning blade, tossed carelessly on the nightstand. Crawford himself walked the shattered edge of a continent in dreams, drawn onward by that shape rolling gently in the swells.

It was a man; he could see that now. A drowning man, and if he could but save him everything would be forgiven.

Moonlight fell on Widow's Ridge, as well. When the creature drifted into painless sleep, ten thousand thousand raging cells in Lily Sleep's bones grew still.

They would abide.

Their time would come.

Lily sighed and shifted in her sleep, and fled unknowing down corridors of dream.

Burying the Dead
The Present

Chapter 6

Under a sky the color of polished steel, Henry watched them put his father in the ground.

He stood in blue shadow, the wind snapping briskly at the green funeral home awning overhead and blurring the sermon into incoherent snatches of scripture. Not that he was listening—not that he was doing anything at all, in fact, beyond trying *not* to think. He craved nothing more than silence, a moment of refuge from the steady clamor of his thoughts.

Henry drew a long breath and exhaled slowly, searching for patterns in the plume of smoky air. He stared restlessly at his clasped hands, at the tips of his shoes, at the fragrant ranks of flowers already drooping in the chill air—at anything but the mound of carefully draped earth, the casket gleaming on its runners, the curtained walls of the pit itself. Anything but the grave.

The thing of it was, though, it was still there. No matter how hard you tried not to look at some things, they were still there. No matter how hard you tried not to think about them, you could not *not* think about them. You could push and push and push them away, but in the end it did no good. They always came crowding back. So he stood there, seeing without looking, hearing though he didn't want to listen, and for a single disorienting moment, he wasn't sure who was standing in his spot: the man who had come here to bury his father or the grieving twelve-year-old boy who'd come to bury his mother on a muddy summer afternoon more than half a life ago.

Even then—*especially* then—there had been things he could not *not* think about, no matter how desperately he wanted to avoid them. So he had stood before his mother's casket, deaf to the words of his father's homily, his mind spilling over with his own remembered words instead. They came back to him now—

—*go ahead do it I wish I wish you'd*—

—nearly the last words he'd spoken to her in the days before the rain closed in like a gray shroud and he lost her forever.

Henry swallowed.

The circle closed. Time folded back upon itself; you always came back to the place where everything began. So it would end as it had started, with another set of words to haunt him, the last words he'd spoken to his father on the August afternoon when he had left the Run, three years gone. He'd finished packing for the drive to Ransom by noon. His car was already idling in the driveway when he turned to face his father through the taut mesh of the screen door. "I worry about you on the road alone," his father had said.

Henry had merely nodded. "I'll call you when I get there," he'd said.

But he hadn't called, not then, not ever.

He would have to live with that. He would have to live with the fact that he had failed his father, just as he had failed his mother all those years before.

The minister lowered his head. "Let us pray."

Henry closed his eyes, surrendering it all to the familiar litany of prayer: the grief, the sorrow, the dumb, inarticulate yearning for—what? Grace? Absolution? A chance to make things right? It didn't matter. It was all a sham anyway, prayer. Nothing listened. Nothing ever had.

The minister closed his Bible. He touched Henry's arm and leaned close to speak into his ear—"He was a good man, Henry, a *good* man"—and then it was over.

Asa Cade clasped his shoulder. "You okay?"

"Yeah," Henry said, "I'm fine." He glanced into the other man's eyes, watery behind half-rim glasses, old ivory spun through with blood. "Let's get out of here."

Asa nodded and they turned toward the cars. The crowd enveloped them, names and half-familiar faces and questioning eyes, endless iterations of the same half dozen sentiments—*we'll miss him, I know you'll miss him, he was a good man, we miss him already*—all the old phrases, reliable and heartfelt and somehow inadequate in the end. Penny Kohler took Henry's hand, her eyes welling. "God bless you, Henry," she said, and Henry, forcing a smile, promised to stop by the church and see her—soon, he pledged, soon—before the crowd swept him away.

They had reached the funeral home limo when someone called out after them.

"Asa!"

They turned together. In the man who stood there—tall and darkly handsome, his hair falling to the shoulders of a tailored overcoat—Henry saw the ghost of an angry child, his fist upraised.

Spikes of rain nailed down a July sky.

Henry Sleep felt a shiver of old guilt.

"Perry," he said.

The other man nodded. When he spoke his voice was neutral. "Henry." Then: "I was sorry to hear about your father."

"Thank you."

They stood there for an awkward moment, blowing clouds of frosty breath while the limo idled at the curb. Touching Henry on the shoulder, Asa nodded toward the car.

Perry stepped forward, his hand outstretched. "Asa—"

The driver was opening the door.

"Perry," Asa said as he ducked into the car.

The door swung shut behind them.

"What was that all about?" Henry asked, but Asa didn't seem to hear him. He reached into his jacket and produced a silver flask. He loosened the cap, his fingers trembling, and the smoky musk of bourbon filled the car. Henry turned to look out the window. Perry was still standing at the curb, staring expressionlessly into the smoked glass, when the limo glided away.

Odors thronged the house, the succulent aromas of the food layering the dining room table, fried chicken and casseroles and bowls of potato salad, rolls in heaping mounds, chocolate pie and upside-down cake; the moist heat of too many people, two dozen neighbors and church members and childhood friends circulating through the downstairs. Cindy Cade scurried through the swinging doors from the kitchen, cradling a dish of deviled eggs.

"Eat," she told Henry. "Eat."

But the day had stolen his appetite. He felt nauseated, the very air around him athrob with the fluid quality of a nightmare, simultaneously familiar and subtly twisted: He recognized the faces behind the outstretched hands, the voices sounded familiar notes, but time and distance had so altered them that he could not call up their proper names.

Bill Richardson, his neighbor, cornered him in the kitchen. Balding and gawky at six-four, Richardson held a plate high as he edged through the crowd. "How are you, Henry? You doing all right?"

"Okay, Bill. You?"

"Fine, fine. Listen, Sarah and I, we're sure sorry about your dad."

"Thanks."

Richardson gnawed a celery stick. "You planning to stay in town, are you?"

"I don't—"

"You're in Georgia, right?"

"North Carolina."

"Right. Willie—you remember Willie?—he's got a thing in Raleigh. Six figures. We're just damn proud of that kid."

"That's great."

Sarah, Bill's wife, appeared at his elbow.

"Well, listen, I know this isn't the best time, but you haven't thought about what you're going to do with the house, have you? Me and Sarah—"

"Bill!"

Richardson turned to glare at his wife and Henry took the opportunity to steal away. He poured himself a cup of coffee and slipped out to the deck. Night had fallen. The clouds had drifted east, disclosing a careless jeweler's mat of stars. A stream tumbled noisily along beyond the denuded oak.

Henry placed his coffee on the rail. He blew into his cupped hands, loosened his tie, felt the night gather cold around him. The interior clamor dwindled to a faraway buzz, like cicadas on a summer day. His tension began to slough away.

"That you, Henry?"

Asa Cade's bony silhouette unfolded from a bench in the shadow of the house.

"I didn't know my father had so many friends."

"Hell, son, he didn't. He didn't have half so many." Propping his foot atop a bench, Asa fished in his jacket for the flask. In the dark, he smelled faintly of bourbon. "Warm your coffee a little?"

"I'm fine."

The door opened, disclosing a triangle of bright yellow light. A shadow fell over them.

"Asa," Cindy said. "Is Henry out there?"

"Henry's right here. You go on now."

Asa glanced back at her, fumbling with the flask, and Henry watched her face tighten with something more than cold.

"Oh, Asa."

"Just leave me be."

"Asa—"

"Just leave me be, I said!"

She swallowed and turned away. The door shut gently behind her.

"Goddamn it." Asa sighed and took a slug off the flask. He wiped his mouth with the back of his hand.

"You okay?"

"Fine," Asa said. "I'm fine." He made a dismissive gesture. "Half these goddamn people didn't even like your dad."

"I always thought Dad was hard to like myself."

Asa grunted. "Sure proud of you, though."

"He could have told me that himself."

"Maybe, maybe not." He worried a Marlboro from his breast pocket and set it alight, the glow firing the angular planes of his face. "For a man who made his living with talk, your daddy found it awful hard to say what needed saying. He never got over your mama dying."

"Who did?"

Henry could feel Asa's eyes probe at him.

"Well, I guess that's true."

They stood silently for a while, staring into the dark.

"I hate this," Henry said. "All these people mooning around, like vultures picking over a corpse."

Asa shrugged. "They're curious, that's all."

"Yeah, well, you know what, Asa. I'm curious, too." Henry turned to face the older man. "Maybe you can tell me what happened."

"Wish I knew myself, Henry."

"Was he sick?"

"Sick?"

"Did he have cancer or something? Is that why he did it?"

Asa took a final drag off the cigarette and flipped it into the night. Henry watched the ember spin away and crash to earth in a shower of sparks.

"As far as I know he was fine, Henry."

They stared at each other for a moment. Cars were starting out front, people beginning to slip away. Asa took a sip of bourbon. He licked his lips. "It was a hell of a shock to me, too, you know."

"Was he depressed?"

"What is this, some kind of inquisition?"

"I just want to know the truth."

"I don't know the truth."

"What do you mean you don't know? You were his doctor, Asa. You were his best friend."

"And you were his son, Henry!"

It felt like an accusation. Henry sipped his coffee, reminded suddenly of the dream, that nightmare pursuit, his father stepping forward to meet him. *Come home, Henry. It's time.* But the fact was, time had gotten away from them both. Time had left Quincy Sleep seven feet of cold earth, left Henry a roomful of books, a decade of strained phone calls, a house where he couldn't sleep at night for dreaming. His hand crept up to touch his cheek, the faded spots of inflammation.

He shivered. "You believe in ghosts?"

Asa held Henry's gaze for a long moment. "Tell you the truth, I don't know what to believe anymore."

"You've had too much to drink, Asa."

Asa laughed. "I can't seem to drink enough these days."

"Yeah, and why is that, Asa?"

"Are you accusing me of something?"

"Should I be?"

Asa's hand shook as he lifted the bourbon and took a long drink. When he lowered the flask, it slipped from his fingers and tumbled over the railing. They stared down at it for a moment, leaking whiskey into the frost-rimed grass below. "Goddamn it," Asa said. "I mean, goddamn it all to hell." He struck the railing with the heel of his hand. He turned away, sucking on his lower lip.

"Asa?"

"Yeah, yeah," he said. "I'm okay. I mean, Jesus Christ, Henry." He stared down at the flask. When at last he looked up, his face seemed drawn and old, two decades past his sixty-odd years.

"Let it go," he said. "Your father killed himself."

The words were out before Henry realized what he intended to say, what he'd been thinking maybe all along, unknown even to himself: "I don't believe it."

"Doesn't matter what you believe. Don't you understand that? Take a week and wrap things up. Put the house up for sale and go. *Go*, you hear. There's nothing for you here now. Your dad is gone and you're not going to do anybody any good mucking around in it. You're not going to bring him back."

"Are you tangled up in something, Asa? Was Dad? Tell me."

"There's nothing to tell."

"That thing between you and Perry, back at the cemetery. That was nothing, too?"

"Nothing to do with you." Asa shook his head. "Old Zach Holland died not long ago, and Perry got his hands on the family jewels. He had this idea of opening up the mines. I put a little money in it."

"I thought those old mines played out forty years ago."

Asa laughed bitterly. "You'd be surprised what's left in those old mines." He sat down leadenly, fumbling for a cigarette, and Henry suddenly had a sense of just how drunk he was.

He turned away in disgust. "I'm going in."

"Henry?"

Henry paused and looked back at the other man, staring out into the night, his bony features limned red as he lit his cigarette. Asa exhaled a long stream of smoke.

"What is it, Asa?"

"Go on back south, you hear? Steer clear of this mess. Cindy and I, you were the child we never had. She couldn't take it if something happened to you, too."

Asa and Cindy were the last to leave. The night had turned colder by then, wind carving through the ridges to the north. Cindy tarried in the shelter of the porch as Asa walked out to warm up the truck, a black shape under the trees, moving with the overprecise gait of a drunken man.

"Don't judge him, Henry," she said.

"Judge him? For what?"

"You have to ask?"

"He's had too much to drink, that's all."

"That's all?" Her voice was flat, so utterly free of affect that he felt compelled to turn and look at her, her cheeks pallid and her gray eyes fierce behind a shiny glaze of tears, fierce and haunted, too. The word had an aptness about it that sent a hot spark tumbling into the dry kindling of his heart. The whole town seemed haunted.

"Forty-seven years I've known the man," Cindy Cade was saying, "and not once did I ever see him drink more than two beers in a sitting. These days, he's stone drunk more often than he's sober. I don't think he ever sleeps anymore—"

His hands came up unbidden and grasped her shoulders.

"What do you mean?"

"Dreams," she said. "He has bad dreams." She shook her head, then pulled away from him to stare out into the driveway. "I'm losing him, Henry."

Together, they watched Asa climb into his beleaguered pickup. The ancient engine coughed before it caught with a roar.

"Is it money?"

"Money?" She turned to gaze at him, so close he could feel the smoky vapor of her breath. He caught a fleeting whiff of her perfume, a wisp of lilac, as though a breath of spring had for a single instant seized him up. And then the wind tore it away.

"He said something about investing in Holland Coal—"

"Asa Cade never had any money to invest. He gave every red cent of it away. He always has." She laughed. "But they're in *something* together. Him and Perry Holland. Your dad too, for all I know. A few weeks ago— this wasn't long after Christmas—Perry Holland shows up, takes Asa off into the night. Without a word to me, you understand. Not a word. That's what I've had ever since, nothing, and Asa didn't used to be a man who kept things to himself."

Two short honks interrupted her.

Henry glanced toward the pickup, idling in the circle. "Go on," he said. "Take care of him."

He walked her to the base of the stairs, and there she turned to face him once again.

"He's afraid for you," she said. "I know that."

"Afraid for me? Why?"

"I don't know. But be careful, Henry. I keep thinking maybe . . ." She hesitated. "I keep thinking maybe somebody hurt your father, maybe Asa knows it. It's worth keeping in mind, anyway. Good night."

He stood there and watched the pickup's taillights dwindle in the trees, feeling the cold light of the stars upon his shoulders, engendering within him something colder still, the white arctic light of a dread he couldn't name. Slowly he climbed the stairs to the house. It was warmer in there, but it didn't help much.

Chapter 7

Gravel crunched under the tires as Henry pulled the Volaré into the lot of the Tipple, a low-slung cinder block bunker with a flickering Budweiser sign over the door. He shut off the car and sat there, listening to the engine tick and thinking about Emily.

Their last moment together had been branded into his memory—the heat of the August noon, the sense of doomed foreboding as he mounted the porch steps with the contract from Ransom in his hand. The job offer had come late, a one-year instructorship, renewable. Not much of a job at all, really, but he couldn't expect much more without a Ph.D. And anything was better than another month in the Run, another month with his father. Emily had met him at the door. He never went inside—he knew the smell of sickrooms well enough—but he could hear the drone of her mother's oxygen machine through the screen, a steady hum intermixed with the babble of the television. *Come with me, Emily,* he had said. *We can have another life.*

She had laughed out loud. *What do you think I ought to do with this one?* she had asked. And as he started back to his car, she had said something else:

If you leave, Henry, don't come back.

But here he was.

Sighing, he opened the door and pocketed his keys. It was after ten, the night moonless and glacial, with a needling wind that augured snow. The cold reminded him of his father, more than twenty-four hours in the grave, and he thought about that for a moment, the cold, cold earth, while he studied Crook's Hollow and felt it all swing back to claim him, his place in the world—the ridges black against the sky, the Tipple, the old coal camp, a maze of rusting trailers and crumbling company houses weathered the color of stale sin. In the valley below, the Run glimmered faintly, a broken crown in a narrow cleft of hills.

Home.

If you leave, Henry, don't come back.

He blew into his hands and started for the bar.

Inside, nothing much had changed. Not the long shallow U of the bar, paralleling the back wall; not the smell, a yeasty reek of beer and smoke; and not the crowd, a largely masculine brew of denim, baseball caps, and Marlboro Reds—the kind of men who worked with their hands and drove the rusting eighties-vintage pickups and muscle cars in the lot. They sat at tables or shot pool at the far end of the room, narrow and oven-warm, like a cave with central heat. None of them spared Henry a glance as he slid onto a stool at one end of the bar.

"I'll be damned," said Frank Bukowski, wiping his hands on the bar towel. "Look what the cat dragged in."

"I was wondering if you still ran the place."

"Too ornery to die," Frank said. A gaunt sixty-year-old with flesh the texture of old leather, he hadn't changed any more than his bar had. He leaned across the counter to shake Henry's hand. "Sorry to hear about your dad. You okay?"

"I'm hanging in there, Frank."

"What can I get you?"

"Just a beer."

Frank tilted a mug under the tap. "You still down in . . . where was it, Georgia?"

"North Carolina," Henry said. "And no."

Frank put the beer down on the bar. "Home for good, then?"

"For a while, I guess."

"That's good, Henry. I'm glad you're back."

They were silent for a moment, listening to something Nashville pump out of the jukebox, all drum machines and pop production.

"Emily still working for you, Frank?"

"Five nights a week. She's running tables tonight."

"She didn't make the funeral."

"Didn't she? You stop in to scold her?"

Henry sipped his beer.

"Been a while, hadn't it?" Frank said.

"Coming on three years."

"Maybe I wouldn't be so hard on her. Her mother's taken a bad turn just lately." Frank rapped on the bar. "Better get busy before some thirsty redneck throws down on me. It's good to see you, Henry."

"Frank."

"Yeah?"

"I got a question for you."

Frank tilted his head.

"If I wanted to know something about the old Holland coalfields, who would I ask?"

"Something on your mind, Henry?"

"Something I heard, that's all."

"See the old fellow in the corner?" He nodded at a man sitting at the far end of the bar, by a countertop peanut dispenser. A stack of quarters stood on the bar before him.

"Ray Ostrowksi," Frank said. "Ray's your man."

"What's Ray drinking tonight?"

"Same thing he drinks every night." Frank reached a bottle off the rack. "Turkey, the high-octane variety."

"Expensive taste," Henry said.

"Funny thing, that," Frank said. "Old Ray, suddenly he can afford it."

Halfway around the bar, Henry ran into her.

One moment he was shouldering through the crowd, holding his beer in one hand. The next, some weight-room hero in a skintight T-shirt and a Red Man cap stepped aside, and there she was, clearing a table. A shock of recognition, almost imperceptible, passed through her when she looked up. He could see it. Then she nodded, a time-lapsed photo of the woman he remembered from three years back, the high school girl he had dated more than a decade ago. What was it Frank had said? Her mother had taken a turn for the worse. Maybe that accounted for the fine wrinkles at the corners of her eyes, the first strands of gray in the mass of dark hair at her shoulders. Yet the sinewy lines of her body were the same, and the frankly appraising look in her eyes.

Otherwise they gave nothing away, those eyes.

"I was wondering when you'd be in," she said.

"I wanted to see you."

She put her tray on the table and stood before him, maybe five-four, a hundred fifteen pounds, drying her hands on a towel. The hands were chapped, the nails clipped short and unpainted. "I guess it didn't occur to you to wonder what I might want."

He let that ride.

The guy on the jukebox was singing about how his wife done up and left him, she took his pickup and his dog.

"Well," she said. "Now you've seen me."

She picked up the tray and slipped past him toward the bar.

"Emily."

She glanced back at him.

"I was hoping we could talk," he said.

"I close tonight."

"I can wait."

She stared at him expressionlessly for a moment, and then the crowd shifted, swirling her away.

"Ten High, that's what I used to drink," Ostrowski said, his tongue sliding over the hard consonant in *that's* to the sibilant beyond. He glanced over at Henry, leaning against the bar beside him. "You ever drink Ten High?"

The voice was high and girlish, at odds with the man

it belonged to, a squat, grizzled toad with rheumy eyes and blunt, capable-looking hands. He wore work boots and jeans, a faded flannel shirt tight over his gut.

"No," Henry said.

"Life's too short to drink bad liquor." Ostrowski lifted the glass, took a slug, and set it into the ring it had left on the bar. He studied Henry. "Strangers buying you drinks usually want something, that's my experience."

Henry smiled into the grizzled face. "I was hoping you would answer some questions for me."

Ostrowski didn't smile back.

"About what?"

"Holland Coal."

"What's there to know?"

"I was hoping you could tell me."

Ostrowski thought that over while he plugged a quarter into the peanut dispenser and twisted the handle. Lifting the door, he scraped a handful of peanuts out of the slot. "You want to know about Holland business, maybe you ought to ask a Holland," he said.

"Perry?"

"Can't ask Zachary, now can you?" Ostrowski said. "Old Zach is just as dead as a doornail."

"So now Perry controls the mines."

"Controls? Hell, them mines is closed up forty years gone. Nothin there to control."

"I heard Perry was opening them up again."

Ostrowski finished his peanuts and bought another handful. "Fuckin nuts," he said. "Got a spot on my right lung the size of a quarter. Spent forty-seven years in the mines and never had a problem. And *now* I got black lung." He shook his head. "Quit smokin, the doctor says. So I sit here and eat fuckin peanuts and the doctor bitches about my blood pressure instead."

He swiveled in his stool to face Henry.

"What did you say your interest in all this was?"

"Just curious."

"Nothing to be curious about there. That's just idle talk."

"Talk?"

"That's right. A speck of truth and a whole raft of bullshit. What's your name again?"

"Henry Sleep."

"That was your daddy ate the barrel of his own gun the other day?"

"That's right."

"Hell of a thing," Ostrowski said. He waved at Frank and pointed at his glass. "Let's have another one."

"Put it on my tab," Henry said when Frank came back with the drink.

Ostrowski raised the whiskey in silent toast. "You been away for a while?"

"Most of a decade."

"Maybe you forget what it's like around here, you been away so long. People in the Holler, they never had nothin but those mines. When they closed up, there weren't nothin left."

"That was forty years ago."

"Don't tell me how long ago it was. I was there. Spent the next four decades workin up Copperhead, little bitty bug holes where a man can't even stand up. And I was one of the lucky ones. I *had* a job."

Henry sipped his beer. "So what's your point?"

"People want to believe them mines are opening up again, that's all. But that's just wishful thinkin. Nothing there to mine anymore."

"So that's the raft of bullshit. Where's the speck of truth?"

Ostrowski took another drink of whiskey and wiped his mouth with the back of his hand. "Well, there *was* a little work up there a month or two back."

"Mining?"

"Nah. Turns out old Jeremiah—that was Zach Holland's father, the one what lived to be about a hundred—did a half-ass job of shuttin down them mines. Just slapped up a fence and blasted the mountain without even bothering to see was the tunnels closed. Never saw such a thing. Anyway, with his dad gone, Perry got to worryin about kids foolin around up there."

Henry swallowed. "Kids?"

Ostrowski waved his hand. "Kids," he said. He fumbled another quarter into the slot of the peanut dispenser and twisted the handle. Peanuts spilled across the countertop before him. "I guess the EPA—the . . . what's the name of that thing . . . the Environmental Protection Agency?"

Henry nodded.

"I guess they done some kinda inspection and told Perry to clean up the site. Anyway, I'd just started collecting my pension from up Copperhead, so one thing led to another."

"He hired you?"

"Me and a few other fellows. We fixed that fence up there, pushed a little of the dirt around, that's all."

Henry turned his glass thoughtfully. "Asa Cade was telling me—"

"Who?"

"Asa Cade."

"The doctor? What's he got to do with this?"

Henry tracked his finger through a ring of condensation on the bar. "He said he put some money into the mines—"

"In Holland Coal?"

"That's what he said."

"Nothing there to put any money into," Ostrowki said.

"I got the sense my dad might have put some money in it, too."

"Is that what this is about?"

Henry said nothing.

Ostrowski shook his head. "I know you're grievin, son, but that don't make any sense at all."

"I thought maybe—"

Ostrowski lurched toward him, one elbow propped on the bar, his face solemn behind its three-day growth of beard.

"Thought *what*? Ain't nothin left up there to mine. Why do you think old Jeremiah shut em down in the first place?"

He slumped back in his seat. He picked up his glass, sloshing Wild Turkey across the bar.

Henry straightened. "Mr. Ostrowski—"

Ostrowski waved his hand. "There weren't nothin to it," he said. "Just a little make-work, that's all it ever was."

Chapter 8

Last call was at one. At one thirty Frank killed the juke-box and turned on the house lights. Henry stuck around. He'd spent more than a few nights helping Emily shut down the Tipple during that final summer in the Run. Now, while Frank and Emily closed the bar, he racked the chairs and swept up, feeling once again that strange sense of time slipping around him, as though he had collapsed into a former life, a former self, the Henry Sleep who had left all this behind for a job he had known even then was nothing and nowhere, running away, just marking time. Maybe—just maybe, he thought—he could do things right this time.

He went to stow the broom in the storage closet. When he came back, Frank was untying his apron. "I reckon I'll get on," he said.

"I'll lock up," Emily said.

"Good night, then." Frank clapped Henry on the shoulder and held his gaze for a moment longer than he had to. Then he let himself out, and they were alone.

Emily dialed down the overheads and slipped a disc into the house system. The room washed away on a velvet tide of tenor sax.

Henry took a seat at the bar. "So you're into jazz now," he said.

"Sonny Rollins," she said. "There's an actual song called 'There's a Tear in My Beer'—did you know that? I'm not kidding. It's on the jukebox." She shook her head. "God, I hate country music."

And that was vintage Emily. In high school, when most of Henry's friends had been spinning scratched vinyl platters of Mellencamp and Springsteen, Emily was grooving on twenty-year-old Motown soul—Marvin Gaye, Mary Wells, and Smokey Robinson and the Miracles—artists so monumentally alien to kids in the Run that entirely by accident she achieved a kind of oddball mystique, a short-lived antimatter cool. Yet even then—especially then—she stood at the margins, wry and aloof, hungry for something more than everyday wonder.

She had also stuck with the college courses long after the high school guidance counselors steered most kids from the Hollow into the vocational track. By all rights, she should have been an outcast, a thrift shop apparition among the designer jeans and Izod sweaters of the town girls. Yet she had a way of rising above all that, town kids and Hollow rats alike, serene and autonomous, watching silently from the perimeter of the classroom, the edge of the bleachers. When she and Henry went out together, they went out alone, and even now, that was how he always thought of her—self-contained and observant, with a smile that cut two ways.

It was that smile she gave him now, rueful and mocking and all too self-aware. Wiping her hands on a bar rag, she said, "You want a beer, Henry?"

"What are you having?"

"Club soda."

"Make it two club sodas."

"I got a little too attached to my after-hours cocktail there for a while," she said. "Cocktail*s*, I should say. Half a bottle of wine to send me off to sleep."

"So you quit?"

"That's right." She set the drinks down in the bar. "Last June."

"Was I—I mean, did I—"

"Don't flatter yourself, Henry. I got used to you running away a long time ago." She leaned her elbows against the bar and pushed her hair back, studying him.

"I'm back now," he said.

"Yeah."

"So what's it going to be, then?" he asked.

She laughed. "You called this meeting."

"Because I *do* want to apologize. When I went away, I thought it was what I had to do. It had nothing to do with you—it never did. My feelings about you never changed. It was about me, me and Dad, and this"—he shrugged—"this place. The Run."

"The Run."

"Do you like it here, Emily?"

"I don't think about it like that. It's just where I am, where I have to be right now, you know?"

He nodded. He *did* know. Six months, a year ago, he wouldn't have understood what she meant, could not have fathomed what forces might keep her here. But now . . . well, now he had something to keep him here himself, didn't he? No matter what Harold Crawford or Raymond Ostrowski or anyone else had to say.

"What are you thinking about?" she asked.

"Honestly?"

"Sure, Henry. Let's try honesty for a change."

He met her gaze squarely. "My father."

"The funeral go okay?"

"I expected to see you there."

She lifted her eyebrows and gave him that smile again. "Things don't always turn out the way you expect," she said.

She let that sink in for maybe two measures of Sonny Rollins on tenor sax, and then she reached across the bar. Delicate as a butterfly, her hand alighted for a moment on his own, and then she drew it away.

"Jesus," she said. "I used to think about this. How I wanted to be the next time you walked through that door. I always knew you would. But it's not easy being a bitch, you know." With one finger, she fished a chunk of ice out of her drink and sucked it thoughtfully.

"I wish you *had* come," he said.

"Yeah, me too." She laughed softly. "I had every intention of coming, even though I want to be angry at you."

"You have every right to be."

"I do. But somehow it's hard all the same. And a funeral isn't really the place, is it? So I was set to come. I had an outfit picked out and everything, and then . . ." She shook her head.

"Then what?"

"You really want to trade sob stories, Henry?"

"Seems like the only kind anybody has to tell just lately."

"Well, you probably know most of this one."

"Your mother?"

"Frank told you?"

"He mentioned it."

She looked at him, but he had the sense she was looking right through him, at something else, he couldn't say what.

"I'm not really an alcoholic, I don't think," she said. "Things just got so hard with Mom there for a while. It just got to be a way to . . . get away."

"So how is she?"

"I put her in Ridgeview last November. November the twenty-first."

"What happened?"

"The emphysema took a turn for the worse. This was not long after you left. There had been bad patches before, but it always seemed to improve in a month or two. This time it didn't. Her mind started slipping about the same time, got to where I couldn't leave her alone. I was afraid she'd burn the house down or something. It was like somebody turned a switch, she got old all at once." She paused, studying the bar, then shrugged. "I looked into private nurses, but . . ."

"Too expensive?"

"Unbelievable. And Ridgeview's no bargain. Between Medicare and what I make here, I can just barely manage." She drummed her fingers on the bar. "I had started taking some classes, over at Sauls Run Community. Just your basic requirements, you know? I couldn't decide on a major." She looked up at him, a self-mocking smile flickering on her face. "I'm thirty years old and I don't even know what I'm interested in. Anyway, I had to give it up when Mom got bad."

"And then Ridgeview?"

"Right. Mom's had some trouble adjusting. She forgets where she is. The other day I started for the funeral, but the phone rang just as I was walking out the door. I ended up at Ridgeview most of the evening, barely made it to work."

"She okay?"

"She's well taken care of. I keep telling myself that." He nodded.

"So anyway, how did the funeral go?"

"About what you'd expect." He paused, uncertain whether to continue. "You read about . . . what happened . . . in the paper?"

"Yeah. But it didn't make much sense."

"It doesn't make much sense to me either."

"Did he leave a note or anything?"

"No. But there was someone in the house when I got in Thursday night—"

"Like a burglar?"

"Like a burglar."

"That's weird." She ran her finger around the rim of her glass. Then she looked up. "Any idea who?"

"No. Whoever it was, he ran when I came in. Nothing's missing. And I had this bizarre conversation with Asa Cade."

"What do you mean?"

He hesitated a moment. And then: "Asa acted like I'm accusing him of something. Cindy says she thought he and Dad might have been mixed up in something."

She raised her eyebrows. "In Sauls Run, West Virginia?"

"That's what I keep telling myself. She mentioned Perry Holland. I thought maybe he had opened up the mines again."

She shook her head. "Not that I know of—and I would know, working in this place. There was some short-term stuff up there in November—"

"Yeah, I talked to a guy tonight."

"Ray?"

"That's right." He sipped his club soda. "Well, I can't believe Dad was involved in anything either, but I'm going to stick around for a while, look into it."

"Henry Sleep, amateur sleuth."

He laughed. "Something like that." He hesitated. Then: "I was thinking maybe we could spend some time together."

The succeeding silence seemed brittle, a razor-thin sheet of ice with Sonny Rollins skating his sax lightly over the surface.

"Yeah," she said.

"Emily—"

"The thing is, Henry, last time you were in town, you stirred up my whole life, and then you just"—she lifted her hands—"went away. I'm not sure I'm strong enough to handle that right now."

"I'm not planning to go anywhere."

"No, but you're not planning to stick around either, are you?"

He said nothing.

"Are you?"

"I don't know. I'm staying for a while, anyway. Until I figure out what happened to Dad."

"And then?"

"And then—" He shrugged. "Then, we'll see."

She nodded.

"So what do you want me to do, Emily? I care about you. I want to spend time with you. Is that so awful?"

"No, it's not so bad at all. But let's don't rush things, okay? Let's just take it a day at a time."

The music filled the silence, tenor sax snaking through an unpredictable groove.

What was it she had said to him? *I got used to you running away*. It was true, he knew. All his life he had been running: from his mother's slow misery and death, from his father and his father's pain, most of all perhaps from the dreams. From Emily, too, he supposed. And what had she done to deserve that?

Maybe you didn't get what you deserved. Had Emily

earned *this* life somehow, running beer in a run-down saloon, a mother crippled by emphysema, a father dead before she ever really knew him? Had his mother deserved her cancer, for that matter? That, more than anything else, had destroyed his faith in his father's God. Maybe that same doubt had wormed away inside his father for all these years—had led him finally to the ice-cold consolation of the gun. Maybe he was a fool to consider any other possibility.

Across the bar, Emily was smiling.

"What?" he asked.

"You remember the first time you ever saw my house?"

Henry laughed.

He did remember—he didn't think he would ever forget actually. December, the year his mother had died. He had been twelve, helping his father distribute the proceeds from the Christmas food drive. He had not known that the scabrous house in Crook's Hollow had belonged to Emily Wood—had never thought of what her life might be like outside of school. But she had opened the door at his father's knock, and Henry had stepped back in shock, the grocery sack slipping in his hands.

She blinked twice, said nothing.

Henry blinked back, squeezing the rough paper bag between his fingers. A small, hard-faced woman with a tight coil of gray hair stepped out of the darkness behind Emily.

"Can I help you?" she said.

"My name is Quincy Sleep, ma'am. I'm pastor over at the First Christian Church here in town."

"We don't take no charity, Reverend." The woman had dropped a hand to Emily's bone-thin shoulder, and Henry, following the motion with his eyes, inadvertently met Emily's lucid gaze. He lowered his eyes, flushing. He still remembered how he had felt in that moment—dirty somehow, as if he had spied her naked when she didn't know he was looking.

"Well, there's no need to think of it like that, ma'am," Quincy Sleep was saying. "Think of it as a gift—"

"We don't take no charity." The woman's fingers had gone white-knuckled around Emily's shoulder.

"Of course." His father had glanced at the number by the door. "I see we have gotten the wrong address. But I do hope you'll join us for services." With a strained smile, he steered Henry away. At the end of the crumbling sidewalk Henry stole a last glance over his shoulder. The door was still open, Emily and her mother framed within it, and for a moment Emily's eyes, fathomless and gray, had caught and held his own. An arc of recognition, electric, had jumped between them then, but she had said nothing. Nothing at all.

Remembering, Henry shook his head. "I felt awful."

"*You* felt awful!" She laughed. "God I didn't want to go to school the next Monday."

"It's funny, though," he said. "That's one of my clearest memories of my father."

"Is it?"

"Yeah. We were in the car afterward, and I wanted to know why your mother wouldn't take the groceries. I was building this model at the time—it was a ship, a battleship from World War II. It had about a million pieces."

"A million."

"At least." He smiled. "Anyway, instead of answering me, he asked me why I wouldn't let him help me with the ship."

"What did you say?"

"I didn't know. It just seemed important somehow that I do it on my own. And what he said was—" Henry lowered his voice, assumed a dead-serious demeanor. " 'Well, maybe that's how that woman feels.' "

"He said it just like that?"

In the deep voice: "Just like that."

They laughed together, and Henry felt something give way inside him, a hard knot of emotion he hadn't known was there.

"But what I really remember," he said, "is what he told me next."

"Yeah?"

"Yeah. He pulled the car over and then he looked at me and said, 'There's all kinds of food in the world, Henry. There's the food you eat. But there's also food for the mind—books and music, say—and there's food for the spirit, too. Sometimes,' he said, 'food for the spirit is more important than regular food. You follow me?' " Henry turned the club soda in its circle. "The thing is, I *didn't* follow him, not then."

"And now?"

"I'm not sure, but I think, maybe, he meant that it's not what happens to you that's important—it's how you react to it. You know what I mean?"

"Yeah," she said. "Yeah, I think I do."

Then nobody said anything at all. They sat there in the stillness of the bar with the light guttering over them, listening to Sonny Rollins blow the blues. After a while, she reached out and laid a hand over his.

"It's not easy letting go, is it?" she said.

Chapter 9

Henry rested uneasily that night—what remained of it—his slumber broken by the old dream of the labyrinth, his tireless pursuer. Again he fled through nightmare corridors, dragging breath into constricted lungs; again, he turned that final corner to be confronted by his father's ghost. Quincy Sleep stepped forward to embrace him and Henry stumbled away, remembering how that figure had touched him once before, the icy burns upon his cheek—

He sat up, sweating despite the chill, the covers clammy in his lap. Aquinas, curled at his feet, lifted his head and peered at him through inscrutable eyes, his tail thumping softly against the comforter. Then he tucked his head back between his paws and slept.

Henry slept again as well, a restless, thrashing sleep haunted by dreams of a different order: Emily, her face remote and unforgiving. *If you leave,* the dream Emily told him, *don't come back.* He woke unrested and late—toward midday—with the words still echoing in his mind. He almost reached for the phone right then, wanting to confirm the sense he had walked away with the night before—the sense that they had reached an accommodation, that there was hope yet. Instead, he got up and dressed quickly.

He spent the afternoon in town, tangled in his father's estate—lawyers and bankers and bureaucrats, like vultures, all of them hungry for a little taste of the flesh. He got home after dark to find a message from Emily

on the machine. She had to work tonight, but maybe
they could spend the day together tomorrow.

He dozed in front of the television and woke disoriented to the doorbell. His first thought was Emily, that
she had managed to get off work early. But when he
opened the door, a tall, bearish man stood on the porch.

"Hello, Mr. Sleep," the man said. "My name is Benjamin Strange, from down the *Observer*? I left you a message. Maybe you got it?"

"I got it. You have any idea what time it is?"

The man—in the dim light of the porch, Henry
thought he might be sixtyish—glanced at his wrist. "Just
after ten, by my watch."

"It's late. Just like the first time you called."

"I have my reasons for that, Mr. Sleep."

"Yeah, well, I don't want to hear them, thanks all the
same. Good night."

He started to swing the door shut. Strange caught it
with one heavy hand. He held it, not really applying
pressure, and said, "I don't know what I've done to deserve your hostility, but you should do yourself a favor
and listen to me. That's all I ask, a half hour of your
time."

"I don't have any interest in feeding the local gossip."

"Your father was a prominent man in this town. People are going to talk."

"Let them talk, then. I have nothing to say to you."

"Maybe I have something to say to you, Mr. Sleep.
Have you thought of that?" The hand fell away. "Shut
me out if you wish. But you should know that the day
before your father died, I spoke with him by telephone.
I don't know why he committed suicide, but the nature
of our conversation leads me to believe that maybe—"
Strange hesitated. "The nature of our conversation leads
me to believe that maybe the official story isn't the
true story."

For a moment the two of them stood there on either
side of the threshold, the old man and the January night
on one side, the young man and the warm house on the
other. Then Strange took a deep breath. Henry heard

congestion rattling deep in his lungs, a phlegmy spasm
that give way to a torrent of coughs, raw and moist and
painful sounding.

"You okay?" Henry asked.

Strange held up one hand as if to say, *Sure, I'm fine,
no problem*, but another fusillade of coughs doubled
him over.

Henry sighed and opened the door wide. "You better
come inside," he said.

"Is that better?"

Benjamin Strange took another sip of water. He nodded, too worn out to speak, perhaps. His breath still
came in ragged gasps, and his long, time-scored face was
pale. Henry watched him from across the kitchen
counter, in the pitiless glare of the overhead fluorescent.
Everything about Strange was simultaneously massive
and somehow dwindled: his enormous blunt hands, knotted around the water glass; his heavy head and luxuriant
thatch of iron-colored hair; his thick-featured, intelligent
face. But the hands were liver-spotted and the seamed
flesh of his broad head clung to his skull, making him
haggard, cadaverous. The lips trembled as he lifted the
water to his mouth, and after he replaced it softly on
the bar, his hands trembled as he rubbed his eyes. Tired
eyes, Henry thought. Watery, gray, exhausted eyes,
sunken under a luxuriant sprawl of eyebrows.

How old was he? Not sixty. Closer to seventy maybe.
The barrage of coughs had dissolved Henry's hostility
for the moment; now he wanted merely to move the
man along.

"Can I get you anything else?" he asked.

Strange—"Call me Ben," he had managed to gasp a
moment ago, and now Henry mentally corrected himself—Ben—nodded.

"Scotch," he said.

"You're joking, right?"

"There's got to be some scotch here. Your dad
drink?"

"Moderately."

"Well, he probably has some scotch in the house."

"Are you sure that's a good idea?"

Ben laughed. "It's a little late to rethink lifestyle issues, I'm afraid."

"All right, then." Henry pushed his stool back, went into the dining room, and returned with a bottle. He got a tumbler from the cabinet, filled it with ice, and thrust both glass and bottle across the counter to Ben. "Bourbon will have to do. Anything else?"

Ben's breath was coming easier now. "Please."

"What's that?"

Ben dug through the pockets of the woolen overcoat he had tossed across the other stool; he retrieved a pack of Camels and a brass lighter and stacked them on the Formica. "May I smoke?"

"If you think it's wise."

"Wisdom doesn't have a thing to do with it," he grunted. He placed a cigarette between his lips, lit it, and took a long drag.

"I'll want an ashtray," he said. "And you'll want a glass. By the time I finish talking, I have a feeling you're going to need a drink, too."

"I know it's late, Mr. Sleep. And I know it was late when I called the other night. But I wanted to be certain the police were gone. I wanted to make sure we could talk privately."

"If you have information about my father's death, the police are the people you should be talking to."

"Maybe, maybe not. I trust you've met Sheriff Crawford?"

"Yeah."

"Did you notice anything odd about him? About the kind of things he wanted to know?"

Henry thought about his talk with Harold Crawford that night, the flicker of anger he had seen far down in the other man's eyes when he pressed him on the police report.

"It struck me that he was more interested in what my father might have said to me than who might have broken into the house."

Ben took a final drag off his cigarette and stubbed it out. "Strangely enough," he said, "Harold Crawford and I had a similar conversation not long after your father's body turned up. The very same day, in fact. He showed up in my office with an interest in what your father might have said to me when we talked on the phone Tuesday morning. 'How do you know I talked to him on Tuesday?' I asked. He told me they pulled the phone records after they found the body." He paused and stared at Henry, as if he had imparted information of great significance.

"I don't get it," Henry said.

"I've been a reporter for a long time, Mr. Sleep—"

"Henry."

Ben nodded, smiled. "Henry it is. I grew up in the Run, Henry, but I worked a good chunk of my career— thirty years—in the Midwest. Milwaukee. Chicago. I'm fifty-seven years old—"

Henry's surprise must have shown in his face, for Ben broke off, letting the sentence dissolve in a mirthless laugh. "That's right, fifty-seven. You might call this"— he waved his arms, a gesture that seemed to encompass the entire town—"a kind of premature retirement. For some of those years I worked the crime beat."

"So?"

"So a cop doesn't just haul phone records out of his hat. He has to get an order from a judge, has to take that order to the phone company, usually has to cool his heels while the phone company pulls the records for him."

"So Crawford knew about the phone call before he should have."

"That's right."

Henry thought about it for a minute. "It doesn't necessarily mean anything. Dad might have mentioned it to Asa or to his secretary down at the church. He might have written it in his daybook for that matter."

"Then why would Crawford lie?"

"I don't know."

"Neither do I. Maybe you're right. Maybe it's nothing at all."

"Or maybe my father didn't commit suicide. Maybe Harold Crawford is mixed up in it somehow."

Ben leaned forward. "It's worth thinking about, wouldn't you say?"

Aquinas sprang to the counter between them. Henry glanced away, breaking the hold of Ben's avid gaze.

"What do you want from me then?"

"Your help for starters. You might be able to answer some questions for me."

"And in return?"

"In return, I'll answer some of yours."

"The thing is, I don't know anything."

"Maybe you know more than you think."

"Such as?"

"Well, background for one. Tell me about your father."

"What's to tell?"

"I mean what kind of man was he? Was he the kind of guy that puts a gun in his mouth?"

Henry watched Ben scratch behind Aquinas's ears while he thought about that. The cat collapsed bonelessly and rolled on his back. Closing his eyes, he stretched, a drugged purr emanating from his throat and chest.

Was his father the kind of man who would kill himself?

The thing Henry remembered best about his father—the core of his personality, and maybe the thing that had finally driven them apart—was his iron self-control. Composed, rational, unshakable—Henry could think of a half dozen adjectives to describe Quincy Sleep, but the words he associated with suicide—hysterical, despairing, depressed—just didn't fit. Henry remembered how he had hated him for the way he had conducted himself at his wife's funeral and in the hard months afterward. The flood waters receded and the grass grew over Lily

Sleep's grave and Quincy Sleep had never talked about it with his son. Not once.

He'd taken refuge in silence and faith.

Or so Henry had always supposed.

"I don't think so," he said now. "When my mom died, Dad weathered some rough waters without blinking an eye. There was some talk then. We had a bad time."

"What kind of talk?"

Henry made a dismissive gesture. "It's not important. The thing is, he could be a son of a bitch, but he was tough. I don't think he would have killed himself."

"I've talked to some people. They tend to concur with your view," Ben said. "On Tuesday morning, the day your father died, he called his secretary at the church. Called in sick. Penny Kohler places that call at about eight thirty. He called me at ten thirty-seven that same morning. I remember that because I had just glanced out the window at the bank clock across the street. They had predicted snow and I wanted to see the temperature. Your dad sounded excited, almost manic, but he didn't sound suicidal."

"What did he say?"

"He wouldn't talk about it over the phone, but he said he thought he had a story for me. A big story."

Henry ran his palm along Aquinas's slick fur. "Those were his words?"

"Something like that."

"Did you set up the meeting?"

"We did. He was supposed to come by the next morning. I tried to get him to tell me more, to give me some idea what he had, but he wouldn't. He said he wasn't sure yet and he needed to go through it again. 'Tomorrow,' he said."

"And there was no tomorrow."

"That's right."

Henry stood. He paced to the window and gazed out, past the ghostly reflection of his face, into the night. "This isn't some kind of sick joke?"

"I've never been more serious in my life."

"And that's it? That's all he said?"

"Not quite."

Henry turned around. "What else?"

Ben shook another cigarette out of the pack and placed it between his lips. He smiled grimly. "He said he had to go, and I told him I wouldn't meet him, not unless he could give me an idea what the story was. I lied, but your father believed me."

"What did he say?"

"He said, 'You want to know what the story is, take a look at the history of this town.' 'What about the town?' I asked him. 'Take a look at how people die,' he said, and then he wouldn't say any more, no matter how much I pushed him. He wouldn't say another word. He got off the phone."

"So did you?"

"Did I what?"

"Take a look at the way people die here?"

Benjamin Strange picked up the brass lighter, leaned back on his stool, and propped his knee comfortably against the edge of the bar. Snapping up the flame, he set the cigarette alight and dragged deeply. He smiled broadly through the cloud of smoke when he exhaled. He didn't even cough.

"As a matter of fact," he said, spreading his hands, "I did."

Chapter 10

It was midnight, the witching hour.

At the end of the hall, just outside the study where Henry's father had—

—been killed—

—committed suicide, the grandfather clock was banging out the hours.

Benjamin Strange let his hands drop.

"What did you find?"

Strange leaned forward, his eyes glinting. "The thing is, I didn't find a damn thing."

"What do you mean?"

"We installed a computer system at the *Observer* a few years back," he said, "so the first five years or so were a breeze. Subject searches turned up exactly what you would expect in a place like Sauls Run: cancer, black lung, heart attacks, the occasional accident. Car accidents mostly, but a tractor overturned on a fellow in Kopperston a year or two back, and four years ago they had a slate fall up in Copperhead. And of course, there were the other deaths, not many, but a few."

"What other deaths?"

"Killings. A spectacular killing over in Beckley a few years ago, when a kid took a baseball bat to his whole family—that one made the AP—but they were mostly just the kinds of killings you see every day in the newspaper business. Coupla friends come to blows over a card game. A fellow kills his old lady because she burned the toast. I looked back seven years on the computer files and it was all the same stuff. Cancer. Pneumonia. A barroom murder now and then."

"So you didn't find anything?"

Ben waved his hand impatiently. Gray smoke trailed away from the cigarette smoldering between his thick fingers. "Nothing that jumped out at me. I spent the day on this thing. What the hell? We're a weekly, right? When the computer files panned out, I went back into the morgue and started looking through the papers themselves. Two years I went through week by week, and then I searched back another twenty-five years by looking at every third or fourth issue." He coughed and stubbed out his cigarette. "It beat the hell out of me, Henry."

"They were all normal deaths."

"That's right."

"Did you look for a pattern within those deaths?"

"What do you mean?"

Henry shrugged. "I don't know. Like Love Canal or something. An unusual incidence of some rare disease, like the water was contaminated or people were living too close to a landfill."

"That's exactly what I thought. So I went back and did it again—first the five years on the computer, then twenty-five more in the morgue."

"And?"

Ben lifted his hands. "Nada. Nary a thing."

"You're sure?"

"Not anymore. But at the time I didn't have a lot of doubt. I mean, I didn't think I would miss anything if it was there. I didn't compare the Run to any actuarial tables or anything like that—not then, anyway—but I've been in the newspaper business for three decades. The people in Sauls Run didn't seem to be dying of anything unusual, or at any especially high rate. I was tapped for ideas."

"So what did you do?"

"Went back another twenty-five years. Still nothing."

"And then?"

"And then I started thinking about your father—a

small-town minister." He turned his glass thoughtfully
and gazed off at Aquinas, sitting alertly at the end of the
bar, his tail coiled primly about his paws. Ben glanced up
to meet Henry's eyes. "I mean, how could a man like
him stumble on some grand conspiracy, after all?"

"So you decided he was a crackpot?"

"Wouldn't be the first—"

"He wasn't, you know."

Benjamin Strange leaned forward. "Oh?"

"He wasn't your typical small-town minister either."

"How do you mean?"

Henry stood. He paced to the end of the bar and
began to stroke the cat. "He didn't necessarily believe
the things his congregation believed."

"You mean he didn't believe in God?"

"No, he believed in God, just not the same God or
the same kind of God others here believe in."

"What do you mean?"

"Well, you grew up here. People in the Run—a lot of
them anyway—believe in the Bible literally. I'm talking
the wrathful Old Testament God, virgin birth, the resur-
rection of the body. Fundamentalism, you understand?"

"Your dad wasn't that kind of man?"

"Not at all. I don't doubt he believed in God, but only
as some kind of impersonal, creative force, unimaginably
far distant in time. Some kind of . . . I don't know.
Something that could be conceived in scientific terms as
easily as theological ones." Henry walked back to his
stool and swiveled, thinking. "He was an intellectual. I
think he saw Jesus as a great moral and philosophical
thinker, and all the supernatural accretions to the histori-
cal reality didn't bother him. As far as he was concerned,
they were enabling devices that made the ethical aspects
of Christianity available to people. In fact, that was one
of his real passions—the links between pagan myth and
Christianity. He spent his life studying them. If he had
turned the same habits to analyzing the history of Sauls
Run, he probably would have looked at it in a different
way than you or I would. And I don't doubt that he saw
something that he believed to be important."

"The thing is," Ben said, "I *did* doubt. And what's more I went about the thing completely wrongheaded. I was thinking like you. Lead in the water, industrial waste, you name it. I was sure that he had uncovered some messy thing like that." He extended a long finger. "That was the first problem."

He took a long breath, gazed longingly at the cigarettes for a moment, and then raised another finger. "The second was in the sample itself. I was getting a false signal."

"What do you mean?"

"The newspaper," he said. "It covers the entire county, sometimes even state news, right?"

"So?"

"So your Dad didn't tell me to look at how people died in the county. He told me to look at how people die in this town."

"That doesn't make any sense."

Ben leaned back, gloating a little, obviously enjoying himself. Now he did tug a cigarette out of the pack, but he didn't light it. "It makes perfect sense when you realize something else."

"What else?"

"I don't think your Dad noticed what was happening in Sauls Run. I think he noticed what wasn't."

"What do you mean?"

"Well." Ben tucked the cigarette behind one ear. "Finally I *did* decide your Dad was a crank—there're thousands of them—and I didn't think much about it until he turned up dead the next morning. And then I decided to take another look."

He pounded a fist against the bar.

"Goddamn it, Henry, it was so obvious once I spotted it."

"What?"

"It's not the way people die here your Dad was worried about. It's the way they don't."

"What do you mean?"

"I mean that I had to throw out all the deaths that didn't occur in the immediate vicinity of the Run—everything from Copperhead and Coal Mountain and that crazy thing in Beckley. All of it. And when I did, I found a couple things. The thing your father noticed, Henry, was not the way people die in Sauls Run, but the way they fail to."

The grandfather clock in the hall uttered a single abrupt chime. Aquinas leaped off the counter and stalked away, his claws clicking against the linoleum in the silence that followed.

Ben reached for the cigarette angled behind his ear and shoved it back in the pack. "Goddamn coughing. If I can just keep myself from smoking, it's not so bad."

Henry leaned forward, clasping his hands. Far down in the bowels of the house, the furnace cycled on. "What do you mean, people don't die here?"

"It's crazy. I keep thinking it's got to be wrong, Henry, but it's not. People die here—I wish to God they didn't, I could use a little help—but they tend to die only of old age or the occasional accident."

"Those are the same things people die of everywhere."

"Sure. But what's missing, Henry?"

Henry stood. He walked to the window and gazed out for a moment, seeing nothing but his own narrow-featured face. In the basement, the furnace shut off with a click, and in the silence, the house seemed utterly empty of life or animation. Only the regular ticking of the clock in the hall came to him. This was the silence his father must have lived in for ten years or more, he thought.

Behind him, Ben stirred. His gravelly voice broke the silence. "Henry?"

Henry had lifted a hand to touch the glass. It felt icy against his fingertips, good and free, beckoning him out of this room, this labyrinth. He dropped his hand and turned to face Ben, and in the space of that single movement it came to him, the thing his father had seen at last, though how or why it had come to him after all the years he had lived in the town, Henry could not begin to guess.

"Violence," he said. "No deaths by violence. Is that right?"

"That's right. How did you know?"

"I can't remember a single murder," Henry said. "Not in the Run itself, not in all the time I was growing up. But you didn't notice, did you, because the paper covered the occasional killings in nearby towns?"

"That's right."

"But that's not so unusual, is it? It's a small town. Most people are friendly—"

"It's a small town, Henry, and like all small towns it's full of gossip and deceit and even hatred."

Henry walked back to the bar and slumped on his stool. "But surely you hear about such things. Small towns go years sometimes without a single murder."

"Years, Henry, yes. But I looked as far back as the *Observer* would take me—over a hundred years, though there are gaps in places—and I couldn't find any record of single killing. There's no way. Not that long, not a century or more."

"But . . . why?"

"Who knows? Maybe something *is* in the water. But I think your father figured it out, and—here's the irony of it—I think someone killed him to keep him from telling anyone else." He leaned forward, his eyes intent. "And that leads me to the second thing."

"What's that?"

"In the last few days, I've done some more research. Not only are deaths by violence practically unknown, but crime of just about any kind is extremely rare. Same with disease. It occurs, but measured against the norms for a population of this size, it's so low as to be statistically insignificant. People here routinely live into their nineties, even to be a hundred or more. They don't so much die, as just wear out—"

"That's not true," Henry said. "My mother. My mother died of cancer. She died of cancer when she was thirty-four years old. I saw it. I was there."

"That brings me to the next point—the really scary point. Listen. For the sake of argument, let's say there's some kind of damping force in action in Sauls Run, some weird radiation or whatever. Who knows? It's basically invisible, but it can be detected by its effects on its immediate environment. So what does it do?" He ticked points off on his fingers. "One, it reduces certain kinds of behavior. People in the Run seem to be far less violent than elsewhere, less likely to commit crimes of any sort, in fact. Two, it extends life span. And three, it reduces disease. Two and three are maybe different aspects of the same thing." He paused. "Now here's the scary thing: Whatever it is, it's been weakening for years."

"What do you mean?"

"There are periodic clusters in the files—intervals when crime flares up, when people die from disease, when people die in general. Each one lasts a couple months, and each time it happens, it's worse. I picked up on it in the summer of 1978—though it might have started earlier. Anyway, deaths—nonviolent deaths, deaths from disease, old age—nearly doubled that summer. At the same time, the crime rate in the Run surged. It was still well below normal for a town this size, but there was a sharp increase. Both rates jumped up overnight and continued high for the next three months or so. It happens again in the summer of 1980—that's when your mother died, right?—and again in the fall and winter of 1987. There was a whole cluster of rapes in the Run that fall. They finally caught him, a guy named Earl Kimball. At the trial, he said something like, 'There was a demon inside me. I kept it caged up for a long time, but it finally got away.' "

"That's just one guy," Henry said. "That could happen anywhere."

"But there's more. At the same time, the death rate skyrocketed—old people, sure, but a lot of young people. Crime, too: There were a couple robberies at gunpoint, two or three child abuse cases. It made me look back in the files, again. Those things had never been reported in the Run either. In the surrounding areas, sure, but not in town. Not until then."

"And it follows the same pattern?"

"Exactly. The rates for all those things skyrocket over-night, and drop off almost as fast. And each time it happens, it's a little bit worse." Ben shook a cigarette out of his pack, tapped it on the counter, lit it. He placed the lighter on the counter and slid it across to Henry. "Take a look."

Henry picked up the lighter and read the engraving:

WHAT A LONG, STRANGE TRIP IT'S BEEN.

"That was what I got when I retired eight years ago," Ben said. "A lighter, can you believe it?" He laughed. "I worked all my life on papers. It's all I ever wanted to do. And I wasn't bad at it, you know? But the lifestyle got me. I spent too much time in bars. I smoked too much. Fifteen years ago, I had a precancerous lesion in my mouth. The doctor took it off right there in his office, didn't even put me under. But he told me to stop smoking." He shook his head. "You ever been in a place you don't want to be and you can't get out of it? Not because you don't know how, but because you don't have the courage? That make sense?"

"It makes plenty of sense," Henry said.

Ben gave him a long look. "Well, that's exactly how I felt then," he said. "I dicked around for another five or six years, tried to quit without really trying too hard, and one day I'm coughing up blood. I'm afraid to go to the doctor, so I dick around a little more, and finally it's so bad I have to go."

He smiled grimly. "There's a shadow on the X rays. Doctor says he can probably get it, but I know better. I *know* the way you know things, and what that shadow looks like to me is death. It looks like a skull in the center of my chest. So they open me up, and turns out I'm right, there's nothing they can do. Doctor gives me six months, maybe a year."

"And that's when you came here."

"That's right. I turned in my notice, collected my lighter, and headed for points south. My family's gone, but hell, I always liked the Run. I thought, well, let's see how the old place is holding up. So I roll into town, settle into a hotel room, and lo and behold, before the week's out, I can breathe a little bit. Another week, I can breathe a little more. So I make an appointment with a doctor, drop my file on his desk, and ask him to take an X ray. Guess what?"

"The tumor's gone."

Ben smiled. "It's smaller, anyway. Doctor has no idea why. He's been tracking it ever since. It finally reached a point where it was pretty clear I was going to outlive my savings if I didn't go back to work. So I talked to Emerson MacCauley down at the *Observer*, and he put me on staff, even rented me the apartment over the office. Which brings us up to date."

He ground out his cigarette.

"In the last two months, death rates are back up, and maybe illnesses are, too. I called a guy at Ridgeview—the nursing home? He says their statistics are off the chart the last couple months. People who've been there for years are suddenly popping off like firecrackers, and they've had to start a waiting list for people wanting in. Strokes, heart attacks, you name it. And the violence has escalated, too. This time—for the first time—we've got people killing each other. In addition to your father—and the police are calling that a suicide—there have been two other killings in town in the last year. A guy named Boyd Samford shot his wife when he found out she was fooling around, and—this one is worse, maybe—a kid up in Crook's Hollow killed an old bum—"

"Ian Barre?"

Ben nodded.

"Christ, Ian's been wandering around the Run as long as I can remember. He's totally harmless."

"It was a fourteen-year-old that did it. He ran into Ian up in the woods and shot him with a pellet gun. He shot him twenty or thirty times and just left him there to die. Nobody even knows why." Ben hesitated. "That's not all, of course. I guess you've figured that out."

He held Henry's gaze for a long moment, and then he looked away.

Emily Wood's face popped into Henry's mind. *Like somebody flipped a switch*, she had said. *Like she got old all at once.*

"The cancer," he said.

Ben nodded. "Yeah. The cancer. It's back."

Chapter 11

"So what are we doing today?" Emily asked when he picked her up the next morning.

"We're going to church. I want to check out Dad's office."

"Sleuthing?"

He smiled at her. "I suppose."

"Not much of a first date."

"When you think about it, it's hardly our first date."

He paused at the sidewalk, staring at their cars—his battered Volaré and her rust-eaten GMC Pacer—nosed over the corrugated gray ridges left by the snowplows.

"Who's driving?" he asked.

"Your heat work?"

"Yeah."

"You are."

As he pulled out, she said, "It's a good thing we're not going to a class reunion."

"We could always rent a limo," he said.

Penny Kohler met them at the church.

"It's just not the same without your father around," she said as they settled in the conference room. Though Henry supposed Penny must have changed over the years, he could not recall that she had ever looked otherwise: a diminutive, energetic woman who hovered just this side of fatness. She patted Emily's hand. "He would have been pleased, Henry." She shook her head. "I don't know how I'm going to get along without him."

"Has the church started the search for a new minister?"

Penny grimaced. "We're putting a committee together. I don't know how I'm going to do it."

"He meant a great deal to you, didn't he?" Emily asked.

"Oh, honey, I don't even know how to tell you. I don't have any family left, you know. But I could always count on Quincy, eight o'clock sharp every morning, Monday through Friday, and always a smile on his face."

Henry felt a dull tug of resentment. *I could never count on him to smile,* he thought. *I could never count on him for anything.*

And now another voice spoke up within him. *You never gave him a chance,* it told him. *You shut him out.*

"Henry," Penny Kohler said. She took a deep breath. "I have a confession to make, Henry."

"What's that?"

She paused, as if gathering her courage. "In the last year or so, your father and I became . . . close. You can disapprove if you want, but it made him happy—it made us both happy, Henry—and I hope you don't think it defiles the memory of your mother. It wasn't like that at all. It was very wholesome and I'm glad that we had a chance to be together, if only for a little while."

"Of course, Penny. I'm glad for you. He was lonely after Mother died."

"Oh, he was, Henry, terribly lonely. But he never complained. I know things were hard between you, but he always spoke of you. *Call him,* I used to say, *for God's sake call the boy*—I actually said that, and him a minister and all—but he always just said, *I don't want to intrude on Henry's life.* You could see that he wanted to call, but he was stubborn. He was a good man, but stubborn."

"I could have called, too."

"Oh, I know, honey. But it's all water under the bridge now. Don't you punish yourself."

Henry said, "Did he seem depressed or anything before he died, Penny? Had his behavior changed?"

A shadow passed across the older woman's face. "You don't think he killed himself, do you?"

"I don't know what to believe," Henry said.

"Well, I never for one moment believed it," she said. "Two or three weeks before . . . before he died, he changed. He wasn't sleeping well and he . . . withdrew, if you know what I mean. He was always kind of . . . to himself, you know. I wish I could find a better way to describe it. He would spend hours in his study. But that all changed—not the time he spent alone, but the *way* he was . . . alone."

"How?"

"Well, it's hard to explain. He was so independent that you might not have noticed if you didn't know him well. But I've known him for more than thirty years and I noticed it." She glanced at Henry. "He just went away. If you said anything, he would answer the way he always had, but there was something about his eyes, this faraway look, like his mind was somewhere else. You understand?"

Henry nodded.

"My, this is awkward." Penny paused. "The night it started, just after Christmas, I was at your father's house." She hesitated. "We were watching the news when the doorbell rang. Your father and I were always very careful—you know how people talk—so I went upstairs. I could hear Asa's voice, and he knew about us, of course—Asa thought we should get married and to heck with what anyone said—but there was someone else along, so I stayed out of sight.

"A few minutes later, Quincy came up and said he needed to go out for a bit." She laughed. "I went to the window to watch him leave, and what I saw surprised me some. Asa wasn't in his truck. They were getting in a little foreign car—"

"Perry Holland's Jag," Henry said.

"That's right," she said. "How did you know?"

"Cindy Cade. The same thing happened with Asa."

"Where was he going?" Emily asked.

"Well, that's the thing, isn't it? He wouldn't say. He

was gone for hours. I had slept a little, but I woke up when he came in. I suppose it must have been three o'clock or so. And this is the odd part. He was dirty."

"What do you mean, dirty?"

"My father used to work in the mines," she said, "years and years ago, back before old Jeremiah Holland shut them down, and when your father came in that night, he looked just like my daddy looked after a shift. He had black streaks on his hands and face. His clothes were ruined. But that's not the half of it."

"What else?" Henry asked.

"His eyes," Penny Kohler said. "He looked like he was in shock. I asked what happened, where he had been, but he wouldn't say. I thought maybe there had been an accident up in Copperhead—they call in ministers, you know, to help with the families—but he would have told me, wouldn't he? And it would have been in the paper." She leaned over the table. "So he had to have been up at the old Holland mines. That's why Perry Holland was along that night. That's what I think."

And Henry, thinking now of the labyrinth of his dreams, said, "I think you're right."

"Well." Penny Kohler stood, rubbing her palms together briskly as though she had dispensed with some necessary but unpleasant task. "You wanted to see his office?"

Henry had few memories of the office.

In the years before his mother had died, he had rarely come here. In the years after, he had never wanted to— had never wanted to come to the church at all, in fact, and once he grew old enough to assert his will, never did.

"I'd like to see you there occasionally," Quincy Sleep had told him the summer after Henry had finished his master's.

"I'm not sure I believe in all that anymore," Henry had replied.

But if God was not here, Henry thought now, his father wasn't either. Despite the photo on the desk—a snapshot of Henry and his mother taken when Henry was seven—the room exuded a brand of impersonal luxury Henry associated with college deans, all plush carpets and upholstered furniture. A computer on a walnut table cycled patiently through a screen saver. Books lined two walls; file cabinets stood on a third, under a portrait of Alexander Campbell.

"So what are we looking for?"

"I'm not really sure. Anything unusual, I guess."

"And that would be?"

"I'm hoping we'll know it when we see it."

If it was there, they didn't. An hour and a half of receipts and old sermons later, Henry stood and stretched. Emily looked up from the desk.

"You want a Coke?" he said.

"Diet."

"Back in a minute."

The machine was in the basement. On the way, Henry glanced into the sanctuary, dim in a wash of bloodless January light.

He stepped inside. What beauty the church possessed lay here, in the tall stained-glass windows and the towering ceiling of burled walnut, ribbed with great beams like the underside of a hull-shot galleon, ancient and threaded by tides. Indeed, something oceanic haunted the room, something vast and still and endlessly patient. Numinous, that was the word. A line from Dickinson came to him—the bit about a certain slant of light on winter afternoons.

Henry knew that slant of light. He knew it well.

If his father lingered, it was here. As he sank into a velvet-cushioned pew, Henry could almost hear his honey-eyed tenor.

What happened? he asked the air. What happened to your faith?

And whom he was addressing—his father or himself—he could not say.

Emily found him there.

"Good thing I wasn't dying of thirst," she said.

"Sorry." Then: "You find anything?"

"Church business. That's all."

She slid into the row behind him and crossed her arms on the back of his pew, making a pillow for her chin.

"That's what I expected," he said. "Anything important he always kept at home."

"Important?"

"Anything he valued for his own interest. The church office was for church business—counseling, correspondence, whatever."

"You've been through the stuff at home?"

"Some of it," he said. "There's a lot there."

They were silent for a moment.

"What are you thinking about?" she asked.

"Pascal's Wager. You know Pascal?"

"He's a philosopher, right?"

"French. Seventeenth, maybe eighteenth century. The date doesn't matter, I guess. Anyway, given the choice between belief and nonbelief, Pascal said the wise man wagers that God exists. If he wins, he wins eternal life. If he loses, he's lost nothing but two or three hours on Sunday mornings."

"Kind of underestimates God, doesn't it?"

"How so?"

"God can't tell the difference between mock faith and the real deal?"

"Maybe, maybe not. Dad used to say faith and doubt were facing sides of the same coin. You can't have faith unless you have doubt."

"What do you mean?"

"Faith is trust in something you can't see, something you can't know for sure. If you know, then you don't have faith, you have knowledge." He paused. "You remember Mrs. Traven?"

"Fifth grade? How could I forget?"

"Dad first mentioned Pascal to me when Mrs. Traven went over evolution. I remember him saying that evolution was a fact, while the Bible—a lot of it anyway—worked through metaphor. I'll never forget what he said: 'Facts and truths are very different things, Henry. Metaphors can be truer than anything else.' It didn't make any sense to me then."

"Does it now?"

"Yeah, actually. But it's pretty cold comfort at times like this." He laughed. "You know, that's the only kind of conversation Dad and I were capable of. I keep thinking that I never knew him at all, and now I never will."

"What do you mean?"

"He lived this whole secret life I knew nothing about. He missed me." He said again, "He missed me."

"Did you miss him?"

"I guess I did," he said, "but I didn't even realize I did. I hated him so much. I was so *angry* at him."

"Why?"

"I thought he—" He broke the sentence off.

"You thought he what?"

"After mom died, I had this fear that they would come and take him away. And now it looks like someone did." He laughed. "It's all so crazy. Maybe he *did* commit suicide."

"Do you believe that?" she asked.

"No. What do you think?"

"I'm keeping an open mind," she said.

"Maybe that's a good idea."

Something stirred at the door to the sanctuary. Henry looked up. Penny Kohler stood there, backlit by the hall light.

"I'm going to lock up now, Henry," she said. "Are you all done?"

"Yeah," he said. "Yeah, we're done."

Chapter 12

No matter how far you run, the past reaches out for you, if only in your dreams.

You thought he what? Emily had asked.

Yet she must have heard the rumors.

Henry had heard them himself, in whispered taunts on the playground the fall after his mother had died. He'd sensed them in the veiled glances of strangers, in the weighted silence that fell when his father came into a room. But even before that—before the rumors, before the long years of listening to his father pace the midnight house—in the days just after his mother's death, the terrible suspicion had blossomed inside Henry's head.

Seventeen years of living with it, seventeen years of never speaking it aloud.

I thought—I thought—

He got home at dusk. Snow spat from an overcast sky, wind-driven flakes of grit, like particles of sand against his face. The lock surrendered to his key. Inside, the house was still and cold.

He climbed the steps. When he reached the landing, the furnace cleared its throat, but the cold did not retreat. It seemed to radiate from the spare bedroom, the room his mother had died in. He had a sense of skating over thin ice, slipping through into the black waters underneath. A flood of almost physical memories enveloped him: the medicinal stench of the sickroom; his father's voice raised in anger; the rain. The endless, all-encompassing, omnipresent rain.

He opened the door, flipped on the light.

Dust and abandonment, seventeen years of silence.

Everything else had remained the same: the narrow bed, rails raised on one side, crisp linen turning the color of ivory; the skeletal I.V. pole and the locked drug cabinet; the roll-away table and the crystal vase where his father had every day placed a single perfect rose.

He took a long breath.

He crossed the room and sat in the armchair.

Nothing had changed. Dear God, nothing had changed.

Where the fear had begun, where it faded into guilt, he could not say.

It had grown inside him, cancerous as the seeds that had germinated in his mother's bones. No one had ever told him that his mother was dying. Awareness took hold of him slowly, derived from the gradual accumulation of evidence: the endless conferences his parents held with Asa, emerging from the study with numb faces; the countless visits to doctors; the frantic gaiety in his mother's voice, the heat when she embraced him.

In her final months, her eyes retreated into hollow sockets. Her glossy hair grew greasy and matted, and she forced his father to hack it off. Her flesh melted, unveiling the skeleton underneath. Her room stank; her moans pierced his sleep.

Asa and his father were arguing in the study.

"She has to go to the hospital, Quincy. I can do something for her pain there."

"She'll stay here, in her house."

"Quincy, please—"

"She doesn't want to go, and I don't want her to."

"Hire a nurse, then. At least hire a nurse."

"*We'll* take care of her! You and I and Henry!"

That had been the end of it.

Henry had watched in silence as Asa demonstrated

how to inject the IV and clear the line of air bubbles; he looked on from the door as Asa counted out ampoules of morphine and locked them away in the cabinet. Asa explained the dosages, demonstrated how to fill the hypodermic, pointed out the port for the IV push. If something passed between the two men then, Henry did not recognize it.

His mother worsened, fought bedsores, fouled herself.

When his father napped, Henry prayed that she would not call for him. When she did he dragged himself to the door, then performed the requested task—fetched her a glass of water or held the rose close so she could smell it—as swiftly as possible. Most days he sneaked away to explore the woods and streams with Perry, to skip stones across the placid surface of Stoney Gap Lake.

One afternoon, she summoned him. He stared at her, her eyes burning in shadowy pits.

"The key, Henry," she whispered, extending a palsied finger at the locked drug cabinet. "Please."

"I can't. I don't have the key."

"You know where it is."

"Dad has it." But he had hesitated a moment too long; she saw the lie in his eyes.

"Bring it to me, Henry."

"I can't. Dad said never to touch the IV."

He shook his head. He stepped away from the bed.

Tears slid down her face. "Please."

"No. I can't."

"I am your *mother,* Henry! You will *obey* me!"

"I can't!"

"I'll do it myself then."

"Fine!" he had screamed. "Go ahead! Do it! I wish you'd die, anyway!"

That night his father didn't come down to dinner. Henry ate alone and went to bed.

She died the next week.

When Henry returned to the house that day, his

clothes splotched with mud and coal dust and his bicycle wedged in the trunk of Harold Crawford's police cruiser, a bleak, steady rain was coming down.

Asa Cade was drinking whiskey in the kitchen.

"Where's Dad?"

"Upstairs."

Henry slipped out of his muddy shoes.

"Henry—" Asa paused. Henry listened to the rain batter the roof and windows. "Your mother—"

"I know."

He went on along the hall then, pulling up the cuffs of his jeans so as not to track mud on—

—Mother's—

—Persian runner. He mounted the stairs in silence.

The door to the sickroom stood ajar.

His father slumped in the armchair, his face cradled in his open hands. His mother lay on the bed, her hands upturned atop the sheet. Her face was gray, the terrible pallor of soggy newsprint.

The room stank.

He turned away, went into his bedroom, changed into dry clothes. For the longest time, he stared out the window at the rain falling through the leaves of the great oak at the back of the house, puddling on the deck, swelling the stream that ran along the edge of the yard. He heard someone on the steps.

"Quincy?" Asa said. "We need to call the funeral home."

His father mumbled something; he couldn't make it out.

Asa said, "You can't just let her lie there like that."

"I won't have anyone see her like this, Asa. Tomorrow is plenty soon enough."

"Quincy—"

"I'm going to clean her up first. Tomorrow."

"All right then."

He heard Asa on the stairs once more. Presently, the front door opened and shut. A car started in the driveway.

He stood there and watched the rain.

*   *   *

That night, Henry had listened from his bed as his father worked in the sickroom.

How must that have been? he thought now. How would it feel to strip the soiled clothes from the body? To wash the slime and shit from the flesh you had known in passion?

Henry closed his eyes as another memory spoke.

That night, for the first night in his life, he had dreamed of the labyrinth, his relentless pursuer.

In the ashen light of dawn, Henry crossed the hall.

His mother lay on her back, her best Sunday dress loose around her shrunken frame. Yet a measure of beauty had returned through his father's ministrations; her porcelain flesh seemed clear and depthless, her expression composed. Her mutilated hair had been washed and combed into something like order. Crazy hope surged within him; he could not quell it. He reached out with trembling fingers—

Her flesh was cold.

When he lifted the blinds, it was still raining.

The inundation had continued throughout that night. Swollen streams gushed out of the hills and into the valley below. By midnight, Mill Creek had overflowed and Cinder Bottom had become a river, sweeping everything—trees and power lines and panicked cattle—into a black torrent. By three in the morning, Stoney Gap Lake had begun to lap over its banks, and before dawn, Harold Crawford and his fellow deputies had begun evacuating sleepy townsfolk to higher ground. At one end of Sauls Run, the courthouse stood well above the waters. At the other, Holland House brooded atop its rocky promontory. Between them stretched a flat brown ocean from which buildings, telephone poles, the high arc of the Stone Bridge emerged like the drowned playthings of some Brobdingnagian child.

On Widow's Ridge, Henry found his father deeply asleep in the bedroom he had shared with Henry's mother. The room reeked of alcohol.

Downstairs, he fixed himself a sandwich and watched television until three, when the power went out. Somehow that seemed significant to him, the picture shrinking to a white hot point, until finally it snapped out of existence, leaving nothing behind at all.

"The whole damn town is flooded," Bill Richardson said. "I don't know how you're gonna take her there."

Quincy Sleep folded his hands into fists. "Well, she can't stay here, can she?"

"I guess not."

"I guess not. So we're going to have to move her."

"I just don't like to leave Sarah and Willie alone in this storm, that's all."

"Sarah and Willie are going to be fine, Bill," said Sarah Richardson from the doorway. "It's only raining."

It was four thirty. Henry's father had been awake for maybe half an hour, most of which he had spent on the phone, first with Asa, then with Bill Richardson. Henry had not supposed that Sarah Richardson would accompany her husband when he came, yet here she was, her plain face tight.

"Get the station wagon, Bill," she said now.

Bill Richardson sighed and disappeared into the rain.

"I'm sorry Bill's such a twit," Sarah said.

Quincy Sleep made a dismissive gesture.

"Henry, would you like to come over and visit Willie while your father is gone?"

"No, thanks." He stood beside his father, looking out into the sullen July afternoon. The Richardsons' station wagon turned into the drive. Bill got out, opened the hatch, and trudged up the porch stairs. Rain streamed from his hair and clung in droplets to his eyebrows and nostrils. His eyes narrowed into angry points.

"All right then." He shrugged through the doorway and started upstairs, Henry's father at his heels.

"Henry, why don't you come into the kitchen with me?"

"No, thanks."

A moment later, Bill appeared at the landing, backing

down the stairs. Henry's father followed. They lugged
the sheet-wrapped corpse between them.

"Henry," Sarah said from the kitchen, "come here
now!"

He ignored her as the men descended, breathing heavily, now and again pausing when one of them began to
lose his grip. He followed them through the foyer, across
the porch, down to the car, and stood at the base of the
steps, watching through the shifting veil of rain as they
loaded their burden into the back of the station wagon.
Bill slammed the hatch.

"We'll be back in a little while," Henry's father said.

"I want to come," Henry said.

Sarah spoke from the shelter of the porch. "Honey,
you're going to stay here with me."

Only the rain moved, a shimmering curtain. Henry
could smell the fecund bouquet of the drowned soil. He
could feel the weight of his father's gaze upon him.

"I really don't think—" Sarah said, but Henry's father
interrupted her.

"Come on, then," he said.

They drove in silence. Henry sat between the two
men, watching the storm whip the trees into frenzy.
Debris-choked torrents churned in the ditches. In low
places, pools had overspread the pavement, forcing Bill
to slow the station wagon to a crawl.

Henry fidgeted, the last words he'd spoken to her—

—*go ahead, I wish you'd die*—

—reverberating in his mind. He whimpered softly, half
expecting a rustle of sheets from the backseat, a cold
hand dropping heavily upon his shoulder.

Bill turned onto the courthouse square, slipping past
the Grand Hotel. At the apex of High Street, the wipers
slapped back a curtain of water, unveiling the valley.
Holland House loomed on the far ridge, ghostly as a
ruined castle on a storm-racked coast. Everything else
had been submerged, streetlights and roofs thrusting like
wreckage through the depths. Water lapped across the
lower reaches of the Stone Bridge.

"There we go," Bill said, pointing at a knot of men gathered by a rowboat bobbing at the water's edge. They coasted down the rain-slick street. Just short of the water, Bill swung the wagon around and parked.

Men materialized like apparitions as they got out into the driving rain. "I'm awful sorry, Quincy," someone said.

"Let's go," Bill said from the back of the wagon.

"Shouldn't the boy wait in the car?"

A tall man in a rain slicker hunkered down before Henry. Asa's craggy face peered from beneath the yellow hood. "You okay, Henry?"

Henry swallowed, nodding.

Asa squeezed his shoulder and stood. "The boy's fine." He glanced down the street, where the water lapped at the pavement. "You holding that boat?"

"I got it."

"We'll take her from here, Quincy," someone said gently, but Quincy Sleep shook his head.

"I'm going to do it myself. You and me, Asa."

"That ain't necess—"

"He can do it if he wants to," Asa said.

Together, he and Henry's father leaned into the station wagon and tugged forth the corpse. Henry gasped as the rain quickened, molding the sheet to his mother's features.

"Easy now," someone said as they shuffled across the rain-blackened pavement, and Henry saw that it was the man who waited with the boat, a heavyset figure standing thigh-deep in water and clinging to the gunwale with one gnarled hand. "It's slicker than owl shit down here."

Quincy Sleep moaned. "I can't do it."

"We're just going to take her across town to the funeral home, Quincy," Asa said. "It's nice and dry there. We're going to take good care of her."

Henry's father sobbed convulsively as they waded into the flood. Muddy water sloshed around their ankles. The big man stepped forward. "Easy now, I'm telling you that asphalt is slick." He swung the boat around.

"Just lift her in nice and easy. We'll make her real comfortable."

The water had risen to their thighs. They lifted the body to place it in the boat, and Asa disappeared abruptly, as though a bottom-dwelling carnivore had dragged him under; Henry's father went down after him, the body slipping away. Henry cried aloud. He stumbled back from the water's edge.

"No!" he screamed. "No, Mommy, no! I'm sorry! I didn't want you to die. I swear I didn't!"

The body bobbed up like a dry cork, half wrapped in the sodden sheet. One arm had slipped free. A porcelain hand rode the surface, fingers drifting languidly in the current.

Asa Cade exploded out of the water, coughing, followed an instant later by Henry's father. They stumbled, grappling with the body.

Henry screamed again, lurching away.

That was when one of the men at his back—he would never learn who it was—swept him into a swift embrace. The last thing he saw before the stranger dragged him to his breast was his mother's face as they heaved her into the boat. Her flesh looked bruised in the gray light and her mouth fell slackly open. But the thing he would remember always—the thing that would haunt him in the moments before he slept—was her eyes. Her dead and staring, her vacant and accusing eyes.

Of the next hours, Henry remembered only snatches—Asa's hands on his face, a moving car, a glimpse of wind-lashed trees. Only the most tenuous thread of awareness tethered him to his body. A little while later he woke to the gentle ministrations of a woman—her cooing voice, her sure hands as she stripped away his wet clothes and dressed him in dry pajamas. For a moment, that fuzzy sense of separation departed, driven away by the swift certainty that he had been dreaming. His mother lived; it had all been a bad dream. Then recognition dawned: The voice wasn't his mother's; it was Sarah

Richardson's. The vision of his mother's face as he had
seen it last—
  —*those eyes, those dead and staring eyes*—
  —exploded into his mind.
He cried out, tried to claw his way out of the
woman's—
  —*his mother's*—
  —arms, but she dragged him back into her chill
embrace.
  Sarah Richardson's voice again, low and soothing.
  Then darkness.

He woke to the stillness of deep morning. Rain pattered at the roof and window sashes, and Bach played
downstairs—a stream of crystal notes, almost visible in
the gloom. He listened for a while. Nothing frightened
him now—not the rain or the dark or the vision of his
mother's corpse bobbing like a cork in the flood waters.
That all seemed distant, boyish and unimportant.
  Presently, he got up and walked into the hall, following that trail of notes, lambent against the dark. Down
the stairs he went, the night house drifting past as in
a dream.
  The study door stood ajar. Henry floated to the door
and pushed it open. The room extended immeasurably,
a tunnel of books clamoring with strings. At the far end,
his father sat in a maroon leather armchair, in the circle
of radiance shed by a single stand-alone lamp.
  How long he stood like that, looking at his father, he
would never know for certain. But in that time, he perceived with a clarity far beyond his twelve years the
broken spirit of the man at the other end of the room.
It was not visible in his father's calm expression, his head
tilted against the back of the armchair and his eyes
closed as he listened to the music; nor was it visible in
his upright posture or his dress, a neat flannel shirt and
carefully pressed blue jeans, immaculate even at this
hour. Rather he saw it in the entire composition of the
scene, the juxtaposition of the man and the half-lit room
in which he sat, the music and the hour. He saw it most

of all in the man himself—not bowed or bent, but tired, as if he had been carrying a burden for a thousand miles and had only now laid it aside.

For the first time, he saw what his father would look like when he was old. And abruptly it all fell into place, the interlocking pieces of a puzzle he had not even known he was working—his mother as she decayed into kindling, Asa as he locked away the shining ampoules of morphine, his mother once again, lunging at him, a sheen of agony in her eyes. *Stay close by today,* his father had said the morning Lily Sleep had died. *Stay close by.*

His father had known. His father had known when she was going to die.

Henry must have made a sound, a gasp of recognition, for his father looked up.

"Henry?" he said. And then he must have understood the odd expression on his son's face, for he said no more.

For a single dreadful moment, they stared at each other in shocked recognition. Then his father reached out and drew Henry to his breast.

"I'm sorry," he said. "I'm so sorry."

Sauls Run
1987

Chapter 13

A monster stalked the Run.

Fall came fast that year, summer fading overnight into the slap of pads from the high school football field and the brassy clamor of the marching band. Yellow school buses prowled the winding roads, and the ridges burned with color. On a moonless night, the monster put in his first appearance.

Deputy Harold Crawford took the call, the code— 261—striking sparks of recognition from his days with the LAPD. Rape. He had seen such things before, but not in years, and never in the Run. The scene, a decrepit Crook's Hollow walk-up, shook him more than he liked to admit. He could feel the girl's haunted eyes upon him as he took her statement in the county ER, and he felt a small shiver of excitement, shot through with shame. It reminded him too much of a certain moonlit warehouse, that nasty little rush.

As a witness, the girl was useless. The guy had come through an unlocked window; it had been dark; he had been wearing a ski mask. Average height, she said. Average build. He had even worn a condom. She remembered only two things that might prove useful: the knife he had held to her throat as he did it, a six-inch switchblade with a pearl inlay, and something he said, the only words he had spoken the whole time he labored over her.

"What's that?" Crawford asked, his pen poised over his notepad.

The girl looked up and held his gaze.

"A demon," she said. "He asked me to help him. There was a demon inside him."

Crawford was wrestling his own demons that fall.

He dreamed bloody dreams, and more than once he found himself walking that broken strand. The drowning man lay always at the horizon, always just out of reach. The black water beckoned. Delbert Grubb was growing hungry again, and Crawford didn't think a dog would sate him this time around.

Crawford's father had served two masters, the Book and the Fist, and as a boy Crawford had learned to know them both. But the Fist had failed him. The Fist had led him to the girl, to the black alley where LeMarius Oxford writhed in agony; it might lead to worse places yet. So he turned to the Book. Waking swollen with desire from slaughterhouse dreams, Crawford offered up prayers to his father's God. Fifteen years ago, when he had fled L.A., God had granted him surcease—had brought him to the Run, had dammed that dark tide before it sucked him down, had made him a good man. But now Crawford's prayers fell on deaf ears. God had retracted His grace and His glory, had turned His face from Crawford in this hour of his need.

A black seed of anger began to germinate in Crawford's heart. Still the dreams came.

Most nights, Crawford fled sleep, cruising the back alleys of the Run, watchful for a demon-haunted man slipping like a wraith among the shadows.

By mid-October, the monster had claimed two more victims, leaving nothing but words for Crawford to hunt him down by. The phrase—

—*a demon, he said there was a demon inside him*—

—tolled in Crawford's mind like a funereal bell, ominous and faintly familiar—and not alone because it reminded him of Delbert Grubb, the past he had tried to forget, his own demons.

But if twenty years of police work had taught Crawford anything, they had taught him not to stare at facts straight on. Don't look for the answer, he reminded himself. Let the answer come. Strange shadows flicker at the corner of the eye. The undermind knows things the overmind does not. So he dropped the phrase into the cauldron of memory and turned to other things. It would bubble up soon enough. It always did.

Meanwhile, the seasons turned. Two weeks of sunshine bright as heartbreak scrubbed the fall sky clean, and then, all at once, the trees dropped their colors. Halloween arrived in a scent of leaf fires. Jack-o'-lanterns leered from darkened windows and grammar school goblins stalked the streets under Harold Crawford's watchful eye. By midnight the goblins were abed, the jack-o'-lanterns extinguished for another year.

A taste of winter tainted the air, and the earth itself lurched a night closer to autumnal sleep. High in its alpine fastness, unknown to Harold Crawford, an uneasy sleeper writhed in dreams.

Below, Crawford kept his watch, pondering demons.

Delbert Grubb showed up the night of November thirteenth.

The monster was up to four by then. Crawford gave his days to a frenzied search for leads, his dreams to gore and tears, the girl twisting underneath him, the hungry grin of the blade. Waking in the graveyard of the night, he showered the stench of the abattoir away, dressed in a clean uniform, and sought the streets.

"I thought you'd never show," a voice said from the backseat as he slid behind the wheel of the cruiser.

Crawford felt a spider climb the knuckles of his spine. He squeezed the wheel until his joints turned white. He closed his eyes.

"Now is that any way to greet an old friend?" said Delbert Grubb.

"You're dead. I killed you a long time ago."

"Do I *look* dead?" the voice asked, and almost against his will, Crawford felt himself turning in the seat.

He stared into his own face across a gulf of years.

If Delbert Grubb was dead, he didn't look it. Through

the lattice of the cage, he looked vigorous and unchanged and *alive,* his big face square and grinning
under a cap of close-cropped hair. In the glare of the
dome light, his eyes glittered like shards of glass, cold
and unafraid of cutting. Crawford saw himself in those
eyes—and knew suddenly that no matter how far he ran,
no matter how fast, Delbert Grubb would always be
there, waiting patiently inside him, biding his time. Delbert Grubb owned a piece of his soul. It was more than
Crawford could bear, and to save himself the agony of
staring it in the face, he swung shut the door, plunging
the car into darkness. He twisted the key savagely and
goosed the cruiser onto the twisting two-lane macadam.

Down through the Run they rode, skirting the edge
of Stoney Gap Lake and slipping past the municipal lot
where Crawford had spent his first night in the Run all
those years ago. And that brought it all back.

"Glad to see me, Harold?" Delbert Grubb whispered
close at his ear. Crawford could feel his breath, warm
against the back of his neck.

"I never wanted to be like you."

"You never had a choice. You and I, we're one and
the same, and I won't be denied, old friend. Not tonight." Delbert Grubb rattled the mesh, and when Crawford glanced in the rearview mirror, he grinned. "You
can't keep me caged up any longer."

"I never wanted to cage you up. I wanted to kill you.
I wanted to burn you out of me."

"Well, *something* kept me caged up, something in this
shit-pot little town. You ever wonder about that, Harold? You ever wonder what it was?"

Crawford said nothing.

"I know you have. Because *I've* wondered, and what
I wonder, you wonder. We're two peas in a pod, old
friend."

"Shut up," Crawford said

The tires sang a different note as the car crossed the
Stone Bridge. On the other side, Crawford headed
north, searching the shadows out of habit.

"You'll never find him, Harold."

"Find who?"

"The man you're looking for. The rapist."

"I'll find him."

"When? After he's done another one? After he's done ten? After he's started cutting them? You'd like that, wouldn't you, Harold?" Grubb pressed his face to the cage. "*Ooooh, help me, help me. I got a demon inside me!*" He laughed. "You've heard that before, haven't you? But you can't quite place it. You know why?"

Crawford said nothing.

"Because you don't want to, that's why. You like it. You like what he's doing."

"That's a lie."

"Is it? What about the dog, then? What about Boy?"

"You shut up about that."

"*Make* me."

The cage rattled in its frame. Glancing into the mirror, Crawford saw that Grubb had wormed his fingers through the grid and dragged his face so close that the mesh tattooed his cheek. He whimpered, doglike, fearful, one moist eye rolling. "You remember this, Harold? Huh? You remember this?" He twisted his features into a mask of tongue-lolling desperation, and time slipped, plunging Crawford into killing heat. The dog scrambled away, gray coils of intestines unspooling at its guts. Excitement welled up within him, pressure building at his groin.

"What about Boy?" Grubb was whispering. "You—"

Crawford's foot came down hard on the gas. "Shut up, I said—"

"—liked the way it felt—"

"—shut up, shut up, shut—"

"—didn't you? You got off on it. You came in your fucking uniform like a boy and you *liked* it!"

Crawford slammed on the brakes and twisted the wheel hard left. The road whirled around him, streaks of darkness and light. The car shuddered to a stop, the engine stalling.

Crawford drew a deep breath.

Silence.

"Even if you find him, Harold, even if you stop him, it won't bring them back. Not the girl and not LeMarius Oxford, either. You can't save them."

Crawford felt tears slipping down his cheeks.

"Please," he said. "Please—"

"Let's take a little ride," Grubb said.

Crawford plucked the guy out of an otherwise empty rest stop on I-77 at just after one that morning. Delbert Grubb told him how to do it: Just turn on the blue lights, he said, just step out of the car and take him.

Crawford did it as the guy came down the walk from the rest rooms. The guy was slim and neat, with close-cropped blond hair, maybe thirty-five. Worried about a ticket, you could tell.

"Is there a problem, officer?" he said.

Crawford just stood there, silent, a titanic battle raging within him. He could sense Delbert Grubb watching him from the cruiser, could feel deep at his core that tidal pull of rage and desire.

The guy took a step forward, his wedding band glinting in the orange glare of the halogen streetlamps. Looking at it, Crawford felt a sick wave of vertigo crash over him, as though he had fallen free of the spinning planet. Out on the highway a truck downshifted for a grade. Grubb's voice—

—let's take a little ride—

—rang inside his head, and the world rocked down around him once again. He felt abruptly stronger, settled and sure.

"Are you al—" the guy started, but Crawford lifted his flashlight.

"Problem with your car, sir. You check these tires?"

"There's something wrong with my tires?"

Crawford waved the flashlight. "See there?"

The guy stepped closer to his car, a Pontiac Sunbird, Florida plates, and Crawford knew suddenly how it was going to happen, knew it to the core of his being, knew it in his sinew and his bones. His senses sharpened, his surroundings snapped into razor-edged focus. He caught a hint of the guy's cologne, his nostrils flaring. The pavement shimmered in a wash of molten orange. The air tasted of highway, of diesel and iron.

"What?" The guy leaned forward to take a closer look, and with one smooth motion Crawford reversed the flashlight in his hand and brought it crashing down.

The guy never said a word, just folded over and settled, sighing, to the pavement. Two minutes later, Crawford was back in the cruiser, pushing hard for home.

In the end, they were together, he and Delbert Grubb, there in the barn with the big doors flung open to a deluge of gossamer moonlight.

"Scream," Delbert Grubb whispered, and the guy screamed. He screamed for mercy and for God and for Mommy, screamed his hatred and his fear and sorrow, screamed to twenty-six acres of nothing—of fallow farm and woodland and unblinking stars.

"No," Crawford whispered. "No—"

But when Grubb leaned forward and handed him the knife—

—*you always liked the wet work, Harold*—

—Crawford bent to the task at hand, feeling the throb of a big engine waking up inside him and knowing that it was this he had been longing for in silence for so long.

Afterward, he was alone.

Alone as he dug the grave. Alone beneath a dawning sky as he wrestled the meat into the hole. Alone as he shoveled black November earth into the dead man's face.

And then he heard a stirring in the leaves behind him. Delbert Grubb grinned.

"One more thing, Harold," he said. "The line you've been trying to remember? The bit about the demons?"

Crawford dropped the shovel and straightened up, his hands blistered and aching at his thighs.

"You talked to the guy eight or nine years ago. A child abuse case. It never went to trial. Remember?"

And Crawford did. He remembered it all: the Crook's

Hollow trailer park where it had happened; the girl; and the guy himself, her common-law stepfather, lean and grizzled and sobbing as he blamed the demon inside him. In the end, the girl had changed her story, the sex suddenly consensual despite her stepfather's confession. Crawford remembered the magpie gleam in her mother's eyes when she came to tell him, like a crow toying with a shiny piece of foil. He even remembered the guy's name.

"Kimball," he said. "Earl Kimball."

"That's right, Harold. And that's the way we'll work it. You scratch my back, I'll scratch yours. But remember this: It's never going to bring them back, not the girl and not LeMarius Oxford, not our poor friend there in the dirt."

"Maybe not," Crawford said. "But it's a start."

Somewhere in the ridges above him, the creature writhed in agony as the pain built to a crescendo and slowly died away.

Crawford turned to his work. When he looked up again, Delbert Grubb was gone. He would be back, though. Crawford understood that now.

It was midmorning by the time he made his way upstairs to bed, his shoulders aching, his hands blistered from the shovel. He lay awake for a long time, and when he fell at last into a thin, uneasy sleep, he dreamed once again that he was walking along that broken shore. The black figure heaved in the distant tide, and as Crawford drew closer, he found himself possessed once again by the wild hope that he might yet save the drowning man, that everything might yet be forgiven. He plunged into the surf, the dark water rising around him. With trembling fingers he touched the figure at last. Bloated and noxious—long past any hope of salvation—the corpse turned its ravaged features to the sky. Crawford found himself staring down at his own decaying visage, into the blasted face of all his hopes and dreams.

Prelude to a Storm
The Present

Chapter 14

He woke to darkness, in the grip of dread: a thunder of wings, the old familiar rush of fear and guilt.

Perry, he thought, *Perry—*

"Henry?"

Hands touched his shoulders and face. Henry thrashed, blind with terror, and then the sound of the voice erupted like a flare inside his mind, illumination, her voice and the scent of her body, the taste of it against his tongue. The hours just past came flooding back to him. Frustrated and exhausted from a day of sorting and re-sorting papers—his father must have kept everything—Henry had arrived at the Tipple late. He'd wanted a nightcap, that's all—a nightcap and maybe an hour of company. But Emily, flushed and harried from running drunks, had brightened when she saw him, and Henry felt an answering shift, a tectonic realignment along some hidden emotional fault line. He had come back to the Run because of his father, he realized suddenly, but Emily was one of the central reasons—maybe *the* reason—he had elected to stay.

The insight rendered Henry nervous and overdirect. After the bar had emptied, he'd simply blurted the words out, like the proposition of some overeager hustler on the make. *Come home with me,* he'd said, wincing at his own clumsiness, and forestalling her reply—

—not yet, it's too soon—

—with an upraised hand.

Just think about it, he said.

She had slipped a Gene Ammons disc into the stereo and turned away. Muscling cases of beer out of the storeroom, Henry had kept his eye on her, trying to read her answer in the set of her shoulders. She was wiping down the bar when he finished rotating the fresh beer into the coolers.

Emily, he had said.

I can't.

I'll go, then, he said. He embraced her, but she held herself apart, her spine rigid under his hands.

Outside, the air was frigid, the sky starless, pregnant with snow. He sat in the Volaré for a moment, waiting for the heater to melt the frost riming the windshield. When he wheeled the car around toward the street, she was standing in the doorway.

He rolled down the window, and she bent to peer in at him, her breath fogging the chill air.

Can I trust you not to hurt me this time? she had said.

You can trust me to try not to.

She stared in at him for a long moment, and then she nodded, almost imperceptibly. *All right, then. I'll follow you.*

And now she was here, coaxing him into this embrace—

"Shhh, it's just a dream, shhh—"

—and everything got tangled up somehow, the flutter of her pulse beneath his lips and the nightmare world inside his head, the black corridors of dream.

Then she was warm beneath him and none of that mattered anymore.

Henry closed his eyes.

The first time had been awkward, a tangle of knees and elbows, old lovers getting reacquainted. This second time was sweeter, and in the moment of release, Henry slipped the traces of nightmare. Afterward, he felt the pull of sleep like gravity, dreamless and deep.

"You said a name."

The words jarred him awake.

"What?"

"In your dream. You said Perry Holland's name."

He lay still for a moment, thinking of that long-ago

July, the sky boiling with storm, Perry's dark hair slick across his skull. He recalled kneeling to push his way into the wormhole, dust motes whirling in the wavering glare of the flashlight, and . . . and—

Nothing.

He could sense the memory, embryonic, almost formed, waiting to be born.

"What is it, Henry?"

She had rolled to look at him, her face earnest in the shadows.

"Just a nightmare."

"You have a lot of nightmares?"

"Not really." He hesitated. "The same one over and over, actually."

"How long has that been going on?"

"Years. Most of my life, I guess. Two or three times a week."

"And you've never told me?"

"I've never told anyone."

She was silent. Then: "You have nightmares about Perry Holland?"

He laughed. "I—not exactly. Years ago, when I was twelve, Perry and I were fooling around up at Holland Coal. It was the day my mother died."

"The day of the flood?"

"Yeah, and—it sounds crazy—but something else happened that day. I don't know what. I just *lost* several hours somehow, most of the afternoon—just gone. Perry and I, we got caught in the rain. I had found this hole, a shaft into one of the old mines. The last thing I remember is worming my way into that hole. Perry was right in front of me. And then . . . nothing." He shrugged. "That night, I had this dream, this nightmare. I'm lost in the mines and something's after me. I don't know what. And I'm looking *for* something, too, and I don't know what that is either." He paused. "That's the dream, more or less. I've had it ever since, but it's worse, a lot worse, when I'm here in the Run."

She put her head on his shoulder, let one hand trail across his chest.

"So you keep running away."

"Not only from the dream, I guess. From whatever the dream means."

"You want to tell me about it?"

He thought about it for a moment, thought about those awkward high school years they had spent together, caught between the Run and Crook's Hollow, and afterward that single summer and the words she had used to end it: *If you leave, don't come back.* Yet he *had* come back, and she had given him another chance. *Don't blow it,* he thought.

Aloud, he said, "Yeah, I want to tell you everything."

But the words were hard to find. Even as they took form in the air around him, irretrievable, he wanted to draw them back. What possessed a kind of crazy logic in his own mind—his father's death, the dream and its variations, the obscurely sensed but inarticulate connections between them—

—it's time, Henry, come home—

—seemed bizarre when spoken aloud, even in the dark. By daylight, he knew, it would sound stranger still. By daylight, it would sound insane. Yet as the night grew colder and a light snow dusted the mullions, he forced the story out. He didn't know how long he talked—forty-five minutes, maybe an hour—but when the last word dropped into the dark like a stone, the ripples rolling away into silence, he could feel the full strangeness of the tale—ghostly visitations and wingéd unseen pursuers—bearing down on him. He drew a breath, waited, said, "It's crazy, I know—"

"It *sounds* crazy," she said, "but that doesn't mean it *is* crazy."

"What do you mean?"

"Facts and truth," she said.

"I don't understand."

"Remember what you told me at the church? Facts and truths aren't necessarily the same thing?"

His father's words.

He remembered all right. How old had he been when

his father had said that? Ten? Eleven? They had been sitting on the deck, gazing down through gauzy autumn dark as the lights in the town below began to wink to life. In those days—before his mother died, before his father retreated into silence—they could still talk about the things that troubled him.

Emily touched his hand. "For the sake of argument, let's assume that it's *not* crazy. How does it all connect in your mind?"

He hesitated.

"Don't think about it. Just answer the question."

"The mines," he said, "it all connects with the mines."

"Because of what happened to you and Perry?"

"I don't know."

"Tell me what you remember about that day."

"What I remember?" He punched at his pillow. "I remember *everything,* everything but those missing hours. I remember how my father told me not to go anywhere and how I went anyway. I remember how angry I was. God, I was angry. I remember the rain and Perry's face and the way my clothes smelled drying in Harold Crawford's car, and when we got home I remember thinking it was my fault—"

"What was your fault?"

"Everything. I should have been there to say good-bye. I should never have gone to the mines, never have abandoned Perry—"

"What?"

Henry paused, the dark room wheeling around him. He said the words again, slowly, the taste of them strange in his mouth: "I should never have abandoned Perry."

"Maybe you miss Perry," she said. "Maybe that's what you're looking for."

"I wonder what I'm running away from."

In the succeeding silence, Aquinas mewed softly. He leaped onto the bed and settled between them, purring— a scrap of shadow pierced by shining eyes, like bright and gleaming holes into another time.

Henry took a deep breath.

"I remember," he said. "I remember going down into the tunnels. There was a lot of rubble at first, but it cleared out some. It was damp and we hadn't gone very far before it was cold, too. I remember that—how cold it was even in July. Perry begged me to stop. But I wouldn't. I was so *angry,* and every time Perry spoke it just made me angrier. The whole time Perry was crying, and . . ." He took a deep breath.

"What?"

"I don't know. I just . . . I left him."

"Why?"

"I don't know. Next thing I remember we were outside. We had had a fight and Harold Crawford was there. My mother was dead. I knew it as soon as I saw the police car. Nobody had to tell me. I knew it the way I knew—the way I knew—Dad—" He paused for breath, swallowed.

"The way you knew what, Henry?"

"Nothing."

"At the church the other day, you were talking about the day your mother died. You said you were afraid someone would come and take your dad away, too."

"It's just the way kids think—"

She clutched his hand. "Don't run away from this."

"Jesus, Emily, don't you remember the talk—"

"Yes, I remember the talk but, Henry"—she massaged the tiny muscle between his thumb and forefinger, working the tension away—"you have to say it. You have to face it."

"He killed her," he whispered. "I think he killed her. And everyone in town knew it."

She took his face between her hands and held his gaze. "Maybe they did, but no one—*no one,* Henry— ever blamed him."

"I did," he said. "I blamed him. And at the same time, I was so afraid they were going to take him away."

"No one was ever going to take him away from you," she said.

"But someone did," he said.

*   *   *

In the silence that followed, the gray room itself seemed subtly altered, strange, the knotted sheets, half visible, twisted into shadowy whorls and ridges like some alien landscape.

"I'm not crazy," he said.

She studied him for a moment, her face sober.

"I was ten when my father died, Henry. It wasn't even remotely my fault, but I felt responsible all the same." She rolled onto her back and rubbed her temples with the heels of her thumbs. "I *know* how it feels. Like you didn't measure up somehow."

"This is different."

"Is it? All I'm saying is the past doesn't go away. It has consequences. Your mother didn't just die, Henry. She suffered an enormous amount of pain and you had to watch that. You felt powerless, betrayed. And all that other stuff—your suspicions about your father, the flood, whatever happened between you and Perry—all that stuff hitting you at the same time, you'd be crazy if it *didn't* make you a little crazy."

"You think I'm *imagining* that my father was murdered? That it's some kind of huge psychological projection?"

"Not necessarily. I'm just saying that it makes a kind of sense. That maybe it helps you feel better about yourself if you believe he didn't kill himself, if he *was* murdered. That way you get a chance to save him, to hunt down his killer, to make it up to him."

"To make what up to him?"

"Whatever it was between you two. To forgive him, maybe."

He shook his head. "It's not that simple. I haven't talked to Perry in years. Why did he show up at Dad's funeral? And what about Asa, with these mystery investments in Holland Coal—when everybody knows the mines have been closed for decades? Or Penny Kohler. She says Dad went to the mines that night. She's almost sure of it. Everywhere I look the mines come up. Once or twice, I can accept as coincidence. But this—this is a pattern. Dad saw something up there, something that shook him up enough that he called Benjamin Strange—"

"He might have been calling about the church social, Henry."

"He said it was a big story. Why would Ben lie about that? *Something* is going on here, Emily. Somebody was in my house when I got home. I could hear him breathing."

He paused, that phrase—

—*I could hear him breathing*—

—resonating in his mind. He felt a fleeting moment of recognition—something about the ragged, laborious nature of the intruder's respiration—but before he could catch hold of it and take a closer look, Emily was speaking.

"But it's all so crazy. Murder and conspiracy—and then, if that's not enough, some kind of mystical force that wards off violence and disease."

He sat up and switched on the lamp.

"What about your mother, Emily—"

Her face hardened. "My mother doesn't have anything to do with this."

"Maybe she does. Not directly, but if there *is* some kind of force, if it *is* fading away, that would explain some things."

"Like what?"

"Like why she got sick. You said it happened overnight, like somebody threw a switch."

"I said it got *worse*, Henry. She's had emphysema for years."

"But the way you describe it, it fits the pattern."

"How?"

"It was a chronic condition, but she basically held her own against it, right?"

"Sometimes she took a turn for the worse."

"But that's the pattern. Those downturns, I bet they correspond to the periods Ben was talking about—the times when crime and illness surged."

He reached out to her, but she flinched away.

"I don't want to talk about this, Henry, okay?"

"Emily—"

"Look," she said abruptly, "I can't do this right now. Mom . . ." She took a breath, then looked up at him. "The doctors say it's just a matter of time now. Probably sooner than later. At first, I thought, maybe if we spent some time together, maybe it would help, but this . . ." She shook her head. "But this is— If I got my hopes up and—and something happened— If it didn't work out— I don't know if I could take that."

Her voice broke. She turned away, dislodging Aquinas.

The cat stalked away, the room silent but for the faint tattoo of his claws against the hardwood floor.

Emily's shoulders heaved.

"Hey," Henry said.

She shrugged his hand away. "This was a mistake."

"What?"

"I just can't do this. This is too fast." She sat up with her back to him.

"Emily—"

"This was a mistake." She stood, reaching for her clothes. "I'm not ready for this. I'm sorry."

He watched, paralyzed, as she dressed and hurried out of the room. And then something shook him awake, a shrill internal voice—

—*don't blow it this time*—

—that propelled him from the tangled sheets and into the hall, still struggling into his clothes. She was at the base of the stairs before he caught up with her.

"Emily—"

The look in her eyes—not anger exactly, but hurt and fear, a hurt and fear so deep he couldn't fully plumb it, as though he had touched some central place inside her, a nerve chafed raw over long years—stopped him cold.

"I didn't mean to upset you."

"You *need* so much, Henry. You always have. And right now, with Mom and everything, I just don't have that much to give. You understand?"

He nodded.

"I'll call," she said, "when I can. Okay?"

"Yeah, okay. That's fine."

She let herself out and he held that image in his mind for a moment, her slim figure poised against the dark, snow spitting down around her from the enormous pressing vacuum of the sky. Then the door shut, and he was alone in the silent house. In the dim kitchen, he made coffee and sat staring out into a welter of storm and night, his mind filling up with things he didn't want to think about. It was dawn nearly before his own words came back to him, barbed with a truth he hadn't even noticed.

I could hear him breathing.

Chapter 15

By the time Henry angled the Volaré into a spot on the courthouse square the next day, the snow had tapered off to flurries. He killed the engine, silencing the radio in the midst of talk about a second front rolling in later in the week. Beyond the windshield, the bank sign cycled through a litany of time (1:07 P.M.) and temperature (28° Fahrenheit).

Henry tugged on his gloves before he got out of the car. At the door of the *Observer*, he paused momentarily, steeling himself for the confrontation to come.

"Mr. Sleep!"

He turned at the shout.

Harold Crawford hurried across the street from the courthouse, waving his arms. He dragged in a long breath as he stepped onto the sidewalk. "I'm glad I caught you. It'll save me a phone call."

"You have something?"

"The lab work on your burglary. Nothing we can use, unfortunately." He paused. "You notice anything missing at the house?"

"No."

"All's well that ends well, then." He blew into his hands. "How are you bearing up?"

"Fine. I'm doing fine."

Crawford shook his head solemnly. "It's just a hell of a thing." He reached out and shook Henry's hand. "We'll keep working on it. I promise you that, Mr. Sleep. Meantime, you holler if we can do anything for you." He pushed his hat back on his forehead as he turned away. The gesture reminded Henry of the man who had driven him home nearly two decades gone, the young deputy nervously chewing at his lip as he turned to answer the boy's question:

It's my mom, isn't it?

I'm sorry, Crawford had said, and Henry could still recall the sympathy in that voice.

On impulse, he said, "Sheriff, there is something else."

Harold Crawford wheeled around to face him.

"My father," Henry said.

"What about him?"

"I was wondering. When you did your investigation, did the subject of Holland Coal ever come up?"

"Holland Coal?"

Crawford took a step closer, and Henry felt a twinge of doubt. Memory gripped him: the look on the sheriff's face when he had asked to see the case file, something like anger rocking down behind those eyes.

"I don't recollect anything like that," Crawford said. "Maybe I should look into it. Who is it you've been talking to, exactly, Mr. Sleep?"

And Henry—thinking abruptly of Crawford lumbering back into the lives of Asa and Penny, people who had suffered enough in all this mess—seized the next name that came into his head. "Raymond Ostrowski," he said.

"I see." Crawford glanced at the newspaper office and nodded. "Well, I'll check it out, Mr. Sleep, but it's hard to see what it could mean. Those old mines have been closed long as I've been in these parts. Like I said before, this kind of thing, it's awful hard to solve."

He held Henry's gaze for a long moment, and once again Henry had the disquieting sense of something else behind those pale blue eyes, the hateful regard of a serpent maybe, icy and remote. Then Harold Crawford turned away.

Henry watched him all the way across the street.

Grateful for the warmth, Henry shucked his coat inside the newspaper office, a long, narrow storefront tiled in green and white. The receptionist directed him to Ben's office, in the back corner, past a disused layout area complete with old-fashioned pasteup boards and a common work space where a lone reporter sat staring glumly into a computer terminal.

The door to Ben's office stood ajar.

"Working hard?" Henry said.

"Hardly working."

Ben sat with his feet propped on the radiator, staring out the window into the alley. Small and cluttered, the office smelled faintly of air freshener and cigarettes. On a table to one side of the desk, a computer cycled through screen-saving patterns. Beside it stood a radio tuned to talk. Ben silenced it as he spun in his seat to face Henry.

"You been listening to this stuff?" Ben asked.

"Not really."

"Heavy weather coming in."

"I didn't come to talk about the weather."

Ben looked up.

"Something on your mind, Henry?"

"You lied to me."

Ben sighed. "Yeah, I guess I did. You want to come in and talk about it?"

Henry closed the door and sat down. He watched as Ben raised the window sash and fished a pack of cigarettes from his shirt pocket. "You mind?"

Henry shrugged.

Ben lit the cigarette. "They give me hell for smoking in here."

They were silent for a moment.

Henry said, "You know, for some crazy reason, I trusted you."

"Well, you should have."

"Why? You broke into my house, practically killed—"

"Don't be dramatic, Henry. I knocked you down—and doing it just about killed *me*. By the time I reached my Jeep, it was all I could do to breathe. Drove half a mile, pulled over, and coughed. I thought I'd never quit coughing."

Henry leaned forward. "Why?"

"Well, I have cancer—"

"Goddamn it, Ben—"

"Hell, Henry, it wasn't personal—you know that. I was just following the story. When I heard you out there, I didn't know who the hell you were—but I sure as hell didn't want to wind up like your father." He dashed ashes out the window.

"All that stuff you told me the other night—is that true?"

"Far as I can tell."

Henry dug the yellow scrap of paper from his pocket and tossed it on the desk. "You took something from my father's office," he said. "I want it back."

Three yellow sheets. Henry didn't know what he had expected—something more complete, he supposed, something with a nice tidy explanation. Certainly something more than three crumpled sheets haphazardly covered in his father's cramped hand.

Folding them over, he started to stand.

"Maybe you should take a look at them first."

"I've got plenty of time to look at them."

"Don't be a fool, Henry. I can help you."

He hesitated. "They were on the desk?"

"*In* the desk. In a file full of tax receipts."

"Hidden."

Ben shrugged. "Maybe." He flipped the cigarette out the window. "Why don't you take a look?"

Henry thumbed through the papers. On the first page, his father had scrawled a list of surnames and dates—perhaps twenty of them—but he couldn't see a pattern. He looked up at Ben.

"Whose names?"

"Various folks unlucky enough to get themselves murdered in the last forty years or so. The dates check out."

"None of them were killed in the Run?"

"Not a one. The paper reported them all, but none of them died here. I suppose that's what he was checking."

The second page looked more familiar, notes toward a

sermon maybe, or one of his father's obscure theological speculations: lists of biblical references, some hasty notes on Hebrew etymology.

"You make anything of this?"

"Greek to me," Ben said. "Or Hebrew. Maybe it's something else altogether. It just got mixed in."

Henry flipped to the third page, a second list of twenty or so names and dates. Here there was no mistaking the larger pattern. The dates fell in clusters—'78, '80, '87, December '96—and Henry recognized a couple of the names—Kimball and Samford—from his previous conversation with Ben.

"I've tracked it further," Ben said. "Seventy-three and sixty-six. Random intervals, but the pattern holds—death and crime rates skyrocketing overnight and dropping off just about as quick. Each time it happens things get a little worse, but people always stopped short of killing each other."

"Until now."

Ben nodded solemnly. "That's right. Until now. Sort of makes you wonder what's going to happen next, doesn't it?" They were silent for a moment, and then, his voice soft, Ben said, "Your dad did the heavy lifting, Henry. It was just a matter of checking the names and dates."

"So you lied about that, too."

"Christ, Henry—"

"He do the research here?"

Ben sighed. "I don't think so. Library, I suppose."

Henry rattled the sheets of paper. Below the list of names, his father had sketched a crude circle. A series of x's had been scrawled in black ink at varying distances from the perimeter. Two red x's appeared within the circle. "What about the sketch?"

"That's where it really gets interesting," Ben said.

The diagram of the circle and the black x's, it turned out, was a rough map.

"It took me a while to figure that out," Ben said, "but it was fairly obvious once I had thought about it. If no murders had been committed in the Run in a century or more—maybe never—it makes sense to try to plot the effect, to figure out where the borders are."

"But he didn't use a map."

"He didn't have to. He grew up here, right?"

"He lived here just about his whole life."

"So he knew the town, knew the lay of the surrounding country. And because he was only interested in getting a rough sense of the pattern, he probably just sketched it from memory."

"So why's this especially interesting?"

Digging through a stack of papers on the desk, Ben produced a second map of the region, a real map. "Take a look," he said, unfolding it.

Standing, Henry saw that here and there Ben had plotted x's like those on the sketch. There might have been forty of them, in green ink, scattered over the nearby towns; beside each, Ben had noted the date, recording them as far back as 1937. In the Run itself, three red x's appeared, one in the southeast quarter of the town, off Mill Creek Road—that would be the Samford murder—another on Widow's Ridge—

—my father's x—

—and a third in the wooded strip between Crook's Hollow and the abandoned Holland Coal property, where Ian Barre must have died.

Around the town, hugging the edges of the closest of the green x's, Ben had drawn a thick black circle. All three of the red x's fell inside the circle, as did the whole of Sauls Run and Crook's Hollow, the abandoned mines, and a stretch of the rugged and sparsely settled country to the north.

Ben smoothed the map with knotted fingers. "It comes to an area roughly fifteen square miles in diameter. Some of the murders"—he jabbed a finger at the map—"here and here—come close to the edges of the town, which is part of the reason nobody noticed this for so long. But here's the interesting part. If you plot the center of—"

But Henry had already noticed it—noticed it with a species of sick dread.

Holland Coal, he thought.

So Raymond Ostrowski had lied. Something *was* going on up there, something more than a little EPA-dictated cleanup.

He closed his eyes and took a long breath. When he opened them again, he collected the crumpled yellow sheets, folded them twice, and slid them into an inner pocket of his jacket.

"That's everything you know?"

Ben lifted his hands. "That's all of it."

"I'll be going then."

He pulled on the jacket and opened the door. Halfway through the maze of empty desks—even that lone reporter was gone—he heard Ben speak again.

"Henry—you have to understand. I didn't know who to trust."

He turned to stare at the older man, framed in the doorway of his office. "I do understand. Perfectly." He paused. Then: "I spoke to Crawford today. They couldn't match your prints. So you needn't worry about that anyway."

"Godamn it, Henry, give me a chance here. If we work together—"

"I'll think about it."

He turned away.

Outside, the Run lay quiet. Henry stood by his car for a moment, thinking of Holland Coal. So it was true, he thought. Somewhere in his past, in the abyss of his memory, the labyrinth of dreams, lay a link to his father's death—a link he could not yet begin to fathom.

Chapter 16

He tracked Ostrowski down the following day. Around one—a safe three hours before Emily's shift—he turned the Volaré north toward the Tipple. Yet he couldn't help thinking of her as he got out of the car, the bruised sky an answer to some indefinable ache within him.

Last night he had almost called her—had actually lifted the receiver, started punching the number. But that wise inner voice had counseled otherwise. Give her the distance she craves, it told him. She hadn't broken it off, had she? She had only asked for time.

Besides, what was the hurry?

The dead were dead.

If he had anything, it was time.

He had cradled the receiver and surrendered to his restless dreams. Now, stepping into the Tipple with Frank looking up from his paper there behind the bar, Henry resolved to put her out of his mind, to focus on the matter at hand. For now anyway, for just a little while.

But Frank hadn't seen Ostrowski for days. "He comes in spells," he said, "and then lays off for a while. You might try his place up on Breedlove Road."

Breedlove Road was a narrow country lane that dipped and climbed through the barren hollows west of town, and on his first pass that way, Henry missed the place entirely. But as he swung back toward the Run, he glimpsed it high in the shadow of a ridge, just as Frank had described it: a rusting trailer on a cinder block

foundation, half hidden by pine and barren hickory. The
rutted drive wound around back, where the trailer
sprouted an additional room, a tumorous growth of
weathered shanty boards and tin. Henry parked the Volaré in the lee of a dented Dodge Charger and killed
the engine.

Dogs whimpered quietly as he got out of the car.
Turning, he could see them, a moil of lean hounds in a
run forty yards back under the trees. They regarded him
solemnly through the interlocked diamonds of the chain-
link enclosure.

"Anybody home, guys?" he said.

When he stepped toward them, the dogs scattered like
a covey of startled quail, fleeing to the hidden reaches
of the run. Odd. Henry peered into the trees. There was
something there, slumped bonelessly in the shadows at
the far corner of the kennel, but he couldn't quite make
it out. It might have been an empty sack or an outcropping of stone. It might have been a dog.

"Hey," he called, but if the thing *was* a dog, it didn't
move. Henry felt a faint, uneasy stirring in his guts. He
hesitated, thinking about walking up there for a look.
Then the wind picked up, shivering him as it cut down
through the trees. The hell with it. He hadn't come here
to stare at a dog run.

Pulling his jacket closer, he turned away. The yard
was barren and strewn with debris—a dented washing
machine, a rusting sink basin, a mound of broken cinder
block. Two cords of wood had been stacked against the
bole of a great oak, and the weathered tarp that had
been used to cover them snapped with every gust of
wind. Despite the slovenly surroundings, however, the
addition looked basically sturdy, the work of a capable
if inelegant carpenter.

He knocked on the door.

"Mr. Ostrowski," he called. And louder: "Hey, Ray!"

He knocked again, waited, then moved over a few
paces to peer through a dirty window. A wood-burning
stove glowed in a far corner, dimly illuminating a clutter
of Dumpster-quality furniture: a sofa and recliner, an

industrial cable spool turned on end as a table. An open bottle of whiskey stood on the cable spool, and a black-and-white television flickered nearby, bathing everything in its ghostly luster.

Henry pecked on the glass. "Hey, Ray! I know you're in there!" He rapped again. "Come on, Ray!"

Henry smacked the wall with his open palm, then stalked back to the door. "You lied to me, Ray! You lied about Holland Coal!" He pounded at the door, splinters digging into his fist. "That all you lied about? How come you can suddenly afford Wild Turkey, Ray? You want to tell me that? How come you're drinking such fine goddamn whiskey all of a sudden?"

He slammed his fist into the door one last time, feeling the ache of release in his shoulders, as though something bottled up for ages had finally been uncorked. Frustration, he supposed. Maybe even rage. Rage at all the lies, the half-truths and evasions. At his own long list of failures and inadequacies. The aching lacuna of memory.

He reached for the doorknob, felt it give beneath his hand, and paused.

Fuck it.

Twisting the knob, he swung the door wide, a wedge of storm light, thin as gruel, pouring itself across the dusty, rough-hewn floor.

"Ray?" he said.

An icy band of metal kissed the hollow of his neck.

In the woods to his back the dogs began to bay.

In the moment of frozen terror that followed, Henry could hear everything: the dogs subsiding into mewls and the bright hard click the gun made as the hammer locked back and the whiskey-tainted respiration of the man who held it, his boots scuffing the denuded soil. The man took another breath and Henry could smell him, too, the whiskey and more: cigarette smoke and the yellow tang of unwashed flesh and the stench of dog on his hands.

Henry swallowed coppery spit. The world steadied around him, and deep inside himself he found that ada-

mantine core of rage, unaffected. The rage pried open
his mouth, and using a voice that was nothing like his
own, spat words into the chill air:

"Was it you, Ray?"

Silence, then, the wind whickering among the trees.

He imagined the bullet smashing through his skull,
what it would feel like, what his father must have felt.
For a single reckless moment, his voice wild—

"Was it?"

—he thought he wouldn't mind dying here in the ice-
rucked dirt before this open door.

A heavy shove sent him stumbling into the room. The
door slammed behind him, plunging everything into a
chaos of poisonous twilight, the television chasing
shadow across the room. He fell to his knees, twisting
to face Ostrowski, squat and grizzled and coming on, the
revolver like a toy in his big hands. Henry scrambled
away. A lamp went over with a crash. Splintered boards
drew him upright and gasping, the frigid barrel of the
pistol tight under his chin, pinning him to the wall like
a bug.

"No," Henry gasped. "No—"

He swallowed, and they were still, frozen in the moment, no sound in the room but the heave of breath in
their lungs and the faraway babble of the television. His
mind seized upon it, for a moment could think of nothing else: just the absurdity of dying this way, in a half-
unfashioned shanty filled with Weather Channel drivel.
Then even that sloughed away, leaving only the two of
them, the gun wedged under his jaw and Raymond Ostrowski's face like a strained flag, his eyes maddened
and afraid.

"Please—"

Henry's mouth had gone dry. He paused, trying to
work up enough spit to get the words out—

"Don't. Please don't."

Ostrowski's eyes cleared, seemed to catch hold in the
moment. "You," he whispered.

Ostrowski drew a long breath and released it, wincing,
and then the cold pressure of the gun retreated. Ostrow-

ski looked down at it, clenched in his big hand, and then he looked back up at Henry and laughed bitterly and turned away.

Ostrowski coughed and lit a cigarette.

"What happened to the peanuts?"

"Reckon I'll be lucky to die of that spot on my lungs." He looked at Henry. "It was you, wasn't it?"

"What do you mean?"

Ostrowski grunted. Moving gingerly, like a man made of fine-blown glass, he picked up the bottle and poured three fingers of Turkey 101 into a jelly glass. "The sheriff."

He lowered himself carefully into the faded recliner by the cable spool and stared at Henry on the rump-sprung sofa. They fell silent, Henry thinking of Harold Crawford. *Who is it you've been talking to, exactly?* he had asked, his eyes as cold as sapphire chips in the setting of his face.

"He was here?"

Ostrowski just stared at him.

"I need a little help here," Henry said. "There's something going on here. Maybe Crawford's mixed up in it, I don't know, but I need a little help."

Ostrowski said nothing.

"Please—"

"Anything I say, it's between you and me. Understand?"

"Sure. Absolutely."

Ostrowski grunted. "He's in it, all right."

"How?"

"Don't know. Perry Holland is the one talked to me."

"Last fall?"

"November it was, not long after old Zachary took ill and Perry Holland got to runnin things. He came in the Tipple one night, said a fella up Copperhead mentioned my name. That EPA shit—that's what he told me, and it sounded reasonable enough. Lord knows I could use the money."

"But it's not true."

"No. I hadn't been up there more than a day or two and I knew that."

Henry said, "He wanted you to open up one of the mines, that right?"

"Maybe you want to tell me how you know that."

Henry said nothing.

Grimacing, Ostrowski leaned over to stub his cigarette out. "Way this works, I tell you something, you tell me something back."

Henry took a deep breath. "When we were boys, Perry and I, we sneaked into one of the old mines. We got lost there."

"What happened?"

"I wish I could remember." He lifted his hands. "I have these dreams."

Ostrowski laughed. "Funny you should mention dreams."

"Why's that?"

"Old-timers—fellas had worked them seams since before the big war—used to say Holland mines had haints in em. Said they'd heard tales of em from old times, back round the turn of the century."

"Ghosts?"

"Haints," Ostrowski said, as though speaking to a dense child. "Spirits. Nothin you could lay hands on, but you could feel em in the air. Men who worked them old shafts—they was all gone by then, of course, but people used to talk about it—they was prone to dreams, it was said."

An icy hand clutched Henry's spine. He leaned forward on the old swaybacked couch.

"In my dreams, it's like a maze, these run-down tunnels, these rotten crossbeams—"

"That's right," Ostrowski said. "It was them old shafts Perry had us workin in. Mines these days, you got a machine that drills holes and you put these bolts up there, eight feet long. Winches the rocks together, supports the roof. These old shafts, they musta been near a

hundred years old. They had wooden beams instead.
Slow going, it was, 'cause them old ceilings can come
down on you just any time.''

Ostrowski fumbled for his cigarettes, suddenly pen-
sive. "Another funny thing. Them Holland mines played
out forty years ago, but there was still coal in them old
shafts. I've done a lot of thinkin on that just lately.''

"What did you come to?''

Ostrowski didn't answer, his face changeable and
strange in the flickering shadows of the television. When
at last he spoke, he looked up and held Henry's gaze.
"I didn't always used to drink like this. These days, the
whiskey, it helps me sleep.''

Henry took a long breath. "Nightmares?''

"I wouldn't call em that exactly. I'm down in them
old shafts Perry had us workin in—but I'm not afraid
really. I just feel somethin with me down there—I don't
know how to put it exactly. It's like I got too close to
somethin down there, somethin powerful, and maybe a
little of it rubbed off against me. On my mind, you
know, and I'm workin it through when I sleep nights.''

"What about the others?''

"Weren't but six or seven—men like me every one of
em, short a dollar and inclined not to say much if Perry
Holland didn't want em to. But I heard a little talk of
dreamin all the same.''

He dashed his cigarette, turning it thoughtfully on the
rim of the ashtray. "All manner of things—old things
and strange ones—buried down there at the bottom of
the world. Way I reckon it, some old miner stumbled
across somethin down there, and Holland—Jeremiah's
father this woulda been, back before the first war—just
closed them holes and opened new shafts on the north
face. Plenty of coal in those days, no end of it in sight. So
he went where the diggin was easier, and men weren't so
prone to dreams. You boys were probably the first folk
down them old shafts in fifty, sixty years. Maybe even
the Hollands themselves done forgot what they found
buried there, and the coal they left behind.'' He held
Henry's gaze. "Sound right to you?''

Henry shook his head. "Nothing sounds right. Nothing makes sense."

Ostrowski nodded. "That's the Run for you. My daddy used to say the Run was a funny place. Old folk lingered here, he said. People got on unusual well. Holland mines never went union, you know. Bloody Mingo, Harlan across the river—they was like war zones. Holland mines wasn't no safer, the money weren't no better, but the unions couldn't stir up a lick of interest. People here was just content. Shawnee thought that mountain was holy ground. I keep wonderin if that's the reason—and if maybe I rubbed up against some of that down there, some old Indian medicine."

"Indian medicine?"

"Them mountains was old when the white man came," he said. "Full of gods and devils. Rub up against something like that, it's liable to touch your mind."

Gods and devils. Henry shook his head, thinking of the dream. The ever-encroaching dark. The thunder of onrushing wings. He looked up. "How about you? You see anything when you were working down there?"

"No." Ostrowski studied his whiskey for a moment, and then looked back at Henry. "But it never felt just right," he said. "And I was glad when it was done."

It was after three by then, the sky graying down toward dusk. Ostrowski got to his feet and shuffled across the room to punch up the fire.

"When did Crawford get involved?" Henry asked.

"He was sittin up there in his police car one morning when I got to work. That's the first I ever saw him. This woulda been late December, a day or two after Christmas. He and Perry Holland had some words, I guess. *Looked* like they was arguin anyway. Later that day Perry told us we was done. We'd opened the shaft and shored it up more than a mile down. Perry gave us a little extra money. To keep our mouths shut—that's how I thought of it."

He racked the poker and dusted his hands against his pants. Henry watched him walk back to his chair, older than he had seemed at the Tipple. He moved gingerly, his torso stiff, his arms held away from his body. Yet there was something else, too, as if a weight of years had all at once descended upon him. It took him a minute to catch his breath after he settled in the recliner.

"You haven't been back since?"

Ostrowski mulled the question over for a while.

Henry glanced at the television, waited. The room had grown warmer, now, almost oppressive. Sweat trickled at his collar.

Ostrowski said, "I ain't never had nothin. Worked all my life and I ain't never had a thing. You look at this place and you can see it ain't no way for a man to live." He waved his hand, a gesture that took in the entire room and the trailer beyond it, dingy and small and packed to the roof with the stink of whiskey and smoke and bacon grease. Ostrowski leaned forward, taking in a sharp breath. "I want you should understand why I did it. I lived my whole life in places just like this one, or worse."

Henry felt himself go cold inside, cold and empty and remote, the diamond vacuum between the stars. Suspicion—

—*it was you, wasn't it, Ray*—

—flared up inside him once again.

"What did you do?"

"Not long after New Year's Perry Holland shows up here. Sat right where you're sittin now, offered me money to do a thing for him—"

And now he said it aloud: "It *was* you."

"I don't know *nothin* bout your daddy. I told you that."

"What, then?"

"He took me down into them tunnels. He had some blastin caps; he wanted me to set some charges."

"He wanted you to bring the mountain down."

"Not the mountain. A stretch of tunnel is all, maybe five hundred yards. Dangerous work, and it weren't strictly legal, but the money—" He shook his head. "I never saw that kind of money."

"Did he say why?"

"Money like that, a man don't have to say why. But he was strange somehow. Panicky like. I don't have the word."

Wood popped in the stove, and Henry watched a single spark tumble from the grate and wink out. On the television, they were talking about snow.

"Up the Tipple a few nights back, I ran into this fella. They're up there diggin again, excavatin that patch of tunnel I brought down."

"Who?"

"I won't tell you that."

"Why?"

"Same reason I *did* tell you all the rest of it."

Grimacing, he fumbled at the buttons on his shirt for a moment. Then he stood, his shirttails falling back to reveal the sagging and bruise-swallowed flesh underneath. Henry gasped. Every breath must have been pure agony.

"I ain't got no love for Harold Crawford," Ostrowski said. "You want to dig into this, it's your own lookout. But there ain't no cause to drag others in, I guess."

Buttoning his shirt, he turned to stare out the window.

"You're the one sent him up here. I got that figured right?"

"I'm sorry," Henry said, standing. "I didn't mean to."

"Yesterday evening, it was. A warning, that's what he told me. I been layin for him ever since."

Henry glanced over at the old man. Ostrowski's eyes glimmered in the shifting light, and now Henry could see what he was staring at: the dog run, half obscured by the shadows under the trees.

"When I heard your car pull up," Ostrowski said, "I was up there near the kennel, diggin a grave." He shook his head sadly, and Henry thought abruptly of the discarded sack he'd seen in the far corner of the kennel, of the way the dogs had scattered suddenly, as if they were afraid.

"Them dogs is all I got," Ostrowksi said. "Man killed one of my dogs, said I should take it as a warning. I won't forgive him that."

Sauls Run
The Present

Chapter 17

Storm mantled the high ridges, gravid with the kind of weather that wrecks things. Cold that cracks stone and sheaths pavement in ice the color of the midnight sky. Wind that splinters oak and snaps powerlines. Snow that drifts shoulder-high, locking the narrow mountain passes. A hundred-year blizzard, a killing snow.

Nestled far down in the valley, her benighted streets steeped in storm presentiment, Sauls Run dreamed unquiet dreams. Gusts rattled windowpanes, and a dozen sleepers turned, crying out their night fears. In her wedding house, Cindy Cade dreamed young the man she had married these forty years gone, dreamed smooth his brow and his deep-set eyes untroubled. Not more than ten miles away, in the Crook's Hollow house where she had grown to have a woman's cares, Emily Wood churned her covers, chasing phantoms, dream mothers, dying as they fled. Benjamin Strange dreamed of death as well, and woke suddenly in his musty apartment over the *Observer*, afraid to be alone. His hand shook as he reached for a cigarette, and the floor was cold under his bare feet as he sat up to brush aside the curtain and gaze into the square. A single light burned in the courthouse, but the windows of the county jail were dark, and they, too, were filled with dreamers, he supposed, dreaming of their freedom.

Every life a prison, every dream a dream of freedom.

What kind of life is this I've led, he asked himself, to die alone, unwived and without a child?

So the long hours wore on, the dreamers thrashing in their beds. Prosaic nightmares, the bitter fruit of stale anxieties, the bitter fruit of care.

But there were other dreamers, too.

And stranger dreams. Dreams of awe and fear that came to men who had plumbed that ancient mountain well. Dreams of haunts and spirits such as their fathers' fathers must have dreamed, dazzled with the cast-off sparks of an ancient and uneasy sleeper stirring restless in its first death agony as they scratched their puny legacies in earth and stone.

Asa Cade shifted in his bed, blew out the breath of whiskey that bought him sleep but no respite from dreams, and crying grieved a dying light, a beauty that he could not save. And Perry Holland dreamed as well, restless in his house atop its tongue of stone.

Dreamers, all of them dreamers. Henry in the house on Widow's Ridge, in flight through labyrinths of sleep. Ray Ostrowski out on Breedlove Road, alone and aching in his sour sheets. A handful of others, Perry Holland's handpicked crew of miners, uneasy sleepers every one, with a cold dawn waking and rubble waiting to be moved.

And in a lonely farmhouse east of town, Delbert Grubb dripped his cup of nightmare into Harold Crawford's sleeping ear. In near three decades on these streets, Crawford had been a good cop: Men owed him; men feared him. Soon enough, he'd have word from such a man on Perry's gang. Meanwhile, Delbert Grubb bided his time.

The mountains brooded over them all, ancient, wreathed in storm, shelter to a sleeper of their own. Buffeted by agony, that sleeper stirred toward waking— and fell once again into its own uneasy dreams.

Dawn comes slow to the mountains, and work won't wait. Mose Cavanaugh started his pickup in darkness and turned it toward the old Holland mines. On a work day, Cavanaugh might not see the sun at all, and indeed it had barely brushed the ridges when he led his six-man crew into the more permanent gloom under the mountain. Five miles across the ridges, the kitchen help at Ridgeview was already at it, too, mixing batter and setting tables while the nursing staff distributed six o'clock meds. By nine, Ben Strange was at his keyboard, Asa at his rounds.

By ten, the day was well under way.

But the dreams lingered—with Perry Holland in his third-floor library, gazing down at the Run like a jeweled toy in the deep cleft below; with Emily Wood, already at her mother's bedside more than three hours when the clock struck eleven; with Henry Sleep, thumbing through his father's notes and nursing Raymond Ostrowski's words—

—he's in it all right—

—into cold certainty.

They lingered with Harold Crawford, too.

Just after four o'clock, he leaned over a sink in the courthouse to splash cool water across his face. When he straightened up, Delbert Grubb was staring back at him from the rust-stained mirror.

"I'm done with you," Crawford said.

But Grubb only laughed. "I'm your own true self," he said, and Crawford felt that black tide drag him out. His mind reeled, all the faces he had tried so hard to forget leering at him. So much blood. Dear God, so much blood—

"You want it," Grubb whispered.

"No, I don't. I don't want to be like you—"

He closed his eyes, clapped his hands over his ears like a child. But still the voice was there—

—you want it you know you want it—

—it would always be there, it was in his head—

"You're not there you're not there you're not there—"

He opened his eyes.

His own weathered face gazed back at him, his own raw eyes. "Nothing there," he whispered. He adjusted the water until it was scalding and scrubbed his hands raw. When he could stand it no longer, he dried them and tapped the mirror with his fingertips. "Nothing there," he said again and let himself out into the corridor.

But he was fooling himself, he knew. An unseen other walked beside him. Everything he thought or did these days wound back to Delbert Grubb.

Even his instincts as a cop had betrayed him, leading him to Perry Holland's operation in the old mines. Crawford had heard the same talk as everyone else, but the rumors rang false to him. Not a single document had come across Crawford's desk from the EPA. And not many federal dollars came into the Run without coming through the courthouse first. Curious, he'd taken a drive up to Holland Coal, just to check things out. The old adversary had risen up inside Crawford that morning, and Perry Holland could not stand against him. So they had gone down together—Holland and Crawford and Delbert Grubb within him—down and down into those crumbling passages—

Crawford stepped into the sheriff's office. He had vowed not to think of that strange journey, yet he couldn't help it somehow. It explained so much—the sense that the Run had stilled those hungry currents within him, the sense that even now that black tide was rising to reclaim him, this time for good.

He filled a cup of coffee from the percolator behind the counter, sugared and creamed it with trembling fingers, and turned to take refuge behind the door with his name etched on the glass. Thank God for the privacy of that office. It had been a calculated risk, running for sheriff—the solitude of that inner sanctum versus the possibility that someone would link his face in the paper to Delbert Grubb—

He laughed bitterly to himself.

For it had brought him full circle once again, hadn't it, this labyrinth of thought? All roads to Rome, Delbert Grubb looming up at every turning of the way. Once again, Crawford felt the lure of that ominous tide.

"Sheriff?"

"Yeah, Abby?" He turned to look at the receptionist,

a matronly graying woman, her eyes blinking owlishly behind her thick glasses.

"Henry Sleep came in—"

Crawford sighed. "I don't have time for him today, not with this weather coming in."

"He's in your office," she said.

Henry Sleep was looking out the window when Crawford closed the door and put his coffee down on the desk.

"You wanted to see me, Mr. Sleep?"

"That's right."

"Well, those clouds are supposed to dump a couple feet of snow, so I don't have a lot of time right—"

"I don't care."

In the charged silence that followed, Henry Sleep turned around. Crawford thought once again of that grief-stricken boy in the July rain, struck anew by a continuity of feature, of attitude. They shared something unformed about the eyes, boy and man—a certain hesitancy and sadness, a certain—

—*cowardice,* Delbert Grubb hissed inside his head—

—but that wasn't the right word either. Detachment might be more accurate—as if Sleep refused to embrace the world, it having wounded him too grievously, too soon. Yet something else glimmered in those eyes now. Determination, maybe. Or maybe anger.

Something that set Delbert Grubb on edge within him. Crawford stifled the urge to lash out. He sat down. "Is there a problem, Mr. Sleep?"

"I was hoping maybe I could see that file now."

"The file on your father's suicide."

"That's right."

"I think we already discussed departmental policy."

"Maybe you could make an exception."

Crawford shifted the stapler on his desk to get at the stack of papers under it. "Look," he said, glancing up at Sleep, "we can talk about that later, but I just don't have time right now, not with this weather coming in."

Sleep ignored the hint. He crossed the room and stood

on the other side of the desk. Close up, Crawford noticed how tired he looked, how worn. A muscle jumped at the corner of one bloodshot eye.

"Maybe you didn't hear me the first time. I don't care about that."

Crawford felt a surge of anger, that oily undertow, anxious to suck him down. Standing, he took a deep breath. He placed his hands flat on the desk and put his face close to Sleep's. "I understand your frustration, Mr. Sleep, but there's no call to talk to me like that. I've been doing everything I can to help you—"

"I don't believe you."

Delbert Grubb laughed. Audibly.

Crawford jerked like a man shocked, dashing the coffee across the reports lying on the desk. He stared dumbly at the spill for a moment. When he looked up, he saw Delbert Grubb over Sleep's shoulder, lounging against a row of file cabinets in his LAPD blues. Crawford could even smell him, seaweed and brine, dank things rotting along a broken strand. Yet Sleep just stood there, as though he had heard nothing at all.

Because he hadn't, Crawford told himself. Grubb's not there. There's nothing there—

But this time the little invocation didn't work. Del Grubb didn't disappear. He just smiled mockingly and aimed a finger at Crawford, his thumb jutting up like the hammer of a pistol. Henry Sleep shot a glance over his shoulder, as if to see what had captured Crawford's attention. Crawford wrenched his gaze away. With trembling fingers, he snatched up the Styrofoam cup and dropped it in the wastebasket.

"Now look what you've gone and made me do," he said, his voice slipping away from him, sounding too loud in his own ears. Reining it in, he went on. "We've been working on your case every da—"

"Then why can't I get a straight answer out of you?"

"I don't know what you're talking about, Mr. Sleep."

"Bullshit!"

A long time ago, in another life, Del Grubb had gone hiking with a friend, a climbing enthusiast, in the Sierra

Nevada. He had tried a fifty-foot rock face, working a guide rope anchored by his buddy. Maybe two-thirds of the way up—thirty-five or forty feet from the ground— he had slipped, swinging free into space, the rocky shale below wheeling under him for a single heartrending instant before the safety harness yanked him to a stop. That was how he felt now. Like a man who has inadvertently stepped into an abyss. Like a man in free fall, about to hit the rocks.

"Do you think I'm stupid?" Sleep was saying. "You never wanted to know who broke in that night. All you wanted to know was what I might have heard from my dad or Asa Cade. That's all you ever asked about."

"This is ridiculous, Mr. Sleep."

"Is it?" They stared at each other in silence for a moment. "I think you were in something with him, something to do with the Holland mines. You and Perry and maybe Asa Cade. And somebody killed him to keep him quiet. Maybe it was you."

"You got no right to walk in here and accuse me—"

"No right? No *right*? You have the guts to talk about rights? I'm not even close to being done with accusations." Sleep jabbed a finger over the desk. "You're not going to get away with this. I'm putting in a call to the attorney general—"

"Now wait a minute here," Crawford said. "Just wait a minute." He dragged in a breath, swallowed. "Now listen—" he said, aware suddenly that his voice sounded desperate, sounded *guilty*. He didn't know what he was going to say, knew only that he had to speak, had to say *something*. "Now listen here—" he started once again, but this time Grubb interrupted him—

You'll have to kill him, Grubb said.

The shock of the phrase was so visceral, so intensely physical, that for a single panicky instant Crawford believed it had been spoken aloud. He actually stepped back, sending his chair whirling away on its metal casters. It fetched up against the radiator with a clang.

"I won't do it," Crawford said. "I told you I was done with you—"

Sleep whipped his head around, scanning the room. "Who are you talking to?"

You'll have to kill him like you did his father, Grubb was saying from over by the filing cabinets. *You'll have to blow his brains out the back of his head. You'll have to gut him like a fish. You—*

"Shut up," Crawford begged, squeezing shut his eyes. "Shut up *shut up shut—*"

But he felt that dark tide seize him—

—skin him flay him gouge his eyes out—

—those words like oily water drag him under—

"Shut up!"

Silence.

Crawford took a breath. Opened his eyes.

Del Grubb had disappeared.

Henry Sleep had stumbled back a step, his face stricken.

"My God," Sleep said, and looking down Crawford saw the stapler in his thick hand, felt the density of it, comforting and heavy, like a stone kicked up from the Marianas Trench, a hole so deep the light had never plumbed it.

"My God," Sleep said.

Kill him, Delbert Grubb hissed inside Crawford's head, but he opened his hand instead.

The stapler thumped to the desktop, and for a moment they both stared at it, mesmerized. Then Harold Crawford looked up.

"Get away," he said in a hoarse whisper. "Get away from here. Get as far away as you can—"

Then the door slammed, and Henry Sleep was gone.

Far down under the mountain, it was quitting time.

As his work gang started back, Mose Cavanaugh lingered for a moment. They had punched through the slate fall today, opening the tunnel into the galleries beyond—galleries Perry Holland had explicitly told him not to enter. Still, he could not help peering into them at least, probing the moted cone of radiance thrown by his cap light. But there was nothing there, just that old rubble-strewn tunnel sloping away at a gentle curve. Yet he shivered—and from more than the damp, clinging cold.

Cavanaugh had never liked the work, never liked the sense of all that earth looming above him, but when his time had come—he was twenty, then—he had gone down in the mines like his daddy and his daddy before him. It was what a man did. Seventeen years he gave to Copperhead Coal, riding the cage four thousand feet into the abyss, the weight of the planet itself bearing down upon him and the roar of the continuous miner in his ears. He used to dream of it coming down upon him, all that crushing weight.

He spat into the dust.

Three years short of his UMWA pension, Copperhead had laid him off. Yet as much as it angered him, it was almost a relief, not having to deal with the crushing pressure of the claustrophobia, all that swimming dark. But work was hard to come by in the Run, and when Perry Holland had come round, Cavanaugh hadn't been in any position to refuse. Besides, he remembered consoling himself, those old Holland shafts had been slope mines, only half as deep as what he had gotten used to up at Copperhead. Closer by half to sunlight, he had told himself. Maybe it wouldn't be so bad.

But it had been. It was worse.

"Hey, Boss! You comin?"

The voice echoed, doubled and redoubled by the endless tunnels, sourceless and somehow disquieting. For a moment he longed for the metal-screeching discord of a working mine. Something to disguise those echoes. He glanced back at the cluster of figures, their cap lights bobbing in the distance, and raised a hand.

"Be along in a minute," he called. "Hang on."

He turned to peer once more into the dark.

Something down there.

He sensed it somehow, he didn't know how, and not for the first time he found himself pondering his grandfather's tales about these old mines. *Haunted,* he had said. *That's why old Holland shut em down in the first place.*

Cavanaugh had always dismissed those tales as an old man's fancy. As a rule, his mind possessed the imaginative capacity of a cast-iron skillet. Just lately, though, he hadn't been sleeping well. Every night he woke brimful of terror and awe from dreams of tunnels and light—crashing tides of light, vast combers of radiance so bright and cold he could hardly bear to look upon them. Now, half a mile below the daylit surface of the world, the balance tipped imperceptibly toward terror.

He turned to go, suddenly anxious to catch up with his gang. That was when he heard it. A man could afford a touch of deafness on Perry Holland's wage, but by God, there were limits to self-delusion, and he heard something. He *heard* something. His bowels felt hot and loose suddenly, and he strained to see something—anything—in all that dark. But there was nothing there. Nothing at all.

Well, it was done, he thought. Or nearly so. Another day or two to clear out the last of the rubble and shore the top up, and it was done.

So he turned to go.

But all the long way back, he had it in his mind. That sound. A whisper like wind through faraway hills, the stir and feather of an ancient wing.

Emily had dozed in the early afternoon, weary of the odors of ammonia and nursing home food, the incessant babble of the television from the lounge down the hall. Weary of everything, not least of all herself. Sleep had brought no surcease. She had dreamed of Henry and her mother both. Now, waking, she found herself remembering his face as he had stood there on the porch, staring after her. None of it was his fault, yet she had blamed him somehow, held him responsible, as if he had betrayed her into seeking something for herself.

The phrase caught and rattled around inside her head, like a stone in a dry gourd. Something for herself. Just once, something for herself.

She glanced at the bed, her mother so shrunken that Emily could hardly recognize her anymore. She touched the old woman's arm, loose and marbled with veins, and then she went to the window, brushing dark hair from her forehead. Thick clouds hugged the ridges, not moving much despite the wind harrying a scrap of newsprint across the parking lot.

Snow coming. A lot of it, according to the nurses. She ought to run home, throw some things in a bag—

"Emily—"

She turned. The old woman had shifted in the bed. Her eyes flickered open, gray, unseeing.

Emily felt a moment of choking guilt—

—*something for myself*—

—as she poured a glass of water from the pitcher and held it to her mother's lips. The old woman drank greedily before letting her head fall back to the pillow. She seemed to go away for a while. Emily watched everything—animation, expression, color—drain from the seamed face as it relaxed into sleep.

She was still clutching the glass, her mind drifting, when suddenly the eyes snapped open once again. This time they were alert and aware, glimmering with the force of personality. The old woman's hand closed around Emily's arm in an iron grip, spilling water across the counterpane.

"Em," she said urgently. "*Em*—"

And this time she collapsed into something more than sleep.

Knowing it was too late, Emily punched the call button. Then she lowered her face to the old woman's bed and wept. She hadn't moved when the nurses got there a moment later.

With Sleep gone, Crawford fumbled blindly for his chair and collapsed into it, staring at the stapler like a man in a trance. Picking it up, he turned it in his hands. Time seemed to slip around him, and for a split second, he found himself once again across the desk from Henry Sleep, the moment as it might have been.

Kill him, Delbert Grubb hissed, and as if in a dream Crawford watched his arm lash out. A polluted surge of elation washed through him as it smashed into Sleep's face, breaking teeth. Sleep stumbled, his expression comically dismayed, and Crawford caught him a glancing shot to the temple. After that everything blurred together—his crazed scramble over the desk as Sleep crumpled, the stapler heavy as a chunk of primordial stone, the dull thud of flesh beneath each thunderous blow, Del Grubb's little litany—

—kill him kill him kill him—

—singing in his head.

And then, abruptly, the vision faded.

Bile flooded his mouth. The stapler slipped from his nerveless fingers. He was going to be sick.

Lurching to his feet, he stumbled into the outer office. "Sheriff—" Abby said, but he thrust his way past her. The corridor reeled before him, and then he was in the rest room, the door swinging shut as he leaned over the sink and emptied his guts, once, twice, a third time.

In the heaving, breathless moment that followed, he fumbled at the faucet, flushing away the stench of vomit. He rested his head against the icy porcelain.

"Please," he whispered, an entreaty, an appeal, but he could not say to whom. The God of his father's Book, maybe, the God who had abandoned him. The God who mocked his agony. Crawford felt a rush of righteous anger at the thought, a raw hunger for vengeance.

He lifted his face to the mirror.

"Come to me," said Delbert Grubb.

The figure in the mirror beckoned, and Crawford stepped forward to welcome the embrace, the Judas kiss. A final dam crumbled within him; a black tide took him out.

He was drowning.

Outside, the snow began to fall.

The Storm
The Present

Chapter 18

Voices. His head was full of voices.

On the sidewalk outside the courthouse, Henry lifted his face to the sky and felt the snow against his skin, a benediction. But it could not cool the debate raging inside him. It could not still the voices.

It's time, his father had said. *Come home.*

So he had come home. Home to death and mystery and love resurrected, home to dreams and portents. Home to madness.

Get away from here. Get as far away as you can—

Another voice.

And why not? he thought suddenly. Why not just get in the car and drive away? Away from the empty house on Widow's Ridge, from the mess he'd made of things with Emily and the madness Benjamin Strange believed to be the truth. Away from the town and away from the dreams. Away from the past. He owed no allegiance to the dead.

He knew this voice. He'd been listening to it all his life it seemed.

Get away, it said.

With trembling fingers, Henry took out his keys. He got in the car, letting his gaze slip down the arc of the Stone Bridge to High Street, the windswept curve of lake, Holland House atop its wedge of stone.

Somewhere in the town spread out before him, a church tower chimed out the hour of five. Night was coming on.

I got used to you running away a long time ago, Emily Wood said inside his head.

He started the car and backed out into the street.

He wasn't running anymore.

Sprawling and many-gabled, Holland House stood fast and mute against the ridges.

Henry got out of his car.

Wind plucked at him, spilling across the promontory to the water three hundred feet below. Spring would green the sculpted acres, but for now Holland House loomed up from its fallow grounds in all its wintry austerity, impervious and proud, less a house than a craggy outcropping of the hills themselves. Two long wings curved like entrapping arms from the central four-story core, alone lighted, the windows of the library blazing out above him.

As a boy, Henry had visited the house only once. Yet it had made a vast impression on him, hushed and huge as a medieval cathedral, dwarfing every sound. He could not imagine living in such a place, entombed in all those fathoms of silence. He could not imagine growing up here.

He rang the bell.

He waited for a moment, shivering, and then the door swung back. Perry Holland's mother stood within, frail and avian, unchanged. Even as a boy, during that single visit, Henry had sensed something haunted about her, as if the weight of history in the house, its generations of Holland men, willful and unremitting, had rendered her a shadow, without substance, nameless. Had he ever known her name? Perhaps not, yet he remembered *her* anyway, the lines of her face, the expression of mute inquiry in her flat, indifferent eyes. None of it had changed.

He shifted uncomfortably. Wind clawed at his back.

"I'd like to see Perry," he said. "If I could."

The old woman swung the door wider, admitting him into an enormous hall paved with flagstones. Glass display cases lined the walls—antiquated mining tools, he

saw, as exquisitely mounted and lit as museum pieces.
On either side, broad staircases curled gracefully to a
second-floor gallery.

"He's in the library, I imagine," she said. "I'll fetch
him for you."

"Wait—"

She turned, her face hawklike.

"Do you remember me, Mrs. Holland? My name is
Henry Sleep. When I was a boy, I came here once—I
was a friend of Perry's."

Her expression softened. "Perry had no friends. He
was a sweet child, but he became an unhappy boy." She
came closer. "Are *you* unhappy?"

He said nothing, at a loss for words.

"Was that your father I read about in the paper?"

"Yes, ma'am."

"Then you must be, I suppose." She hesitated, as if
she wanted to say something else, but just then a voice
sounded from the gallery above.

"Henry Sleep."

Henry looked up. Perry Holland leaned over them,
his arms crossed on the gallery railing. He wore jeans, a
billowing shirt of red silk. Brushing a lock of black hair
from his forehead, he descended, his boots ringing in the
vast space. "Henry Sleep," he said again, his voice neutral, an acknowledgment, nothing more. "Mother, take
his coat."

Henry watched him as the old woman collected his
coat. Close up, his narrow, patrician face triggered a
flash of memory: the rain-lashed mountainside, the vast
and echoing dark. Old guilt stirred within him.

"Hello, Perry," he said.

They stood in silence, taking measure of one another.

"Well," Perry said at last. "Come up to the library."

They climbed the stairs without speaking, leaving the
old woman below. As they slipped through a door on
the gallery, Henry glanced back at her, clutching his coat
and staring after them, her face forlorn. He thought of
Zachary Holland for a husband, taciturn and coldly
handsome, with eyes that gave nothing away, and felt a

dart of pity for her. What had she been before she came here? And what had Perry—delicate and feckless Perry, so much his mother's child—become with such a man for a father? But he had died, Henry recalled, and he said it aloud—"Your father died"—to fill the space.

"That's right." Perry gave him an inscrutable glance. "Rather suddenly, actually," he added as they mounted a second set of stairs, emerging into a broad corridor. "An aneurysm, that's what they tell me."

Through wide-flung double doors, Henry saw the high, book-lined library, running the length of the central facade. The chandelier sparked reflections in the fanlight windows, a dizzying labyrinth of books and walls, winding away into the storm-darkened evening.

"I'm sorry," Henry said.

"I am, too. I didn't think I would be. We never much cared for each other, my father and I, but I'm sorry all the same."

They faced each other in the doorway.

"It's no easy thing, this losing a father," Perry said.

"Your father was a good man," Perry said when they were seated. "When I was a boy, I used to envy you your father."

"He was a little remote, I thought."

Flames snapped in the fireplace, summoning lustrous reflections from the depths of the furniture, heavy old mahogany, polished to a fathomless gloss. The pleasant aroma of wood smoke enfolded them.

"Well, there are worse things than being remote," Perry said. "My father, he was bitter his whole life. I think he resented the fact that by the time he became master of Holland House so little remained to be master *of*. Hollands used to run this town, he always said. And I think that's what he always secretly wanted. So he lived a long, bitter life."

"How old was he?"

"Eighty-one. People hang on in the Run, don't they? They just hang on and on. My grandfather lived to be ninety years old and they say old Titus Holland—my great-grandfather—he lived to be well over a hundred. He went out shooting on the day he died. Or so the story goes."

"You don't believe it?"

"It's funny. I don't know what I believe anymore."

"There seems to be a fair bit of that going around."

"It wouldn't surprise me." Perry stared into the fire, his features veiled in flickering shadow. After a moment, he said, "What was your word? Remote? Well, my father was . . . cold, I guess. It's the best word I can think of, anyway. I don't think he cared for anyone very much, though he hid it well enough. But you could sense it about him. He had the capacity to be monstrous, and occasionally he was. From the time I was old enough, I always pitied my mother." He looked up suddenly, and fixed Henry with his gaze. "I guess that's all beside the point, though, isn't it? Somehow I don't think you're here to rekindle our friendship. So why *are* you here, Henry?"

"I've been looking into my father's death," he said. "Certain names keep coming up—yours, Asa Cade's, Harold Crawford's." He paused, but Perry said nothing. "The mines keep coming up, as well."

"Well, you've been busy, haven't you?"

"What are you doing up there, Perry? I hear things, but they all conflict."

Perry stood and paced to the long row of windows. "I don't make a very good conspirator, I'm afraid." Abruptly he turned to look back at Henry. "It all comes back to our little adventure up there, you know. Do you remember much about it, Henry?"

"No."

"Nor did I. Oh, I remembered some things well enough—what happened before we went into that hole, the sheer terror of being lost down there, lost and alone. But the heart of it—well, it was all distressingly vague."

Henry stared at his feet, suddenly unwilling to meet Perry's eyes. The words he'd used with Emily—

—*I never should have abandoned him*—

—swam up from the depths of his mind. He swallowed, his mouth suddenly bone dry. "Look, about that—"

"I was afraid of the dark as a kid—did you know that?"

"No."

"Terrified," Perry said. "I felt it closing in around me, suffocating me. I refused to sleep with the lights off. I wept. A sniveling cunt, that's what my father called me." He laughed. "Dad always had a gift for color."

"I was angry," Henry said. "Going in there, it was an act of defiance, a way of letting it out, that anger. You were crying, I remember that, and so—"

"So you left me there. Because you were angry. And maybe you had a right to be. That must have been the worst summer of your life. But it wasn't *my* fault, your anger. It had nothing to do with me. Can you imagine what it was like for me, alone in all that dark? I suppose you can't. It's always about Henry Sleep with you, isn't it?" Perry paused. "I used to have nightmares about wandering those tunnels."

Henry looked up sharply. "So when your dad died and you took over the family affairs, you decided to look into them."

"What if I did?"

Henry got to his feet. Night had closed in and Perry stood with his back to the uncurtained windows, framed in darkness. So he had been wrong, Henry thought. There was some Holland in Perry after all—he could see it in the obdurate set to his face, the cold anger in his eyes.

"It was all so long ago," Henry said. "Can't we put all that behind us? I need your help."

"Where were you when I needed you, Henry? I could have died down there. We both could have died. And you left me."

The fire popped in the stillness.

Henry said, "Why did you have Raymond Ostrowski blast a tunnel you had just finished opening?"

"You really have been busy."

"Here's what I think," Henry said. "Whatever it was

that haunted you, that haunted your dreams, you found it. But Harold Crawford found *you,* and Harold Crawford is dangerous. How am I doing so far, Perry? Have I got it about right?"

But Perry said nothing.

"So you went back to Ostrowski. You had him blast that tunnel, to protect whatever you found down there, to buy you some time to think about what to do with Crawford. Did you tell him it was a slate fall? Is that what you told him?"

"You tell me. You seem to know everything else."

"There's a lot I'm not sure of. Like what's down there, or why Asa and my father got dragged into this, or why my father had to die. But, yeah, I'm guessing you told Crawford there'd been an accident, a delay. And he kept the pressure on to reopen the tunnel. So now you're running out of time again, and you still haven't figured out what you're going to do." He stepped closer, his hands outstretched. "Maybe I can help, Perry. Why don't you let me try?"

"I don't need your kind of help, not after last time."

"Goddamn it, I deserve to know what my father died for."

"I don't know what you deserve, Henry. You're the one that excels in passing judgment, remember? That, and running away. All I know is that I'm done speaking with you. You can find your own way out. Just like I did, all those years ago."

He wheeled around to look out the window and squared his shoulders. A dismissal. Henry waited for a long moment, and then he turned to leave. But at the door, he paused to look back. "And your dreams, Perry? Now that you know?"

Perry Holland turned to face him.

"They're full of light," he said. "My dreams are full of light."

The entrance hall was empty.

Coatless, Henry let himself out into cutting wind and snow, the town barely visible below the escarpment, a paltry sprinkle of stars. He was opening the door of the Volaré when the old woman appeared out of the shadows.

"I brought your coat," she said.

"Thank you," he said, pulling it around him. "That was kind of you."

He reached for the door handle, but the woman didn't turn back to the house.

"What is it?" he said.

"I was listening."

He stepped toward her. In the swimming, snow-whipped light from the library, her sharp face was still and serious; her bright eyes did not move away from his.

"I'm afraid for him," she said. "Please help him."

"He'll have to let me. You'll have to convince him to talk to me. Can you do that?"

"I can try."

"Soon," he said. "Do it soon. Have him call me."

Another thought struck him, an image: Harold Crawford looming up behind the desk, clutching the stapler like an old stone savage armed. He touched her hand, leaned closer. "If something should happen to me, there's a reporter named Benjamin Strange. He's been looking into this. He lives in town, over the newspaper office. You could try him."

Nodding, a bare inclination of her head, she started back to the house.

"Mrs. Holland," he called after her.

She glanced back at him.

"What's your name?"

He thought she might have smiled. "Willa," she said, and then she went on toward the house. Henry watched through dark and whirling snow until the door had shut behind her.

Chapter 19

Henry braked at the bottom of the hill and sat for a moment, watching snow drift endlessly out of the night sky. It steamed off the hood in smoky curls and melted on the windshield, leaving ghostly smudges of water on the glass. He adjusted the heat, basking in the rush of warmth across his hands and face.

He studied the strip of pavement winding past into town. By midnight, the roads would begin to freeze, but it was early still. They might remain passable for hours. A left would take him down Mill Creek Road to High Street, across town, home. A right would lead him into the mountains, to Asa Cade's house. He thought of Asa—Asa with his mystery investments in Holland Coal, Asa with his dreams—and another disembodied phrase came back to him, another voice: *Cindy and I, you were the child we never had. She couldn't take it if something happened to you.* As if Asa had feared something *would* happen unless Henry were careful. Something dreadful. Something like the thing that had happened to his father.

Sell the house, Asa had told him. *Go.*

It wasn't hard to read his insistence as a warning.

Asa had seen what had been done to Quincy Sleep—what Crawford had done, Henry thought, feeling the certainty of it in his bones—and he was afraid.

He was afraid.

Henry felt his groin tighten, his testicles draw close against his body. He touched the gas, easing the Volaré

into the street, toward the mountains, where Asa Cade
awaited him.

The snow had picked up by the time he reached the
house, a seventies-era brick rancher blazing warmly
through a screen of pines. He got out of the car and
trudged toward the house through an inch and a half of
powder, his breath a plume of gray vapor. Wind-driven
grains of snow stung his cheeks.

He pushed the doorbell and listened as it chimed
dimly beyond the door. Thinking of Cindy's words—

—he's stone drunk more often than he's sober—

—he pulled back his sleeve to glance at his watch,
hoping he had gotten here before Asa crawled too deep
into the bottle.

Six forty. Early yet.

He pushed the doorbell again. Crossing his arms, he
stamped his feet and gazed back at the car, its nose
pointed down the long, twisting driveway. Blackness
pooled under the trees.

He rang the doorbell again, then leaned over to peek
through the narrow vertical window by the door.
Through the sheer drapes, he could see the bright hallway, a corner of the dining room. Nothing moved within.
His heart picked up a beat. A vein pulsed at his temple.

"Shit," he said quietly.

Lights blazed in almost every window. Surely they
were home.

Still . . .

He went down the stairs and across the yard to the
carport. Both vehicles were there, Cindy Cade's chocolate Mercedes and Asa's F-150, their rear ends dusted
with snow.

He stepped closer, peering into the shadowy interior.
Nothing.

The night was brighter than he would have thought.
The snow seemed to possess an internal radiance, a reflection of the lights from the house maybe. A silvery
gleam infused the scene, making the interior dark of the
carport blacker still by contrast.

Henry sighed, feeling that vein pulse at his temple.

He stepped between the cars, skating his hands along the chill metal sides to guide him. As his eyes adjusted, the vehicles assumed a shadowy solidity, their noses snug against the back wall of the carport. When he slid his hands along their hoods he found them cold.

He glanced at the gray square of the carport's mouth. The wind hurled a billowing white sheet across the yard.

He should go, before the roads started to freeze.

He had started edging back between the parked vehicles, when something else caught his attention, an odor rising up through the carport's layered scent of gasoline and exhaust fumes. Something burning.

His guts twisted.

Sucking in his breath, he sidled through the foot or so of space between the hood of the Mercedes and the carport wall. As he came around the far end of the car, searching the gloom for the concrete stairs to the side door, his foot snagged a rake propped carelessly in the corner.

It crashed to the floor. He jumped back, banging his leg against the side of the car. In the ensuing silence, the panicked drumbeat of his heart sounded like a cannonade.

Elsewhere there was no sound. No rush of footsteps in the silent house, no voices raised in challenge.

No one snapped on the carport lights.

Wind whispered across the roof of the carport.

He dragged in a lungful of frigid air.

"Jesus," he whispered.

Stepping over the rake, he felt for the first step with his foot and climbed quickly to the door. He was certain that it would be locked, but the knob turned in his palm and he eased it open, wincing as the hinges emitted a low-pitched whine.

A wedge of light fell into the carport and the acrid stench of something burning grew stronger. Narrowing his eyes against the brightness, he stepped into the kitchen and shut the door behind him. He surveyed the room swiftly and then crossed to the range, where a saucepan of soupy cheese sauce had boiled over onto a hot burner. The smell was awful, and the pot itself had begun to blacken. He switched the burner off and dropped the saucepan in the sink, wincing as the handle singed his palm. He wanted to curse, but he gritted his teeth and squeezed his eyes shut instead, for now he knew that something had gone dreadfully wrong here.

Sweat trickled down the narrow valley of his spine, and a metallic taste filled his mouth, the taste of dread and fear, his own black foreboding. Icy panic rose into his throat, and he swallowed deliberately, forcing himself to remain calm.

Focused.

He crossed the room and peeked into the dining room. The table had been set for two—roast beef and vegetables congealing untouched upon a platter, a bowl of steamed broccoli.

He stood there for a moment thinking of Cindy Cade—plump, dimpled, pleasant Cindy Cade—scuttling between the kitchen and the dining room with these items. Worried—he knew she had been worried—but determined to go on as normally as possible, though her husband had begun a slow degeneration into drunkenness, haunted by dreams he dared not share with her.

Henry folded his hands into fists and unfolded them once again. Whatever had happened, it hadn't happened long ago.

Was he alone here?

Panic hammered at him. He slipped through the dining room, pausing in the foyer to peer out into the snowy night where the Volaré awaited him. Then a quick glance into the living room, also empty, and down the hallway into the rear of the house. A bathroom, a glare of white fluorescent, his own startled face surfacing in a silver sheen of mirror. He snapped off the light, kept moving. A spare bedroom, also empty, and beyond that two doorways: to his left, Asa's office, the door slightly ajar; to his right the door into the darkened master bedroom, standing open. He paused here as a series of frenzied thoughts detonated in his mind.

The lady or the tiger?

He squeezed his eyes shut and drew a breath. A faraway voice was chanting hysterically in his mind—*What will it be now, door number one or door number two, door number one or door*—and he recognized that he had stopped thinking in any rational way when he stepped into the kitchen and smelled the flat, unpleasant odor of blackened cheese.

Yet a dread imperative urged him on.

He felt tears, hot against his cheeks, and it occurred to him in some distant corner of his mind, far removed from the hysterical babble—

—door number one or—

—that filled his conscious thoughts, to wonder how long he had been crying.

"I think I'll take door number two, Bob," he whispered to himself. "Let's hope it's the vacation getaway."

He stepped into the darkened bedroom and turned on the light.

Cindy Cade lay on her back just inside the door, three neat holes in her chest, like bloody mouths. There was more blood than he would have imagined. The room stank of shit and urine and an odor like burned rope that he thought might be cordite. Dead, he knew she was dead, she had to be dead, yet he found himself kneeling beside her—he thought he owed it to her—fumbling for a pulse and God God God her flesh was still warm—

He moaned softly, unconsciously, that question—

—was he alone here was he—

—blazing through his mind.

He gasped, letting her wrist slide limply to the floor.

Asa was on the far side of the bed. He did not crouch beside him, did not touch his flesh. Asa had been shot in the face, the impact fanning blood and hair and chunks of bone over the comforter, the headboard, the wall beyond. The nightstand had overturned, spilling change and matchbooks, magazines, an ashtray, a twisted pair of Asa's half-rim spectacles. And something else: a revolver and a box of bullets, just visible inside a broken drawer.

Unbidden, his mind dished up a grim little movie, Asa diving for the pistol as the intruder—

—*Crawford*—

—stepped over Cindy's body—

Henry felt his gorge rise. He stepped around the body, stumbled into the bathroom, and vomited into the toilet. He wiped his mouth with the back of his hand, flushed the mess away, splashed cold water on his cheeks.

Back in the bedroom, he fumbled numbly with the gun. Sooner or later, he couldn't say how long, he figured out how to open the cylinder. He shoved bullets into the chambers with trembling fingers, spilling three or four to the carpet. Sliding the box into a coat pocket, he returned to the hallway, the pistol clutched in his right hand.

He did not bother to shut off the lights behind him. Somewhere between the hall and the front door events became very confused. He seemed to slide away into a black abyss.

The whole thing might have happened to some other man.

He came back to himself behind the wheel of the Volaré. A narrow span of snow-obscured pavement snaked off through overhanging trees. Snow blew furiously out of the dark, catching fire in the twin funnels of his high beams. The road dipped and twisted hard left before him.

Even as he realized that he was going too fast, the rear end of the Volaré slid out to the right behind him. He wrenched at the steering wheel, trying to recall whether he was supposed to brake or steer into the slide, but Asa Cade's shattered face kept swimming out of the snow before him.

Then it was too late.

Henry caught glimpses of sky and snow and barren wind-tossed limbs as the car spun across the icy road in eerie stillness. The silence erupted as it jolted through the underbrush and plunged downhill. Branches cracked and whipped the chassis, metal shrieked, a rear window shattered in a rain of glass. The car slammed against an up-looming tree with a teeth-rattling crash. Henry flew forward, smashing his head against the steering wheel. A beacon flared inside his skull and faded into darkness. He slumped against the cracked vinyl of the front seat.

Outside, snow continued to fall.

Chapter 20

Cold woke him.

Consciousness came back in shards—a numbed awareness of his fingers and toes, a trickle of moisture at his mouth, a faraway throb in his back and shoulders, like a toothache in his bones. Henry opened his eyes. Through a spiderweb of windshield cracks, a stark monochrome world took shape: the black boles of trees, like sentinel giants, a chill radiance of snow. He flexed his fingers, fat and clumsy as sausages.

Then a wash of bloody memory—

—Asa, Cindy—

—sent bright panic jolting through his system.

He moved suddenly, too suddenly, and the toothache in his bones flared into a root canal, sans anesthetic.

Slowly, then. Slowly, trying to ignore the white-water current of his thoughts—

—you're going to freeze to death—

—he took stock of himself. He rolled his head on his shoulders and gritted his teeth against the buffeting tides of nausea. He curled his fingers and toes, grimacing as a thousand needles pierced them. He wiped away the moisture at the corner of his mouth: blood, black on his sleeve.

He looked up. The Volaré listed at the angle of the slope, at rest in a cradle of trees—one beyond the smashed hood, the other wedged under the front right quarter-panel. He lay in the corner framed by the seat and the passenger-side door; beyond the driver's-side window opposite, he could see a distant shoulder of road. Snow fell through the trees, already obscuring the tire tracks and twisted bracken.

Letting his gaze rove over the interior of the car, he recovered the gun from the leg well on the passenger side and slid it into a coat pocket. He found a knit cap in the glove compartment, a single glove beneath the seat. He spent a moment searching for its mate, then gave it up. The residual ache in his bones had begun to escalate into paralyzing soreness. He had to move while moving was still an option.

Clawing at the cracked vinyl, he scrambled up the seat and out the driver's-side door. He slogged uphill toward the road. He fell twice before he gained the pavement. His clothes and shoes were soaked through, and the panicky voice babbling away inside him—the one screaming about frostbite and lost fingers and facial disfigurement—had begun to grate on his nerves.

Yet he could not silence it.

For now, standing at the edge of the mountain road, he could see that frostbite and disfigurement—even death—were very real possibilities. Up here the wind had a keen arctic edge that sliced through his heavy coat and whittled his waterlogged pants into brittle columns of ice. Snow drove at him, abrasive as sand. The road was covered, impassable without chains and four-wheel drive. Maybe even then.

Which left him stranded in the midst of a blizzard, injured, very likely in shock, maybe hunted.

The word echoed inside his head.

Hunted.

He wheeled around, his feet unsteady. Skeletal trees loomed up, a low sky filled with wind-driven snow, the black shoulder of a mountain. To the southwest, just visible through the shifting veils of storm, a faraway twinkle of light.

The Run.

Henry turned up his collar, shoved his hands into his pockets, and began to trudge down the mountain toward the dim and beckoning lights.

*   *   *

At first, he lurched along in the shelter of the overhanging mountain, his hands in his pockets, his face
turned down. Before long, however, the snow had
drifted knee-high there, forcing him to the other side of
the road, where the bluff fell away into a wooded ravine.

Even here progress was difficult. His icy clothes clung
to him. The wind drove a steady, freezing whiplash of
fresh snow into his face. Now and again, he staggered
into the trees for a moment's refuge, but each time an
image of his own lifeless body—his flesh blanched, his
hair frozen in Medusa coils, his eyelashes blistered with
ice—forced him into motion once again.

All sense of time fled. It seemed as though he had
never done anything but walk, that he might walk forever. He didn't even care, by then. He only continued
because he thought he would be warmer walking than
lying down in the snow. For now, anyway. If it got too
much worse, he could lie down. And the promise of this,
of death in the snow, painless and warm, sustained him
to walk for a while yet. Eons later, he had forgotten
ever dreaming such a death. He walked because he had
always walked.

Once, as he drew close to town—he'd been walking
for eternities, by then—a salt truck lumbered by, its
chains chewing at the ice. His first impulse was to flag
it down. Then a bleak image—

—Asa's shattered face—

—rose up in his mind and he retreated into the trees
instead, his heart pounding. Unbidden, his hand had
gone to the butt of the pistol tucked inside his pocket.
Breathless, he watched the truck's taillights dwindle in
the distance. When even the sound of the engine had
faded, he stepped back onto the road, resumed the
nightmare journey.

Eventually, Holland House reared up above him.
Henry shrank into the shadows as unwelcome images
swarmed out of the night. Cindy Cade, her face frozen
in terror, her three wounds like bloody smiles. Asa's
gory face. Last of all his father.

"You can't be here," he whispered when Quincy Sleep came striding out of the snow. "You're dead."

Yet he was. Here. Here, as Henry had so often seen him, clad in washed-out jeans and a flannel shirt.

Henry felt a touch at his elbow, turning him up High Street, the black expanse of the lake behind them. No lights gleamed in the storefronts or the second-floor apartments; the snow lay alike over everything, trackless and serene, over buildings and cars and shrubs and sidewalks, mere shapes beneath the endless blanket of white. Like a dream world. And here his father, here Quincy Sleep, striding beside him after all this time, and after all this pain, untouched by weather.

"Why?" he asked. "Why did you have to die?"

People die, that's all. They just die.

"But I'm frightened . . ."

Henry turned. He could barely see his father through the dark and snow. His legs felt like water underneath him. He said, "I've always been afraid—"

He felt that touch, urging him on. Snow blew and wind raged and still they walked. Ahead, the courthouse loomed above the arc of the Stone Bridge. And then they were on the bridge, Cinder Bottom falling away beneath them, the wind pouring down from the hills. Cold, so cold. He felt exposed here, no shadows to flee to, no place to run.

"You have to help me," he pleaded.

The mysteries are locked inside yourself.

"The dreams . . ."

They were over the bridge, High Street angling up to the courthouse square. His father took him by the shoulders, his eyes commanding. In his mind, Henry stood before a mirror, touching on his face the spots of inflammation, like burns, the imprints of a dead man's fingers.

To stop the dreams, you have to understand yourself.

Henry recoiled, wanting to pull away from the presence who walked beside him. Yet he could not. Slowly they climbed the hill. Something tugged at his elbow. He stumbled back, crouching in the black mouth of the alley as a sheriff's Blazer cruised slowly by, chains gnawing at the icy street.

"I'm afraid—"

Look inside yourself. Dreams are symbols. Symbols are real. Metaphors are true, Henry. Remember.

Then the courthouse square, the blank storefront windows. He stumbled. He was on his knees in the snow; he didn't remember how he got there. He forced himself to his feet, then staggered into a recess between buildings.

He saw a door. Then he was climbing the dim stairwell inside, reeling with dizziness, the presence at his elbow steadying him. At the top of the stairs they paused before a door. He collapsed against it, hammering his fist against the flimsy panel. And then he stopped and only leaned there, weeping.

To stop the dreams you have to understand yourself.

Henry turned his head to look at his father—his father, lost to him for all these years—and he felt well up within him all the mixed emotions, the thousand ambivalences he had felt for as long as he could remember. The hatred and the love and the bone-deep suspicion. The manifold regrets. The grief. Oh yes, the grief.

He heard the sound of a dead bolt being drawn back on the other side of the door.

Henry gazed at his father and wept. Quincy Sleep looked as he had looked always, heavy and thick-muscled as a lumberjack in his faded jeans, his flannel shirt rolled back to reveal the intricate corkscrews of dark hair on his arms. And then he wasn't there at all. In the faint radiance of the bare bulb dangling overhead, the banister and the newel post printed their shadows upon the wall, with all the stairs descending.

"Please," he whispered.

Henry felt the door shudder underneath his weight, opening inward. And then, having lost the strength to stand, he was falling. Falling and falling and uttering these words aloud—"Father, Father"—into Benjamin Strange's sleepy and affrighted face.

Sauls Run
The Present

Chapter 21

For Del Grubb, the storm and its immediate aftermath were an exercise in frustration.

There had been a bit of pleasure at first, to be sure, but he had rushed the business with Asa Cade. He had been locked inside Harold Crawford's mind for too long, listening to that old siren song of rage. Once or twice over the years, he had managed to wrest control from his alternate self—the incident with the young man from the rest stop sprang to mind—but those occasions had merely sharpened his hunger. Nothing allayed it, not even his protracted chat with Quincy Sleep. Sleep had been planning to go public—a move that would have deprived Grubb of the vengeance he craved—and silencing him had been a sweet job, but the hunger had been gnawing at Grubb through all those years locked in the prison of Harold Crawford's mind, and it would not be sated. Well, now he was free—free for good, he could feel it—and it was Harold Crawford pissing and moaning down there in the dark. That was fine with Del Grubb. Just fine.

There had been a bad moment in the courthouse men's room. Looking up from the sink, his nostrils wrinkling with the ammonia stench of urine—

—*Christ didn't anyone clean this place*—

—he had caught a glimpse of his own face staring back at him—his first true moment of self-appraisal in years. The fat, graying man inside the glass looked nothing like the Del Grubb of old, sculpted and hard, with the cold eyes and prominent bone structure of an Aryan king. Only the eyes remained unchanged, and that brought it all home to him.

Twenty-four years, that's what he'd lost.

Twenty-four years with Harold Crawford at the wheel. A weak sister, Delbert Grubb's father would have called this middle-aged sack of shit. Dear old Dad, master of the Book and the Fist, generous in applications of them both. His father had made him sculpted and hard, and at that moment, looking into the rust-stained mirror at the weak sister he had become, Grubb felt the brunt of his father's shame.

His hand lashed out before he even thought it through. Shards of glass rained musically into the porcelain basin. He was lucky he hadn't gashed himself badly. He sucked at a bright droplet of blood welling up from a shallow cut in the heel of his palm, thinking, *Be cool.*

The end game had started, but it wasn't over yet, not by a long shot.

Which reminded him: He had a few loose ends to wrap up.

Back to the main office for a word with Abby—oh, he was cool—and then he was settling behind the wheel of a Blazer in the Public Works garage. Free. He could feel it inside him, that freedom, spreading black and bountiful wings as he took the Blazer out from under the courthouse and into the snow just starting to spin from the forbidding sky. The snow was a good thing, he remembered thinking as he turned the Blazer east, toward Asa Cade's. If the Run got half the snow the National Weather Service was calling for, it would shut down everything for a week. No one would stumble across his handiwork for days. He was looking forward to it, that little bit of work.

He had planned on a little fun with Cindy Cade, a little of the old slap and tickle, and who cared if she was sixty years old? It had been twenty-four long years, she was plump and juicy as a roasting hen, and a man needed a warm hole to poke it in every now and again.

Sometimes, the old five-fingered discount just wouldn't do. Unfortunately, it had gone badly from the first.

Grubb should have seen it coming, should have had a better sense of the kind of terror Asa Cade must have been feeling after Quincy Sleep's little accident. But Harold Crawford had softened up more than Grubb's gut. He'd softened up his instincts, too. They ambled down the hall to Cade's office, he and Asa and Cindy Cade, and Grubb had just started in on his questions— he had a million of them—when Cade had dodged into the bedroom. Said he needed to visit the john, but Grubb never believed that—though Asa Cade *did* look like a man about to shit his pants. Everything had gone to hell in the next few seconds. Asa had gone for the gun and Cindy Cade had got between them somehow. She took three bullets in the clamorous instants before he got to Cade, the gun hot and smoking in his hand.

A botched job for sure.

Afterward, Grubb had stared longingly at Cindy Cade's body, his cock as stiff as a crowbar in his pants, but that was all he had done. He wasn't some kind of pervert who liked to fuck dead women—not as a habit anyway—nor had he come in his pants like Harold Crawford. No, he liked them live and squirming underneath him.

He'd been more careful with Raymond Ostrowski. He found him dead drunk, passed out before the television in a ragged easy chair with a bottle of Turkey in his hand. He had a gun, too, and Grubb took a moment of special pleasure in waking up the fat little fuck and giving him a chance to dry fire it two or three times before he realized the damn thing had been unloaded while he dozed. Then Grubb had taken out his own gun—but he hadn't fired it. No, he'd just swung it around and cracked Ostrowski square on the head with its heavy butt. The next time Ostrowski woke up, he had sobered considerably. It was too late by then. Old Ray had had a bit of a run-in with a roll of duct tape, and he wasn't going anywhere at all.

They were outside, back in the shelter of the woods, back by the dog run. It didn't take Ostrowski but a minute or two to figure out what Grubb had in mind. He blubbered like a baby while Grubb finished off the job he'd started the last time he'd come around, picking off the remaining dogs one by one. Bang bang bang bang bang bang, six shots batting away through the snow. The dogs had remembered him, too. They retreated to the corners of the chain-link enclosure, their eyes rolling with terror, but there was nowhere to hide. Grubb had gut-shot the last one, and they sat out there in the snow and dark for a long time, listening to it die.

Old Ray blubbered the whole time, and Del Grubb had laughed to hear it. Yes, indeed, a good time had been had by all. And he was only getting rolling, too.

In the end, Ostrowski forgot all about his dogs. It just took a closer acquaintance with Del Grubb's knife to help him put them out of his mind for good. The knife also seemed to improve his memory, and when Grubb learned about the little trick Perry Holland had pulled, he felt a slow burn of anger. He'd have to take care of that small oversight, too, before things were over. But first things first—and Raymond Ostrowski was the matter at hand. They'd spent a pleasant hour or two together, he and Ray and his trusty six inches of steel, and if Grubb might have felt a little spasm in his groin along the way, well, even a strong man had an occasional moment of weakness, right? Twenty-four years was a long time, after all. A very long time.

Grubb only regretted he had to rush it there at the end. But the snow had kept coming down and down, and duty called. So he'd finished up and headed back to town, slipping into the mask of Harold Crawford as easily as a politician slipping on his campaign smile. But it had really been Delbert Grubb all along, taking care of the thousand and one tasks a sheriff had to see to in the middle of a small-town blizzard. Delbert Grubb, hungry and waiting.

It was after midnight before he could manage to slip away again. When he had gotten up to Widow's Ridge,

Quincy Sleep's house was empty and dark. For a moment, he feared that Sleep had slipped off just as Crawford had warned him to, but a brief investigation suggested otherwise. If he had gone, he had done so without taking his clothes. He'd probably just holed up somewhere during the storm, and that meant he would turn up eventually. All Grubb had to do was keep his eye peeled and wait for the weather to break. As soon as Perry finished clearing that tunnel—a few days at most— Grubb had some plans for the thing under the hill. The end game.

After that, nothing much would matter at all.

In the meantime, Grubb had to play-act at being Harold Crawford, see to his business, be cool. And that was what he did, too. He spent the next couple of days hauling stranded motorists out of ditches, monitoring highway conditions, and seeing that housebound folks got something to eat. And he did it all with a smile on his face; after all, his was an elected office, even if he never planned to run again, and old habits died hard. Inwardly, though, he chafed—at the continuing absence of Sleep; at the delay the snow would cause Perry Holland's crew; most of all, at the frustrated hunger welling up inside him.

It would be a good death, that last one. He longed for its consummation. In the meantime, he kept silent. He made his official rounds. He stayed cool.

But the waiting was hard.

Benjamin Strange spent the days of the storm waiting, as well. The boy—for so he thought of him, he couldn't help it—had given him a scare, stumbling in out of the snow like that. A scare, and more than a little food for thought, for in stripping away Henry Sleep's ice-encased coat, his hands had found the folded yellow notes that had belonged to Quincy Sleep and something else, too. The gun.

Ben had never liked guns, and he didn't care for this one either, a black short-barreled revolver made by Smith & Wesson. Loaded, too, though it didn't smell as though it had been fired. With trembling fingers he unloaded it and set it aside.

Then he tended to the boy. He finished undressing him, wrestled him into a warm tub to bring his body temperature up, put him to bed. A long welt had risen on the boy's head, and the skin around it gleamed with dull purple bruise, but he couldn't find any other injuries. The head worried him, though. Ben knew just enough about concussions to know he should get Henry to a hospital.

But the matter of the gun kept him from doing so. That and a memory of Harold Crawford that kept coming back to him. After Quincy Sleep had killed himself— *if* he had killed himself, and Ben didn't think he had— Crawford had paid him a visit, using that hogwash about phone records as an excuse. And what Ben remembered most about that interview was the light in Crawford's eyes. Curiosity, he had supposed, and then, as the interview—interrogation was really a better word, wasn't it?—veered oddly off course, he had thought it might be anger.

Standing to go, Crawford had wheeled around to face him. "You'll want to call me, you hear anything else about this," he said. He tapped his hat against one fleshy thigh and held Ben's gaze, that strange light flaring up in his eyes. In that moment, another thought arced like a comet through the night sky of Ben's mind: that it was nothing at all, that light, that for a single unnerving moment he had been staring into a hollow pit at the center of Harold Crawford's soul. Crawford had smiled then, thanking him for his time, and that bleak light had winked out as suddenly as it had sprung to life. Watching it go away was like watching someone put on a mask.

Now, remembering, Ben thought: No, it wouldn't do to get Henry admitted to the hospital. Not until he figured out what had happened, why he had the gun.

Instead, he smoked and kept watch by the bedside. Occasionally, he coughed, expelling a thin pink froth into the towel he held to his weathered face. He was dying. He could feel it in his chest, every breath a battle with the enemy in his lungs. He found himself thinking about the odd cycle Quincy Sleep had discovered. Ben found himself trying to believe it, trying to convince himself he could count upon it to save him. If he could only weather these strange dark months, he wondered, would the wheel turn once again? Would the cancer go into remission?

Ben suspected he'd never have the chance to find out. The sickness was coming on faster now, too fast, and he couldn't help thinking of Henry's mother. The cycle had turned then, too; but it had turned too late for Lily Sleep. She had died anyway. Ben thought about death, like falling down and down into the dark forever, and he shivered.

He wished he believed in God.

Toward morning, Henry grew feverish. Ben leaned closer, anxious to snatch something from the ravings. All he got was names—Emily and Asa, Cindy—but he recognized two of them, the Cades, right off. It was seven o'clock by then. A pale, overcast dawn glowed outside the window, the sky still filled with snow.

Ben found Asa Cade's home number in the directory and punched the number into the keypad. He counted the rings, an even twenty-five of them, before he cradled the phone. Somebody should be there, he thought. A morning like this one, somebody ought to be there. He stared at the gun, lying on the nightstand with the contents of Henry's pockets—the folded packet of notes, a wallet, a handful of loose change. But it was the gun that drew his eyes. His mind locked on it somehow, summoning up the phone call to Asa Cade, those twenty-five rings.

He'd never felt so old or so afraid.

The boy moaned in his sleep.

Ben sat heavily. Flipping open the wallet, he thumbed through the usual detritus—a five and three crumpled ones, a North Carolina driver's license, credit cards, photos. The photos gave him pause: Quincy Sleep, broad-shouldered and smiling in his clerical robes; a faded snapshot of a tired-looking woman with a ten- or twelve-year-old kid he took to be Henry; the senior photo of a high school girl, posed and ill at ease.

He slipped the photo from its sleeve and studied the girl more closely. With her dark, shoulder-length hair and frank, watchful eyes, she possessed a kind of second-glance beauty, the kind of good looks most people pass right over. He liked Henry better for having the good sense to notice her. He flipped the photo over and read the inscription with a little shock of recognition: EMILY WOOD, 1986.

Nothing more.

He glanced at Henry, sleeping restlessly, then back to the photo, then to the gun. He felt a prickle of unease at the back of his neck. Twenty-five rings, he thought. What the hell?

He reached for the telephone book and thumbed it open. Wolford, Womac, Womac, Wood. He stared at the number for a long time and then he picked up the telephone, resolved to count rings again. But someone picked it up right away.

"Miss Wood?" he said. "Emily Wood?"

"Yes."

The voice sounded old and weary, edged with tears, and he thought, *It's someone else; she wouldn't be that old*. But he said, "My name is Benjamin Strange. Do you know Henry Sleep, Miss Wood?"

She was silent for so long that he thought they might have been disconnected. And when she spoke again, there was a depth in her voice that said she was more than a friend. "Is he okay?"

"Can you come?" he asked.

Henry dreamed he stood on the frost-heaved hardpan of a ruined street. As far as he could see—to the rim of jagged mountains, like dragon's teeth—lay only the bombed-out shells of houses, blackened walls, basements like dark mouths in the earth.

On a rocky promontory over waters oily black, Holland House had fallen into decay. Opposite, the squarish bulk of the courthouse loomed up, like the last rotten molar thrust through a diseased gum. Between them, nothing at all. Only gutted houses, ashen ruins, as though a great conflagration had burned here. A bloated moon shed its cancerous radiance across the debris. Wind harried gray stratus across the midnight sky.

A derelict church lay before him, its steeple tumbled down, an abortive aspirant to grace. His father's church. Moonlight danced like teeth along the shards of the stained-glass windows as he crossed the fractured street. A chill, driving rain had begun to fall.

He stopped by the illuminated brick sign. At the top it read:

FIRST CHRISTIAN CHURCH
REV. QUINCY SLEEP

Memory ghosted through him when he glanced at the white placard below, but the innocuous legend he recollected—

—FELLOWSHIP SUPPER SATURDAY JANUARY 21—

—had been replaced by a more ominous inscription:

TO STOP THE DREAMS YOU HAVE TO UNDERSTAND
YOURSELF
YOURSELF
YOURSELF

Just then the wind picked up once again, hurling itself at his back in endless waves. He braced himself against it, sought to turn and run—
—*to stop the dreams you have to understand*—
—but the wind held him there—
—*yourself, yourself, yourself*—
—frozen and immobile, as one by one the letters on the white placard tore free, transforming themselves into sharp-eyed ravens, black as scraps of midnight sky.

They hurtled at his eyes, shrieking in fury, but the wind whirled them away. And then he saw that the backing placard, too, had undergone a transformation: where it had once shone spotless white, it now glimmered oily black, a vertical pane of dark, glossy water.

The baptismal pool.

I don't believe in all that, he had told his father.

A dozen tiny circles expanded and disappeared in the black pool's placid surface, ghosts of the wind-whipped spears of rain. If he took a single step closer, he knew what he would see.

Himself.

The wind shrieked louder still, hurling him forward. The rain drove a thousand stinging needles into his back.

Gravity reversed itself.

He screamed as he plunged headfirst toward the pool. His own distorted face rocketed up to meet him, like the visage of a bottom-dwelling fish. The waters shattered around him with a crash like all the glass in the world breaking at once, and then he was falling, endlessly falling into the heart of an impenetrable darkness, into the heart of the labyrinth.

She could come, Emily said. She had a neighbor who owned a Ford Explorer—snow tires, chains, four-wheel drive, the works. Even so, it took her a couple hours to get there. The power and the phone had gone out by the time she arrived, so Ben found himself studying her by candlelight. She was smaller than she had looked in the photo, maybe five-four and trim, with a few strands of gray in her dark hair and warm crinkles at the corners of her eyes. But her face was wan and tired.

"Where is he?" she asked.

He watched her work with Henry, her hands sure and gentle, as if she had done this sort of thing before. Henry came swimming out of sleep still sodden with fever, his eyes glazed and bleary. She managed to get some Tylenol in him, a glass of water, a few spoonfuls of canned soup. At least the gas was working.

Afterward, he slept more easily.

They stood in the kitchen, basking in the heat from

the oven door, and watched night pour out of the ridges to lap at the islands of candlelight visible in nearby windows.

"He told me this crazy story," she said.

And so he sketched it out for her, watching her face in the flickering radiance of the candles, looking for the disbelief he thought he would see. But her face gave nothing away, as if she had become accustomed to keeping every stray thought and emotion locked inside herself. Surfaces and depths, he thought. And he wondered again how he had managed to get so old and so near death without a wife or children. He thought of them as children suddenly—grown children, her and Henry both—and he wished they could have been his.

"It sounds crazy," he said, but she waved her hand.

"My mother died yesterday, up at Ridgeview. So did two other patients. Three in one day, and the nurse said it had been odd like that just lately, the deaths piling up, a whole generation passing before her eyes."

"I'm sorry."

"It's been coming for a long time." She looked over at him. "But I keep thinking about what Henry said, that maybe he was right. You think I could take a look at those notes?"

Ben retrieved them. He leaned against the counter while she thumbed through them.

"The second page?" she said.

"It doesn't fit, does it?" He drummed his fingers on the counter. "We thought maybe it was something that got mixed in—"

"But it's in the same hand, from the same notebook."

"I was going to look into it," he said. "Just to be sure. I even got some books from the library."

"You still have them?"

He nodded.

"Let's have a look," she said.

The snow began to taper off at midnight. By two, it had stopped altogether. The clouds lifted and the cold reach of heaven smote the mountaintops. The Run shimmered beneath its frosting of immaculate starlight, perfect as a wedding cake.

Emily dozed in the armchair by Henry's bed.

Ben made up a bed on the sofa. He lay still and tried to empty his mind, but sleep was hard to find. He kept thinking about the cancer growing inside him, sealing off the alveoli in his lungs one by one, leaving him less and less to breathe with. He kept thinking about afterward.

So he circled back to it at last: the thing taking shape in the notes, its implications. What had Quincy Sleep told him that morning on the phone? *Imagine a story that changes everything.* The phrase mocked him. Everything.

But this . . .

Who could have imagined *this?* He thought it was madness—and he'd said as much to Emily at the kitchen table.

"Not now," she had replied. "We'll talk about it in the morning. The three of us."

"But—"

"In the morning. Henry deserves to be a part of this."

Now, his angular frame wedged into the sofa, Ben found his lips shaping the word once again. *Madness.* But another voice was speaking inside him, the voice Quincy Sleep must have been listening to in the end. *Why not?* it asked. *Why not?* Ben had no ready answer. The truth was, he *wanted* to believe, wanted to believe the way terminally ill patients want to believe in miracle cures at mysterious clinics in the Caribbean. He laughed softly at the thought, for it came to the same thing in the end, didn't it, this madness? It was the madness of an old man who was afraid to die. And so he fetched up against the cold immutable fact of his skepticism, like a man running full tilt into a wall.

But it was that other voice—the one that whispered, *Why not?*—that chased him down at last into a restless old man's slumber. And it was that voice that echoed in his head eight hours later, when Henry Sleep awoke him.

Why not?

*   *   *

If there was a difference between Harold Crawford and his dark brother, it was this: In his ponderous fashion, Crawford was a thinker. Del Grubb, on the other hand, lived deep in his nerve ends. He acted on impulse, surfing dark breakers of emotion on instinct alone. Those instincts rarely failed him. By noon of the day Henry Sleep awoke, however, Grubb was beginning to think that this time they had.

Crawford was talking in his head. He wouldn't shut up.

The circle is closing, Crawford whispered. *You're running out of time.*

Grubb, patrolling the winter-struck streets, couldn't seem to shut out that voice, and as much as he didn't like to admit it, he couldn't help concluding that his dominion might well be as conditional as Crawford's had been. Everything was still in flux. Though he had temporarily gained the advantage, the titanic battle raging within him had yet to be decided. So he sat back and drove by instinct, letting his hands take him where they would, and he listened. And what it told him, that voice, was this: *The blizzard was your friend. The blackout and the problem with the phones, they were your friends. And now you're running out of friends, because the snow is over. Another day or so, the power and the phones will be working. Another day after that the roads will be clear, and you just might find some slick state agent down from Charleston sitting on the other side of your desk. Sleep said he was planning to call the attorney general, and enough strange things have happened around here just lately that some slick hotshot might decide Sleep's story's worth a closer look. And a closer look would do it, wouldn't it, old buddy?*

Grubb grimaced at the mockery in that phrase.

Crawford laughed. *That's right,* he said. *A closer look and your little charade would fall to pieces. Nobody'll worry about the likes of Ray Ostrowski, but they'll hang you for killing Cade. After all,* the voice added, *they're already asking about him down at the hospital, aren't they?*

And they were.

Cade hadn't come in on rounds. Grubb had told them he had checked in with the Cades, the doctor was just down with a touch of flu—but he wouldn't be able to put them off forever. Sooner or later—probably sooner—some smart-ass with a four-wheel drive was going to head up Cade's way and take a look. *You know what's going to happen then?* Crawford asked him.

Another voice answered the question—*The shit is going to hit the fan,* it said—and Grubb actually flinched when he heard it.

It was his father's voice, speaking in the tone he liked to use just before he went to work with his fists. That was the one thing Del Grubb and Harold Crawford had always agreed on: They hated their daddy. Hated him with the very breath of life.

Motoring north into Crook's Hollow, oversteering with a kind of thoughtless grace when the Blazer spun out in the curves, Del Grubb suddenly felt very much like Job. A great hero of his father's, old Job, crouched out there on the ash heap while God rained down shit from the heavens. *I abhor myself, and repent in dust and ashes*, Job said. It was one of his father's favorite verses, but frankly, the sentiment made Grubb want to puke. Unlike his father, he couldn't see much use in a God willing to shower a righteous man with shit just so he could win some cosmic wager. Maybe that was something else he and Harold Crawford could agree on: One should never pass on a chance to deliver a hearty *Fuck you* to their daddy's God—and to hell with the consequences, pun very much intended.

That right, Harold? he inquired, but the little voice had fallen suddenly silent within him.

Which was fine by Delbert Grubb.

He steered the Blazer to the curb and cut the engine, curious to see where his instincts had brought him. They hadn't failed him this time. Getting out of the car, he felt a bottomless certainty spill through him, a conviction that everything would work out as he had planned. He started up the walk to Mose Cavanaugh's house. It was time to remind Mose that he owed Harold Crawford a favor for keeping his boy out of the penitentiary. Old debts had a way of coming due, Del Grubb thought with satisfaction.

It was time to check on the progress at the dig.

Daylight was fading when Grubb emerged from Cavanaugh's house and climbed into the Blazer. He pulled into the street with one hand loose on the wheel, throwing up plumes of snow as he spun the vehicle south toward the Run. He could see the whole town spread out in the valley below him, and he plotted his course with his eye as he dropped down out of the Hollow.

It ought to be near dark by the time he got to Perry Holland's mansion on the hill, and that was just fine by him. Some work was best carried out in the dark. Settling up old scores, for instance—and he had a score to settle with Perry Holland for his little bit of trickery.

But he'd need a guide first of all, and Perry would do just fine. After all, it had been Perry who led him down there in the first place, Perry who showed him that miracle of his daddy's God.

"Oh, it's open all right," Mose Cavanaugh had told him when he asked about the mine. "We broke through the night the snow started."

That was good news indeed. Even better, Crawford's nagging voice had died away inside him. Grubb's instincts had been vindicated once again.

Grubb felt a flush of high spirits at the news. And that had been a lucky thing for Mose Cavanaugh, a lucky thing indeed. For Cavanaugh had done something stupid as Grubb stood to leave. He had grabbed Del Grubb's shoulder—he had actually *touched* him—and spun him around there in the foyer.

"Listen," he had said. "You want to watch yourself."

Grubb pried the fingers from his uniform with distaste. "Are you threatening me, Mr. Cavanaugh?"

That had rocked Cavanaugh a little; Grubb could see it in his eyes. "No, Sheriff," he said. "Of course not. I just—there's a couple things you ought to know, that's all. Those old tunnels aren't stable. Some places, they're just shored up with timbers yet—wood that's been there the better part of a century. We'll need a week yet to make it safe."

"And the other thing?"

Cavanaugh hesitated then, and to Grubb, who had spent his share of time in interrogation rooms, he had the demeanor of a man about to confess something that shamed him.

"There's something down there," Cavanaugh whispered. "I've heard it rustling around. I've heard it—" He hesitated. "I heard something moaning down there," he said.

Grubb let a hint of doubt creep into his voice. "Moaning?"

Cavanaugh looked up and met his gaze. "That's right."

"Well, I'll keep that in mind," Grubb had said, smiling the way you smiled at a crazy man. And then he let himself out.

Now, cruising slowly over the snowpack, the Blazer's wheels slipping now and again, he thought once more of his father's God. Oh, there'd be moaning, he thought. By the time he was done, there'd be more than moaning in those old tunnels.

The sun had begun to set, turning the snow along the western ridges a smoky red. To Delbert Grubb, it looked as though the mountains had been dipped in blood.

The Labyrinth
The Present

Chapter 22

"What if," Emily said, "the second page of notes wasn't mixed in by accident? What if it was the key to everything else?"

They sat in a wash of cold afternoon light at a table stacked with books and papers. The streets beyond the kitchen window had the stunned emptiness of a city occupied by enemy troops. Plows the size of tanks rumbled through occasionally, and once a Ford Explorer slipped past—furtive as a rebel in government territory, Henry thought, watching its rear end swing as it cornered the courthouse square.

The thought didn't amuse him. His head throbbed, and he felt a bit too much like a guerrilla soldier himself all of a sudden: wounded and hunted. He had filled Ben and Emily in on everything soon after he woke up. Ghosts seemed to throng the kitchen, clamoring for justice as he finished the story, and in the conversation that followed they agreed on calling in state authorities as soon as the phones were back in order. Hoping his luck had turned, Henry even picked up the receiver and rattled the button for a dial tone. A deep and inert silence poured out instead.

He pounded softly on the table. "I just wish we knew *why* it was happening."

Ben and Emily exchanged a glance.

"Actually, Ben and I have some ideas on that," Emily said. That was when she had waved the notes at him— the three yellow sheets covered in Quincy Sleep's careful hand—and said they thought the second page might be significant. "I got to thinking," she added. "Your dad's office at the church was almost pathologically neat. It didn't strike me as the office of a man likely to mix things up."

Henry laughed dryly. "That's true enough," he said, reaching for the notes. "Still, the second page is just biblical references."

"Well," Emily said, "he got involved in this for a reason—maybe *because* of his expertise, not in spite of it. Ben and I got to thinking that maybe the second page *is* connected to the rest of it somehow, so we spent some time yesterday tracking down the references."

"What did you find?"

Emily reached across the table and turned the notes so she could read them. Henry watched her finger slide down the narrow-ruled lines. "They all come from the Old Testament. In this column he cites Genesis and Numbers. In the second column, Isiah, Proverbs, Deuteronomy, Joshua. The first thing we did was actually look up the references."

"The pattern wasn't hard to see," Ben said. "They were all references either to giants or to spirits who inhabit Sheol—the Underworld, the grave, Hell, however you translate it. I guess various readings are plausible."

"That leaves us a long way from the Run," Henry said.

"Maybe not," Ben said. "Your dad's notes deal partly with Hebrew etymology. I'm anything but an expert, but when we started looking into this, some odd things turned up."

"Odd in what way?"

"Odd in that they seem to have connections with what's happening in the Run," Ben said.

"*And* with your dreams," Emily said. "I've been thinking a lot about those dreams."

"So have I," Henry said. "Turns out I'm not the only one that's having them."

Emily exchanged a glance with Ben. "I guess that shoots down my notion that they were some kind of psychological projection, doesn't it?" she said wryly, and Henry was struck suddenly by a memory of the context in which she'd first advanced that theory—not just the conversation itself, but an almost tactile recollection of her skin against his skin, the taste of her lips, even her scent. He smiled and dropped his hand over hers, pierced suddenly with an almost physical ache of longing.

"But it does support our other hypothesis," Ben said. "Who else has been having the dreams, Henry?"

"Raymond Ostrowski and Perry Holland, for sure. Maybe Asa. Cindy said he'd been having bad dreams. And Penny Kohler said Dad had been having trouble sleeping, too."

"All people who had been up to the Holland mines," Ben said.

"Which means it all fits," Emily said to Ben.

"Fits what?" Henry asked.

"The other hypothesis," Ben said. "When we looked at the biblical allusions, we got to wondering if the dreams could be repressed memories of actual experiences."

"But then why would the dreams fade when I'm not in Sauls Run?"

"Maybe it's a matter of proximity," Emily said. "You come too close to . . . whatever it is, the original experience . . . and you have dreams. And you *continue* to have them as long as you stay inside its sphere of influence."

"Inside the circle on Dad's map," Henry said.

"Right."

"The point is," Ben said, "what if *all* of you—everyone who's been into the mines, Asa, Perry Holland, Ostrowski, whoever—what if you saw or felt or *perceived* somehow—who knows how?—something so transformative that you couldn't handle it on a conscious level?"

Henry sat back. "Gods and demons," he said after a moment.

Emily and Ben traded another look.

"What do you mean?" Ben asked.

"Raymond Ostrowski told me the mountain was holy to the Shawnee, that men who worked those tunnels in the early part of the century also complained of dreams." He paused. "How did he say it? That they'd rubbed up against something, some god or demon, and they were working it through in their sleep. Something like that."

"So it goes back that long," Ben said.

"*What* does?" Henry said. "What are these connections you were talking about?"

"Well," Ben said. "Emily told me that you dreamed there was something down there. Something with . . ." Ben hesitated.

"Wings," Henry said.

"Wings." Ben lit a cigarette. The coughing, when it came, was vicious, a phlegmy rattle deep in his chest. When he put the cigarette into the ashtray, he was pale.

"Maybe you ought to cut that out," Emily said.

Ben just smiled.

"Wings," Henry said. "So that's important?"

"You tell me." Ben picked up the notes and dragged a nicotine-stained finger down the page. "The first column cites two passages about giants." He flipped open a book. "Here we go. 'There were giants in the earth in those days; and also after that, when the sons of God came in unto the daughters of men, and they bare children to them.' "

Emily picked up another sheet of paper—this one covered with writing Henry recognized as her own. "The actual Hebrew word translated as giants is *Nephelim*. When you trace that word back to its root—*napal*, to fall—you realize that these giants—these 'sons of God'—are the fallen ones."

Henry took a long breath. Overwhelmed by the smell of Ben's cigarette, he stood. Halfway across the kitchen, the floor cut loose beneath his feet, swinging like a ship at anchor.

"You okay?" Emily asked.

Henry clutched the countertop for a moment, riding

the swells. "Tired, I guess." He paused. "The fallen ones. Well, that sounds a little ominous."

"In a Christian context," Ben said, "it sounds like the host of angels who fell with Lucifer." He lifted his hands. "Wings, right? But that's not all. You said your father was interested in connections between pre-Christian belief and Christianity."

"Like the rest of the Old Testament, the text itself is pre-Christian," Emily said. "Some Rabbinical commentators view the Nephilim not as angels but as . . . associates of God—servants, soldiers, whatever. God's terminators, if you will." She lifted her eyebrows. "They had a sort of semidivine status, but they weren't necessarily evil, not in the way we think of the angels—the demons—who fell with Satan."

"In fact," Ben added, "they probably had little interest at all in human affairs."

"It sounds like you believe in them."

Ben picked up his cigarette and put it down without taking a drag. He shrugged. "Hypothetically, then. The point is, there's at least a hint of a connection to your dreams."

"What about the second column?"

"That's where it gets really interesting," Ben said. "The second list cites passages using the Hebrew word *Rephaim*. In some contexts it means departed spirits, in others it, too, refers to giants. Until the 1920s, most scholars thought the two usages were distinct. That is, they saw the Rephaim as a race of giants, like the Nephelim. But they didn't link that use of the word with the ghost meaning."

"So what happened in the 1920s?"

Emily shuffled papers. "A Syrian farmer stumbled across some ancient tombs, leading to excavations at a place called Ras Shamra, where they uncovered the archives of an ancient kingdom named Ugarit. It was one of the most famous finds of the century—like the Dead Sea Scrolls—because the tablets there not only shed light on scripture, but on some disputed Hebrew words."

"Including the word Rephaim," Ben said.

"The Ugaritic tablets suggest that the two meanings—giant and ghost—may be related. Apparently, the—what? the Ugarites?—the Ugarites worshipped an elaborate pantheon in which the Rephaim, the departed spirits of their ancestors, held special powers."

Ben stubbed out his cigarette as another fit of coughing overwhelmed him. When it had passed, Emily said, "Which brings us to another connection. You ready for this?"

"I don't know what I'm ready for."

"Your dad's notes steer us back to word origin," she said. "This time the word in question is Rephaim. Its history is nowhere near as clear as that of Nephelim, but one etymology traces it back to the Hebrew word *râphâ*."

"And that means?"

"It means to heal," Emily said. She looked up and held his gaze. "It means they had the power to heal."

At twilight, Ben went back to the bedroom to nap—as much because he sensed they needed time alone, Henry thought, as because he needed the rest. Henry appreciated the gesture, but as shadows stole across the faded linoleum, he questioned its wisdom. He and Emily sat at the kitchen table in a silence teeming with chafed emotion. Uncertain how to break it, he found himself toying with a pencil instead.

They spoke simultaneously—

"I'm sorry—"

"I guess I owe you an apology—

—and dissolved a moment later into laughter. Subdued laughter, but the real thing.

Emily said, "I wish the power would come back on."

"I wish the phones would."

The words dissipated their laughter, inviting it all back—the enveloping dread, the ghosts of Asa and Cindy and Quincy Sleep, as well. Henry thought of Crawford rising up behind his desk, clutching the stapler like a bludgeon, and he glanced at the gun lying on the table, taking comfort in its chill promise. He had reclaimed it when Ben retreated to the bedroom. Emily had watched silently while he loaded it, sliding the bullets into their chambers with unsteady fingers. She was silent now, too, her breath frosty in the chill apartment, her face half obscured in gloom.

"How are you doing with everything?" Henry asked.

"You mean my mother."

"Yeah."

Emily riffled a stack of notes. "I keep thinking that if I had believed you, maybe we could have—" She paused, biting at her lower lip.

"What?"

"Done something." She looked up. "Figured this out some way. Maybe we could have saved her."

"You can't blame yourself."

"But, Henry—"

"Look, if I hadn't spent nearly two decades running away from all this, maybe Dad would still be alive. We can sit here and second-guess our decisions all night, but that won't change anything."

"I guess."

"Besides, how can you blame yourself?" He rapped the pencil dismissively against a book and laughed. "I mean, come on, what are we talking about here? Fallen angels?"

"I don't know," she said. "*Something,* though, I believe that."

"Do you?"

"Yes. After Mom died, I went back to the house and opened a bottle of wine. I sat at the table for an hour or more, looking at that glass and thinking, *Why not have a drink? What possible harm could it do now?*"

"Did you?"

"No. I was tempted, but no." She pushed aside a stack of books and laid a hand over his. "I'd been living for my mother so long that I wasn't sure I could find a reason to go on. I think that's what it was. And the whole time I sat there, our conversation was running through the back of my mind. Two other patients had died within hours of Mom, and I kept remembering what you said, that whatever's going on here is getting worse."

He flashed upon Asa's spectacles, twisted in the junk from the spilled drawer, somehow more terrible than all the blood in the world. "It is," he said.

"Well, I decided I wanted to help figure that out."

"What about finding a reason to go on?"

Biting her lip, she twined her fingers through his. "I don't know."

Henry stood, dragging his hand away. Still clutching the pencil, he strode to the window. "So why did you even come here, then?"

"Look at me," she said.

He turned.

Her face was strained and worn. "The worst thing about the night Mom died was that a part of me—a part I didn't even want to acknowledge—was *relieved*. I'd given up my life—I'd given up *myself*—to keep her at Ridgeview. I don't even remember my plans and dreams. If I'm going to be fair to you—if I'm going to be fair to *us*—I have to take some time and get to know *me* again. And then we'll see. I care about you, I know that, but we'll have to see."

"And in the meantime?"

"You can wait if you want to. I'd like you to. I don't want you to run away again, Henry."

Henry swallowed, shamed—

—*I got used to you running away a long time ago*—

—into turning back to the window.

The sky glowed with sunset, a palette of red and orange that shimmered over the ridges, reminding him of the optical illusion that had seized him that night in the scenic overlook—that bright conflagration leaping from tree to tree and finally to the Run itself, huddled in the narrow valley.

Emily's phrase had caught in his head—

—*whatever's going on here is getting worse*—

—and in a brief, almost palpable flash, the kitchen seemed to shear apart, bright shards spinning away as he plunged into the labyrinth of dreams.

His hand flexed unconsciously, snapping the pencil. He stared stupidly at the broken ends for a moment, and then he looked back to the table.

He met Emily's gaze.

"I'm not running anymore," he said.

There was a banging in his dream.

He woke suddenly, disoriented, the cumulative impact of the last few days—the deaths, the wreck, the fever—washing over him in a paralyzing wave.

"What—"

Emily's hand closed over his mouth. Henry gaped at her, her face blanched and strange in the candlelight, and it all came back to him, huddling under a blanket on the sofa and whispering while Ben napped. Glancing at the luminous dial of his watch—

—*7:30*—

—he saw that they must have dozed.

Then the banging.

The door.

Prying Emily's hand away, he reached for the gun and scrambled to his feet. Ben joined him an instant later, breathing laboriously. Another moment passed with the two of them crowded in the foyer while Ben fumbled at the lock. At last, he drew back the bolt and threw open the door.

An old woman stumbled in, her thin face shielded by the plastic rain bonnet tied beneath her chin. Dropping the gun atop a table, Henry stepped forward to meet her. She sagged against him, her chest heaving.

"Are you okay?" he said.

The old woman thrust back the rain bonnet; a cloud of wispy gray hair escaped. Willa Holland looked up to meet Henry Sleep's bewildered gaze. "You have to help me," she said.

For a moment, Henry's mind ricocheted between memories of blinding snow, her hawklike face looming in the dark, and the twisting labyrinth of nightmare. He had been dreaming of it once again. Willa Holland clamped her hands over his shoulders, anchoring him in the moment. "There's no time," she said, and then Emily was shepherding her past him toward the sofa.

As soon as the old woman was seated, the strength seemed to drain from her. When Ben said, "Please, ma'am, what is it that's going on here?" she made no reply. She just hunched shivering under the blanket, her face ashen, her breath coming in long gasps. Emily rubbed her back for a moment, and then the old woman drew a long breath and squared her shoulders.

"I'm sorry," she said. "It was so cold. So cold."

"You walked here?" Emily said.

"My car," she said. "I got stuck on the other side of the Stone Bridge. I should have been here earlier." She took another breath. "He came for Perry an hour ago, maybe an hour and a half. Harold Crawford. The doorbell woke me. I eavesdropped." She laughed humorlessly. "Not for the first time, either. It's not especially dignified, I suppose, but I'm far too old to fuss with dignity."

"They're going to the mines," Henry said.

"That's right." Her hands knotted in her lap. "Perry and you . . . I know you had some trouble—but he's my only child. He's all I have left." She leaned forward, taking Henry's hand between her own. Her chill was catching. Suddenly he wanted to draw away, to run away, but she held him fast, her eyes burning with desperation.

"Go to him," she whispered. "Please."

Chapter 23

Everything was exactly as Henry remembered: the nine-foot chain-link fence surmounted by coils of razor wire, the decaying moonscape beyond. Only the sky had changed, a black, fathomless gulf looming up where he half expected the lowering storm clouds of that long-ago July. Winter clutched the mountains like a fist.

The drive had taken nearly an hour, Ben steering his Jeep with a sure hand over cindered, snow-packed roads, the town dark under the night sky. There had been a bad moment before they got under way, Henry and Emily exhanging words while Ben hunted up some flashlights in the newspaper office downstairs.

"What are you doing?" he had asked as she shrugged into her coat.

"Going with you," she had said, and he had bitten off his response before it escaped his lips. She had made her terms clear enough, and he supposed he could accept them. He owed her that.

He reached into his jacket and touched Asa's pistol, reassured by its cold weight as the Jeep slipped through the open gates. A single set of tire tracks disturbed the pristine snow cover, winding past the weathered brick facades of the machine shop and the bathhouse just beyond, the coke ovens and the slag heaps lifting bony spines above the snow. As they climbed into the ridges, Henry felt that lost summer rushing back to claim him, the boy he had been inhabiting the man he had become.

Had he won anything at all from those seventeen years?

A little wisdom, he supposed. Enough to know that invulnerability was a lie.

Glass shattered, and its shards drew blood.

The sound of the engine shutting off drew him back to the present. They had parked by a Blazer with county tags, in the shadow of the tipple. Reluctantly, Henry followed Emily from the Jeep. Wind swept across the shoulder of the mountain, nipping at his flesh. On the far side of the Jeep, Ben tilted his head and curled a long hand before his face to light a cigarette. Coughing another of those deep, moist death rattles, he straightened up. He shouldered a gym bag from the backseat and slammed the door.

"Let's get moving."

Henry and Emily fell in behind him, as he followed the footprints angling off toward the mine. The creak of the tipple overhead echoed across the derelict coalfields, a lonely and bereft moan that touched something buried inside Henry. He felt time slipping once again, with only the manifest changes around him—the cluster of yellow earth-moving machinery, the open mouth of the mine itself, as flat and impenetrably black as the baptismal pool of his fever dream—to anchor him in the present.

Emily spoke, her words echoing his own foreboding. "Are we really going in there?"

Ben snapped his cigarette into the snow. He dug three heavy flashlights out of his gym bag and passed them around. "It'll get us out of the wind, anyway," he said, and his words sparked another memory—

—*just to get out of the rain*—

—this one rocking Henry on his heels.

Get away, an inner voice beseeched him. *Get as far away as you can.*

Henry shivered. Harold Crawford's voice, he thought, and he saw the man himself looming up over the desk, gripping the stapler in one thick hand, murder in his eyes. His gaze had kept drifting past Henry, as though someone stood at his shoulder, and remembering that now, Henry knew that he was mad. He was mad, he had Perry Holland, and he was somewhere down there in all that dark.

Get away.

But he was done running.

Switching on his flashlight, Henry stepped inside. A sense of the vast weight of the mountain overhead possessed him, and for a single—

—vertiginous instant, paralyzing claustrophobia gripped him. He closed his eyes, but the air blazed blinding white even through his eyelids as another lightning bolt slammed to earth behind him. The assemblage of rock above him groaned, threatening collapse, and then he was moving, terror spurring him deeper into the wormhole. Perry must have fled before him, his fear of the blackness under the mountain eclipsed by the terrific storm without, for the glimmering white soles of his shoes were gone.

The passage grew narrower, and with each concussion of the storm, dust sifted down from above. Henry hurried on, anxious to get free of the avalanche of debris overhead before something shook loose and the whole mass tumbled in, crushing him. Then his hands came down on emptiness. He teetered for a single moment, overbalanced, too terrified even to scream as he tumbled forward, clutching the flashlight in one hand and scrabbling desperately with the other at the stones beneath him. Ten seconds later, he jolted to a stop, his breath exploding in a moment of white-hot agony.

Out of the darkness, a voice: "Henry?"

Gasping, he managed to fill his lungs. He sat up and aimed the flashlight at the voice. Perry Holland's handsome face floated in the murk.

"You okay?" Perry asked.

"Yeah." He clambered to his feet, feeling a little like Alice tumbled down her rabbit hole, and swept his flashlight tentatively—

*　　*　　*

—around a flat shelf of rock, beyond which a low corridor plunged into the heart of the mountain.

Ben placed a steadying hand on his shoulder. "You all right?"

"Fine," he said. "I'm fine."

But he wasn't. He stood there in silence, buoyed on a tide of nightmare, uncertain whether he had for all these years been sleeping and was only just now waking up, or whether he had finally left the world of waking men behind for good.

Emily touched his hand. "Henry—"

"I know."

He went to the edge of the gently sloping platform and flashed—

—his light into the gloom. Outside, thunder hammered at the mountain. The stony columns, which here and there buttressed the low ceiling, groaned.

"Henry? What are you doing?"

Perry's voice sounded hollow as it bounced back—

. . . *doing, doing, doing* . . .

—from the deep corridor that lay before him.

Henry turned and flashed the light at Perry's pale, fretting visage, but he felt nothing, nothing at all.

He was made of glass.

"Let's take a look around," he said.

Without pausing to see if Perry would follow, he edged down the corridor of rough-hewn stone. Ancient wooden beams stretched across the ceiling at intervals. The air tasted sour, like the air in a bottle of flat soda. It was cold too; his wet clothes clung to him as he descended.

"Henry—"

Perry stood at the crest of the corridor, gazing down, as Henry impaled him on the flashlight beam.

"We should stay here."

"Stay then."

"Henry—"

"I didn't come all the way up here to sit. I want to explore. If you want to sit there, I'll be back."

"You could get lost. You could fall. Who knows what could happen."

"You my mother, Perry?"

The words escaped him before he could bite them off. Tears sprang up in his eyes. Nothing, he thought. I feel nothing. I am made of glass.

But there it was: the image of his mother, dwindled to a rack of bones in her sickbed, her face translucent under her mutilated cap of hair. He had inadvertently invited her into his mind by speaking her name; he'd read that demons could be conjured up that way, and now, thinking of his mother, he recognized the truth behind the superstition: She haunted him, her and the sickness that was devouring her from within. If she was going to die, then let her get about doing it. But he wasn't sticking around to watch, no matter what Dad said.

He squeezed his eyes shut.

Glass. I am made of glass.

And then he opened them and descended. He could hear Perry's timorous footsteps not far behind, following, and deliberately he picked up his pace. Passages wound off to either side. Rooms. Several times he passed abandoned tools or piles of rubble, and once a rusting mantrip. Ahead, in the inconstant beam of the flashlight, rails snaked away into the heart of the planet.

"Henry!"

He sped up, the corridor twisting away before him. Perry's footfalls sounded louder, and suddenly Henry realized that he could hear nothing else. For some time the storm noise had been diminishing and he hadn't even noticed. Now it was gone entirely.

They were that deep.

"Henry, *please!*"

The voice trembled on the verge of tears.

He did not respond. Faster. Faster.

And then the sobs came, great, heaving sobs that grated at Henry's nerves. What had Perry to cry for, after all? His parents were alive and well, weren't they?

Hurrying out of view, he ducked into a side passage

and flattened himself against the wall, clicking the flashlight off. The darkness enveloped him immediately, an inky-purple wave of nothingness. His bedroom never got this dark, not even on a moonless night. There, no sooner than the light went out, the eye began adjusting—collecting the bright line beneath the door and the faint glow of the window blind, constructing from these stray illuminations the old familiar room, redone in shades of gray and black.

Here the darkness fell around him in suffocating pleats, like a shroud. His eyes strained to no purpose. He choked back the icy panic climbing into his throat. He could feel nothing.

Glass.

But it was bad all the same, and the whole time he was holding the flashlight right there in his hand. What would it be like for Perry out there, alone in the dark, no light close at hand?

He felt a seed of pity taking root within him—

But just then Perry started up with his puerile whining.

"Please," he sobbed. "Please, Henry, don't leave me here alone, please, *please*—"

For a moment Henry thought the other boy would just collapse, crumple weeping to the floor. But he kept moving instead, afraid maybe of what might be creeping up on him. A delicious thrill of fear zipped through Henry at the thought, and—as Perry drew still closer—he considered leaping out of the passage, giving him a real scare and then being done with the whole thing. The mine was beginning to creep him out, too. But then the character of Perry's whining changed. It grew shriller, more incoherent, a low, mewling plea—

—"Mommy, help me, Mommy, please"—

—that sent a bright stroke of hatred through Henry's heart.

He pressed himself against the wall and bit his knuckle until he thought he might draw blood. Perry passed through the corridor outside, wending his way deeper into the bowels of the mine, and Henry—

* * *

—hadn't said a word. He had allowed the other boy to go on alone. Without even a candle to guide him.

"Jesus," Henry said aloud.

And Benjamin Strange turned, flashing his light into Henry's eyes.

"What is it?"

But how could he ever say? How could he explain?

Henry lifted a hand, warding away the blinding light. "Nothing," he said.

Ben pointed the light at the floor. Glittering motes of black dust whirled in its beam, stirred up by their passage, and Ray Ostrowski's words came back to Henry: *Them old mines ain't played out, after all.*

They stood in a silent circle, their faces ghostly in the backwash of the flashlights.

And in the silence Henry thought of his unforgivable cruelty that long-ago summer afternoon, of how he had allowed Perry Holland to descend alone into the abyss, driven by a rage he could neither comprehend nor control—rage for the mother who had been slowly dying, for the father who had allowed it.

An explanation, but not an excuse.

There could be no excuse.

Henry turned, flashing the light into the black pit that awaited them.

"We may not have much time."

Looking at their drawn faces, he could see the unspoken knowledge they all shared: It might already be too late. Even so, they stood there for another moment, gathering the courage to descend. The silence of the pit—

—welled up around him, formless and immense. Perry's panicked voice had faded, winding deeper into the abyss, ever more shrill and hysterical as it diminished in volume, audible finally only as a distant echo, and then not audible at all.

Once again, that bleak panic surfaced within him, like some loathsome bottom-dwelling creature risen to hunt the midnight surf. Henry dragged down a choking breath. Water dripped somewhere far away. An overburdened column creaked.

His thumb hovered at the switch of the flashlight, but suddenly he dared not drive it home. A grim certainty had possessed him: Something stood in the darkness before him. Something hungry. Something with many teeth. Who could say what might be lurking in this squalid pit? And so he stood, his back to the wall, waiting—

He took a deep breath, and with one sweating finger slid the switch home. Ghostly radiance flooded the chamber.

Nothing leaped from the gloaming to claim its frightened prey. He saw only the rough walls of the surrounding passage and the yawning mouth into the corridor beyond—the corridor into which Perry had descended, fearing the dark, but fearing more to remain alone at the coal mine's shattered summit.

He stepped into the corridor and glanced with longing at the slow ascent. Guilt clutched at him. He had to find Perry.

So he turned his steps the other way, his heart quailing within his breast, and—

—resumed the descent. They didn't speak as they went down, their lights mere pinpricks in the omnipresent dark.

Henry fought to keep his breath steady, to repress the panic hammering at his sternum. He reached out to grasp Emily's hand and listened always for the telltale rustle of that nightmare pursuit.

And still—

—he descended, trying to reassure himself that nothing could live in these tangled passages. Only darkness and time, the slow crushing age of mountains, squeezing coal from lifeless rock.

Oh, Perry, he thought. I'm sorry. I'm sorry.

He clutched the flashlight as a drowning sailor might

clutch a broken spar. The knobby handle pressed into his sweating palm. Overhead—

—the mountain shifted, creaking. A thin rain of dust sifted over Henry's cheek.

He played his flashlight along the ceiling overhead. The roof bolts that had been set by Perry's crew dwindled here, and the beams looked dry with rot, unutterably weary. He wondered how old they were. Decades, Ostrowski had said. Nearly a century.

That creaking again. Another soft whisper of dust, like the wings of a moth brushing his face in the darkness.

Henry shivered.

Benjamin Strange, just ahead of them, paused and lifted his hand. "Listen," he whispered.

And they listened. Through the vast and formless dark it rose up to them—

—a low, faraway sound so familiar and yet so unutterably alien that it halted Henry in his tracks. Not the hysterical tears of the terrified boy who had descended into the pit before him, not the familiar sobs that accompanied a scraped knee or a broken arm, but a sound more ancient—a hushed lament for all things past and passing, for doomed beauty, glimpsed without hope or expectation in the midst of ugliness and fear. Broadcast throughout the lower tunnels by some trick acoustic, the quiet dirge drifted through the sable depths in the voice of a boy on the verge of manhood. Perry Holland's voice.

Henry Sleep paused—

—as seventeen years later his elder self would pause and draw Emily Wood close against his breast.

Somewhere in the abyss below, Perry Holland was screaming.

Chapter 24

Eerie and inconsolable, those strange sobs reverberated through the depths of Holland Coal's abandoned mine, rusting twelve-year-old Henry Sleep nerveless in his tracks. For a moment, he could no more conceive of pushing deeper into the labyrinth below than he could have imagined deliberately hacking off a finger. The muscles of his legs had gone rigid and unyielding; fear petrified his knees and ankles.

For a moment, he just listened.

And such a sound: a wordless keen of terror and awe, it spoke to him on an almost cellular level, to some atavistic knowledge in his bones. Nothing that compelled a human being to make such a sound would leave him unaltered, Henry sensed. Whatever lay below had the power to destroy him utterly, to erase the boy he was, the man he was becoming, and leave in his place . . . what? Who could say?

Yet in the end, he knew something else, as well, even then: Whatever else it might be, it was first and always the sound of a boy weeping. A boy he knew. Perry Holland.

And this thought—the name itself perhaps—recalled him to the moment: buried in this earthen vault while thunder walked the ridges. Alone, whereabouts unknown to anyone in the waking daylight world he had left behind. For the first time in weeks, the knowledge of his mother's impending death and his father's withdrawal into silence retreated.

Perry Holland was lost down there. Lost and alone in the dark. And it was his fault.

He forced himself to begin the descent once again—to lift his legs and drive them leadenly forward, deeper and still deeper, until he could no longer recall the route back to the surface, to sunlight and grass and the life he had left behind.

As abruptly as it had begun, Perry Holland's scream was gone. Cut off, stifled, choked, just *gone,* with all those endless fathoms of charged silence rolling up in its place. Henry jumped as Emily's hand clamped around his arm. Willa Holland's voice echoed inside his head.

Go to him.

They descended, nearly running, three abreast where space permitted, in single file where the tunnels narrowed—Henry first, Emily following, and Ben last of all, his clotted lungs wheezing with effort. Twice coughing fits overwhelmed him, but they pushed on, following the narrow-gauge tracks down a passage that curved slowly deeper.

They paused at last before a low, narrow tunnel that wound off to the right, and there—

—*remembering*—

—Henry switched off his flashlight, signaling for Ben and Emily to do the same.

A winding bolt of night enfolded them. Henry fumbled for Emily's hand, perspiring despite the chill, and clutched it while his eyes adjusted. He waited, uncertain what he had expected to see. Then it was there: a faint, chill radiance, almost imperceptible.

"What is it?" Ben whispered.

It seeped from the narrow aperture in the wall, dim and uncertain, occasionally flickering. Coal dust sparkled and whirled inside it, settling slowly to the floor. Henry's mind spun back into that half-forgotten past. Seventeen years ago, noticing the dark graying toward light, he had paused before this same aperture. It had been brighter then, much brighter, and he had stood before it, switching off his flashlight as he reconstructed Perry's descent through the pitch-black corridors, the relief he must have felt seeing that faraway glimmer of illumination.

Henry's heart thudded in his breast. Stale air cycled through his lungs, thick as slowly coagulating blood.

Dear God, he thought. Dear God.

And once again, unbidden, the nightmare world possessed him: the tangled labyrinth, the breathless agony of pursuit, the thunder of onrushing wings.

By force of will he wrenched himself from the dream. He squeezed Emily's hand once more, his gaze flicking between them: Emily, ashen and determined, her thin lips set in a bloodless line, and Ben, his eyes ablaze with excitment. Looking into those eyes was like brushing aside a veil of weariness and ill health to glimpse the man Ben must once have been, the reporter hot on the scent of a story, a big one.

He touched Ben's shoulder.

"I hope you get your story," he said.

Ben glanced at the mouth of the passage into light and grinned a reckless grin. "Let's find out," he said.

Henry went in first, stooping as the ceiling pressed lower. The tunnel twisted six strides ahead of him. He eased around the corner into the passage beyond, the shorter end of an ell, lower still. The tunnel narrowed into shadows, dark but for the faint alien radiance visible beyond the opening before him.

His heart hammered.

He seemed to have slipped into an alternate time stream. Moments inflated into hours, launching themselves into the past with the slow majesty of dirigibles receding into flawless blue. Every step took a million years. He might have been wading through quicksand.

The strange luminescence flickered, guttering like a candle in a drafty room. The mountain shifted its enormous weight above him, and a tiny breath of sand dusted his face, exhaled from the mouth of a jagged overhead crevice that snaked the distance of this arm of the corridor. No supports at all had been set here—no roof bolts, no rotting wooden props. Perry would have forbidden work crews here. Perhaps no other step had fallen here at all, just Perry's and maybe Harold Crawford's—

Henry swallowed, stricken with an image of Crawford, spouting nonsense—

—*I won't do it I told you I was done with you*—

—as he rose up behind the desk—

And then he stood before the terminus of the tunnel, a bright window into some other place—

—*into the past*—

—no higher than his chest.

He dragged in a long breath. Ben touched his shoulder.

Okay then, he thought.

He hunkered down. He went in.

For a moment he could see almost nothing at all—not Perry Holland, not Harold Crawford, nothing, just that strange shifting funhouse light, a sea of shadow around a dimly radiant core. And then a series of impressions broke upon him, one after the other, like storm waves crashing on a solitary shore. He glimpsed Perry first—

—*dear God let him be alive*—

—slumped in the shadows half a dozen paces away, and then the surrounding space itself, like a cathedral, dizzying in its immensity, a wedge of vacuum driven into the heart of the mountain, narrowing into shade where that frigid radiance failed. Last of all, his eye was drawn to the bright center, the low stone slab and the thing curled, sleeping, there.

Beauty.

Beauty like a physical blow, stark and unforgiving and wholly inhuman, like jagged alpine heights or the black reaches between the stars. Beauty and power and such a cold magnificence that he could not comprehend it. Breath caught in his breast. He had not imagined such creatures existed in the world.

He stood there, trapped like a beetle in the moment's amber, his mind aclamor with thought and memory, tracing out the way it must have happened, the fool's errand that had brought his father to this place, his father and

Asa Cade as well. For the thing was dying—its body wasted, its glamour fading and diminished. So Perry must have sought what help he could. A fool's errand, and he must have known it at the time, for no man— no mere human art, no paltry human faith—could salve such a creature's pain.

Yet what else could he have done? What else could anyone have done?

And then—mere seconds had passed—seventeen years of memory came crashing down upon him. He remembered it all, that first journey into the labyrinth— how he had crept down this same passage, easing past the narrow ell and through the bright aperture beyond; how, then, too, his eyes had fallen first on Perry, rocking against the wall as though he had taken a hammer blow to the stomach, venting that strange and toneless cry of terror and awe; how, at last, his gaze had slipped to the creature at the center of the room, so much brighter then, so gloriously bright.

Stark, unremitting terror had clawed through his guts, leaving in its wake a glittering vacuum. Never again would he believe in his father's God—a sane and merciful God, however distant. God, if God existed, was demented, mad, the Old Testament deity of jealousy and wrath, the fire-and-brimstone monster of the preachers who twice a year pitched their tents in the field off Plug Hollow Road and excoriated the men and women who sought from them salvation. God, if God existed, was an evil God, to bear such beauty in one hand and in the other death—

—his mother's death—

Oh, he remembered. The contradiction had shattered him, like so much precious glass.

Then, as now, the flashlight had slipped from his nerveless fingers. He had reached down and fumbled to pick it up, and he had fled—without pause for thought, without a moment's consideration for the boy he left behind. Flight. In the moment of that shattering disclosure, he could think of nothing else. Just flight. Flight through endless and ascending dark, a glimmer of wormhole light, the storm-lashed ridge beyond. Rain slammed into his face, mud geysered from his pounding feet, and then Perry's hand fell across his shoulder, and he turned, not fighting back, too ashamed to fight, hungry for the benediction of those blows.

Now, looking back, he saw that even as he fled in terror through those black tunnels he had begun the process of forgetting—of transforming the creature into his nightmare pursuer. For seventeen years he had been running and only now, here, buried in the heart of the mountain, could he face the past at last. Only now, when he no longer had a choice, could he tear away the final veil of memory.

And then the thing moved.

He swallowed hard against the knot of awe and terror in his throat as it drew breath and shifted in the grip of some unimaginable dream. Like a man, but not a man, more massive than any man in the world—

—*a giant, there were giants in the earth*—

—cold and terrible in its glamour, the thing curled, fetal in its agelong sleep, and fell still once again, naked but for a bright mantle of wings, white rapturous wings, like a cloak of molten ice.

Chapter 25

Emily's scream startled time into motion once again.

It also saved Henry's life.

Dazzled with beauty, paralyzed with it, he might have sensed movement from the shadows a moment too late.

As it was, he was already in motion when a half-glimpsed figure—

—Crawford was it Crawford—

—plunged from the darkness right of the tunnel's mouth, gathering Emily under one outstretched arm without even slowing down. They barreled into Henry at full speed, but Crawford's lowered shoulder merely grazed him, spinning him off balance. The glittering blade, which might have gutted him had he been standing still, slashed through his jacket instead, exposing the lining.

Henry staggered to the floor as they rocketed past into the circle of radiance. Crawford went down as well, skidding across the stone. Emily twisted free, scrabbling on hands and knees to get away. Crawford was too fast. Moving with the grace of a younger, lighter man—

—an altogether different man—

—he lunged after her. One thick hand closed around her ankle, dragging her back. Emily screamed, flailing at him with her flashlight, and Crawford struck her arm. The flashlight spun away. It shattered, spilling echoes into the silence. Batteries skipped across the stone floor.

In the same instant, Henry came to his knees, gun in hand. Without a single wasted gesture, Crawford dragged Emily into the line of fire, knotted his hand in her hair, and yanked her head back. Then the blade was at her throat. Her flesh dimpled, blanching at the pressure. Her eyes rolled in terror.

For a moment, everything held, a deadly tableau: Ben at the tunnel aperture and Henry clutching the gun, Crawford and Emily tangled on the floor, backlit by that weird shifting glow. And then the creature drew another labored breath and that strange radiance flickered, dimming. Something gave way high in the vault overhead. A glittering cloud of black dust eddied down around them.

All the while, a crazed litany was chiming in Henry's head—

—is it Crawford is it—

He clamped down on it, silencing it. He could see the man clear enough, couldn't he—the same blue eyes, the same bulky frame? And yet, there was a subtle change all the same—a deft certainty in the way he moved, an ache of emptiness behind those eyes. He reminded Henry of a very fine actor, one who looked the same from role to role, but nonetheless somehow—Henry couldn't say how—managed to shift, visibly *shift*, the personality at the core. The man across the room was Harold Crawford—and he wasn't. It was that simple.

Henry inched forward, gripping the pistol in trembling hands. Perry Holland moaned in the darkness at his back.

"Easy," Ben whispered.

"That's right," Crawford said, and the change was in his voice, too—a way of biting off the vowels, so the words were sharper, free of that slow mountain cadence. "You ever want to see your lady friend again, you want to take it very, very easy."

Then he did something so unexpected, so bizarre, that Henry felt the shock jolt through his guts. He leaned his face into the crook of her neck and *licked* her. He *licked* her, a long, lingering caress, his tongue curling obscenely before it slipped back into his grinning mouth. Henry felt the shock of the gesture reverberating through him, shock and anger, too, igniting that molten core of rage.

"She's a pretty thing," Crawford was saying. "I'll keep you in mind when I'm—"

"Fuck you."

The voice was barely his own. The room seemed to spin, his mind exploding with flashbulb memory—his father in the casket, the bodies of Asa and Cindy with their wounds like bloody mouths, and Emily, Emily last of all. Emily. The light in her eye as she bent to meet his kiss. The taste of her beneath his lips. Emily. Bleeding out on the stone floor of this nightmare fissure, her throat slashed to the bone by the bearish monster across the room.

Fuck you, the rage said. He'd lost enough, *enough,* and somehow the rage was screaming in his voice, screaming through tears, "Fuck you, fuck you—" Somehow, it was winding the tension on his finger, dragging the firing pin slowly home—

Crawford let the knife jump a centimeter or two, just biting into Emily's flesh. She moaned as a jeweled droplet of blood beaded up at her throat.

Ben's voice was sharp with warning. "Henry!"

In the same moment, a hand closed over his shoulder.

"Don't do it," Perry Holland whispered.

Henry stole a glance over his shoulder. Perry's face glistened with blood under the mining cap. "It's not mined out down here. There could be gas, anything." He gestured vaguely at the room around them. "With all this dust in the air, you could start a fire that might burn a decade."

Henry drew a breath. The rage held the trigger at the tension point for a moment longer, and then slowly released it. The hammer came to rest with a barely perceptible click.

"That's better," Crawford said. "Now why don't you just drop the gun altogether?"

As of their own accord, Henry's fingers separated. The revolver clattered to the floor by his flashlight. Crawford gestured with the knife, and Henry sent the pistol skidding over the stone, a shimmering wheel of silvery reflection. It came to rest by Emily's foot. She whimpered once again, and Henry met her gaze for a single moment. Then he looked back at Crawford, possessed once again by that strange sense that this wasn't the man he knew. Another personality, colder by far than the deputy who had driven him home all those years ago—

—*I'm sorry, son. I'm so sorry*—

—stared back from behind those chill blue eyes.

The words were out before he had thought them through: "Who are you?"

Harold Crawford laughed. "Oh, that's good. That's very good. I'll let you in on a little secret. It doesn't matter who I am, and it doesn't matter who you are, because when you get down to it we're all just random collisions of atoms, and a man has to take his pleasure where he finds it." He leaned forward to lick Emily's neck once again, and this time he let one hand close over her breast. He grinned. "But since you asked, I'll tell you. You can call me Grubb. My name is Delbert Grubb, and down inside it always has been."

Once again, that rage flickered far inside Henry. He bit down upon it, forced himself to speak calmly:

"And Harold Crawford?"

"A mask," Crawford said. "A convenient fiction, that's all he ever was."

"I don't believe you."

Through the glittering clouds of coal dust, Henry saw a flicker of uncertainty in the big man's eyes. Forcing himself to ignore Emily's panicked expression, her small body rigid in the sheriff's grasp, he tried to reach whatever fragment remained of the man who had told him of his mother's death, the man who had said, *I'm sorry,* who had meant it.

"You're a good man," he said. "Or you were once and you can be again."

"Shut up," Crawford hissed, lunging forward a step. His face paled and twisted. The knife jerked at Emily's neck, drawing forth another bead of blood. "Shut up, shut up, you shut up, I was never a good man, I never wanted to be—"

"No? What about when I was a boy? What about that day in the rain—"

"It was an act."

"You couldn't fake that—"

"You're a fool if you believe that."

"You told me you were sorry," Henry said. "You meant it. You *meant* it."

Crawford's grip tightened. Gravity captured the droplet of blood at Emily's throat. Henry watched it slide down her neck, leaving a bright red wake. He could not turn away.

"This is getting old," Crawford said. "Now what we're going to do—"

But Henry never learned what they were going to do, for an uncanny, pain-racked moan filled the cavern, drowning out Crawford's words. Something gave way with a groan of tortured earth in a distant corner of the fissure, releasing a clamorous torrent of rock. The creature shifted on its stony slab. Crawford shrank back, dragging Emily with one hand. In the same breathless moment, the creature too was moving. Turning in a feathery waterfall of wings, it rose, up and up. With a kind of dread inevitability—

—Henry's heart seized within him—

—the massive head wheeled about on the great stanchion of that neck. It opened its eyes, featureless and blank as hammered silver, without iris, without pupil. Blind, Henry thought, it's blind—

But no. It was worse, far worse, for it *saw*: it saw everything. With a pitiless awareness that passed through him like a flame, it penetrated Henry in a glance. Even had he wanted to, he could not have hidden. Even had he wanted to, he could not have fled. He merely stood there, skewered on the glacial spike of that regard. And then, as impersonal and remote as the white-hot blast of a star, the bright gaze swept past.

Henry sagged, terrified and exhilarated, unable to tear his eyes away. He drank in the sight of the thing, wasted, gaunt, a dream in sculpted flesh: the great wings thundering from the knotted roots of its back, the ropy muscles twisted under flesh scored with a dozen wounds healed to gleaming scars, the polished dome of its skull. Its sex dangled like a club between its legs. Air gushed in the clotted bellows of its lungs.

Crawford cowered before it, transfixed. His mouth gaped and tears glistened like tiny jewels on his trembling cheeks. The hand knotted in Emily's hair opened as of its own accord. She scuttled away like a crab. Henry was there to meet her, to lift her to her feet. He held her fiercely, watching over the dark crown of her head as the light washed over them in waves.

His eyes caught Harold Crawford's gaze, and he saw that it *was* Crawford, now, *really* Crawford, the man he had seen so many years ago, through all the shifting veils of rain.

"I'm sorry," Crawford said, and Henry was so caught up in that strange sense of the past laid over the present like a palimpsest that at first he thought he must have imagined the repetition of those words. But no, it was real. He was saying it again: "I'm so sorry. I'd take it back—if I could, I'd take it all back—"

And then the thing seized Harold Crawford.

It lifted him as a man might lift a child, as a child might hoist some blind crawling insect for closer inspection. Crawford's feet dangled above the floor, kicking impotently. The knife gleamed in his hand. He stared in silence into that enigmatic gaze, so deep and cold you could drown there.

"All I ever wanted was to be a good man," he whispered. "It's all I ever—"

His voice broke. With a protean stir of wings—Henry felt the blast against his face—the thing raised Harold Crawford higher, and still higher. It held him effortlessly, like a rag doll, its face radiant and chill. Crawford extended a trembling hand. His fingers brushed its cheek. The gesture seemed to calm him.

"I even prayed for it," he said, "just like my daddy told me. I got down on my knees and prayed."

Emotions flickered across his face: awe and wonder and a hate so deep and corrosive that it was nearly love. Maybe it *was* love.

"Why did you abandon me?" he asked.

And then he drove the knife into its breast.

Sauls Run
The Labyrinth
The Present

Chapter 26

For Del Grubb, the descent into the coal mine with Perry Holland was an apotheosis.

For Crawford, trapped and voiceless in the straitjacket of his own flesh, it was an exercise in frustration. For more than two decades, he had resisted the siren call of that angry tide. Lashing himself to the mast of his aspirations, he had sought to atone for the sins of his past. With the work of his hands he had fed the hungry ghosts—the girl in the warehouse, LeMarius Oxford, the others, too many others. Compensation, they had cried. Provide, provide. And he had tried: He had sought to do good works, as his father's God commanded. So it was a bitter draught indeed to swallow, this drowning mouthful of his own failure.

And there was worse to come.

Del Grubb suffered insult without grace, betrayal not at all. Before the night's work was done, Perry Holland would bleed for his deceit. But first he'd watch this other die—this servant and attendant of Grubb's father's God, this mystery that Perry Holland had worked so hard to save—and maybe that would be the sweetest vengeance of all, to master such magnificence and revenge himself in the very same breath upon a mortal enemy.

Ah, yes. Grubb's penis stiffened just thinking of it.

For Harold Crawford, imprisoned deep in Del Grubb's flesh, even that was not the worst of it.

The worst of it was this: Crawford was a secret sharer in Grubb's aspirations. Even now, those hungry currents were beating in his soul. At some level, no matter how much Crawford denied it, he and Grubb were one and the same—as Grubb himself had put it all those years ago.

The worst of it was this: When Perry Holland rose against Grubb, anxious to protect the thing buried in all those depths of earth, Crawford too derived some pleasure in striking Holland down. It was a paltry thing, to be sure, that pleasure, shot through with remorse, but it was there all the same.

As Grubb had said: He'd always liked the wet work.

When he heard noise in the corridor a few minutes later, Crawford felt another muted surge of that pleasure. With Holland unconscious, Grubb had turned to gaze in awe at the thing sleeping on its stone pedestal. Another man might have missed the signs—the whispers, the faintest echo of a footfall—but even so enraptured, Grubb heard. He was like an animal, preternaturally sensitive, immersed in the physical. Crouching in the shadows, watching them step into the inner chamber, he congratulated himself on his luck. Sleep was weak, the reporter old and sick. But the symmetry of their deaths appealed to him.

The girl was an unexpected bonus. Grubb didn't know who she was, didn't care. But after two decades of watching Harold Crawford stroke himself to fruitless spasms in his darkened bedroom, taking her might be the sweetest bit of work that night.

Just for a moment, he let his mind sweep him back to the moonlit warehouse, back to the girl. He'd become a man that night. A shattering orgasm had rocked through him when the knife bit into her throat, and he knew he'd found his one true calling. Afterward, in celebration, he'd had her once again, spending in her moist box before the corpse went cold.

Now, Grubb eased the knife from his pocket. The blade licked out, ashimmer with that molten glow. To his shame, Crawford shared Grubb's surge of excitement, the tingle of anticipation in his loins. But he felt a wave of remorse as well. *Watch out,* he screamed. *Get away!* But Grubb was too strong. Nothing emerged but a strangled grunt.

Maybe it was enough, for even as Grubb uncoiled from his hiding place, the girl spun to face him, screaming.

And then Grubb was moving, gathering her to his side as he plunged out of the shadows with the knife. But the stroke that should have finished Henry Sleep went awry instead, and after that, nothing went as planned. In the hurried moments that followed, everything went wrong. Grubb felt his control slipping away when Perry Holland awoke. And while Sleep at last surrendered his gun, he wouldn't surrender his voice, and the more it talked, that voice, the more Grubb sensed his old adversary stirring within him, growing stronger.

Grubb felt suddenly uneasy. Things had gotten out of hand here. Sleep should have been dead, Perry Holland unconscious at the very least. He should have mastered this situation from the beginning, yet now he found himself facing three angry men with that—

—*monster angel servant of my daddy's God*—

—at his back. A standoff.

So he had resolved to act. In action, Grubb found solace; in action, Grubb found strength—that had always been the case, and perhaps it would have been so this time. But then he heard the rattle of those congested lungs, the rustle of those mighty wings, the creature—

—*angel demon*—

—shifting on its bed of stone. Grubb stumbled back, dragging the girl with him as the creature rose before him. Its taloned feet splintered the floor. Its rib-staved breast heaved with exertion. The vast wings flexed and unfurled, wafting to him an unutterably ancient reek of iron and blood and tears.

For the first time in his life, Del Grubb was afraid.

Even as he lifted his gaze, climbing it rung by rung up the ladder of puckered scar tissue on the thing's gaunt chest, Grubb felt his fingers open, the girl slip scrambling away. And then he was staring it full in the face, the features hooked and cruel, the mouth an implacable gash, and the eyes—

—*God God*—

—the eyes, deep sunk beneath the high-crowned dome of skull, the eyes, flat and affectless and cold, a cauterizing sheen of silver burning flame—

Fire swept through him—

Harold Crawford writhed in agony.

—a scorching fire, a cleansing inferno that burned Delbert Grubb out of him, and—

—*too late too late*—

—made of Harold Crawford the man he had always longed to be.

Crawford wrenched his head away.

"I'm sorry," he whispered. "I'd take it back. If I could, I'd take it back—"

Great hands closed about him, clawed fingers tearing at his clothes. Helpless, he found himself dangling before the thing.

"I wanted to be a good man," he cried. "It's all I ever wanted."

Higher and still higher, the thing hoisted him. He found himself staring once again into those terrible eyes, unable to tear his gaze away, and the guilt came bubbling out of him, guilt and recrimination and hate.

"I even prayed for it," he said, "just like my daddy told me. I got down on my knees and prayed."

Why was he pleading? He'd done the best he could. He'd tried; God knows he'd tried. Where was this God, where was his daddy's God? And that question too came gushing out of him, an anguished whisper—

"Why did you abandon me?"

—freighted with sorrow and guilt and all those years of bitter resentment. And even before he realized it, an avenging impulse had fired along his nerves and his arm was moving, plunging the blade deep, deep between the slatted ribs even as the thing lunged toward him, its flesh parting like paper, like seamed and ancient parchment, and through the rent it made came pouring out at him all the light in the world, tides of light, great combers of light, he had never known there was so much light in the world, and that face, those strange hooked features, what was it that he saw there, was it gratitude?

Harold Crawford cried aloud as the great hands closed tighter still about him, a dying reflex, crushing, tearing him asunder. And in the moment he realized he was dead, he was already falling, falling and falling, down to a sunless sea.

The light flared out at them all, bright as a star going nova, brighter. Just as it became blinding, Henry Sleep saw two things he thought he would remember the rest of his life.

The first was a vision of Harold Crawford, his body bent at an angle no man could survive, his face enraptured as he gazed up at the thing that clutched him.

The second was the expression in that alien physiognomy.

Release. He thought it was release.

Then the light went out, plunging them into darkness.

Flashlight beams punched radiant alleys through the murk. Ben reeled back, his eyes burning with the afterimage of that awful vision. Overhead, rock shifted, releasing fresh torrents of dust. Not three feet away, a chunk of stone the size of his fist smashed into the floor. The mountain sounded as if it was tearing itself apart.

"We've got to get out of here!" he screamed.

Ben glanced at Henry, standing in an awestruck huddle with Emily and Perry Holland, and saw him bend to retrieve his fallen flashlight. In the same moment, Holland wheeled to face him. Ben caught a flash of bloodstained face beneath the helmet, the smudged wound at his temple where Crawford must have struck him. They lunged toward him.

"Go!" Holland shouted. "We're right behind you!"

The mountain rolling above him, Ben ducked into the passage. He was around the ell and into the central shaft before the coughing took him. Cursing, he collapsed to his hands and knees as moist, wrenching eruptions tore through him. He spat blood into the dust between his splayed fingers. His vision narrowed, darkening—

Not yet, he thought, I'm not ready yet—

"Jesus, Ben—"

Hands snatched at him. Ben caught a glimpse of Emily, Henry close behind her. Then they were moving, dragging him to his feet between them. He'd managed to hang on to his flashlight somehow. They stumbled on in the wake of the moted beams as the mountain heaved and fell still once again. In the silence, a beam cracked ominously, and razor-edged shards of rock pattered down around them.

"Go," he gasped. "I'm slowing you down—"

"Don't be a fool," Henry said.

"If we can reach the section where Perry bolted the top, we should be okay," Emily gasped.

The same realization struck them all at once.

For Henry, the moment had the crystalline fragility of a dream. Touch it and it might shatter—the labyrinth of tunnels winding around them, the faint plume of his breath, the terror and guilt—

—my fault, my fault—

—rising up inside him once again, old friends. Oh yes, touch it, it might shatter. If you're lucky you might wake up, snug and warm in your bed. If you're lucky you might—

But it was real.

The cold sheen of perspiration on Emily's face, the panic in her eyes—those were real things. The clinging chill, the rattle in Ben's lungs. The clouds of iridescent dust, each breath gritty and particulate. Real. Real. All real.

"Perry," he said.

They stood in a pocket of calm, the mountain quiet.

Ben shrugged them away and tottered a few paces on his own. He slumped against the wall and lifted his face, gray and smudged in the backwash of his flashlight. The words came between inhalations as labored as gusts of storm. "When did you see him last?"

"He was here—"

"—he was right behind us—"

"We were trying to get you up, and—"

Emily held his gaze. "Something gave away. It sounded like a rockslide."

Henry turned away, his head filling with voices—

—*I should never have abandoned him*—

—*he's my only child, he's all that I have left*—

Emily was staring at him. He could feel her gaze, a positive weight against his skin.

Above them, the mountain rumbled threateningly.

"No," she whispered.

"I have to," he said. He looked at Ben. "I'm going back. It can't be far now. Emily can help—"

"Henry."

He turned to face her.

"Please, Henry—"

He took her by the shoulders and pulled her close, the length of her body warm against his own, her eyes frank and hard. "Can't you see, I don't have any choice." His lips brushed hers, chapped and dry, for a fraction of an instant.

"Go, then," she said.

He went.

He descended into the detritus of geologic upheaval: rockslides and fallen stones, that glistening veil of dust. There were noises, too, a legion of whispers and murmurs, the trickle of stone and earth, the endless drip of water into faraway pools. It was all too much like the dreams, and at the thought, panic touched him, panic like a wild bird, a blur of wings and razor-edged beak.

He fought it, choked it off, descended.

The mine rumbled at closer intervals, building to some awful crescendo. Once he scampered into the sheltering arch of a tunnel as the ceiling came down in chunks. Later, he found his path blocked by fallen slate. He clambered over the rubble on hands and knees, his fingers bleeding. At last, after how long he could not say—hours, days, the timeless intervals of nightmare—he found the tunnel, blind now, empty of light.

He went in, around the corner into the shorter end of the ell. There *was* light here, a dim electric illumination—

Something rattled under foot, summoning echoes from the chasm beyond. He nearly tripped. Light cascaded by him, shadows capering along the walls. Blind terror seized him. The thing clanged against the tunnel mouth, spinning into stillness.

A mining cap, its light still burning.

"Jesus," he whispered.

Hunkering down, Henry picked up the cap, dented and misshapen. A sick wave of dismay rolled through his guts.

He stepped inside.

Perry lay just beyond the archway, slumped on one side, his fingers pale and open, beckoning. A softball-sized chunk of stone lay nearby. Henry knelt, his heart pounding. When he touched the body, it rolled bonelessly to its back. Perry moaned. Blood seeped from the wound at his temple, but his serene face was otherwise unmarked.

The mountain rumbled overhead.

Henry slapped Perry's cheek lightly, urgently. "Wake up," he said.

But Perry only lay there.

For Emily, the moments following Henry's departure were frenzied, nightmarish. Each seismic shock brought down a hail of dust and rock, making it hard to breathe or see, to climb at all, much less support Ben, who hobbled along beside her with his arm draped heavily across her shoulders.

"You okay?" he grunted between breaths.

"Fine," she said, and she was except—

Except she kept thinking about Henry, alone down there in all that dark. Except she kept replaying their talk back at Ben's apartment—

—*I care about you, but we'll have to see*—

—and the look on Henry's face as he heard the words. Except—and maybe this was the worst thing of all—she couldn't help thinking that if she had only believed him, they could have done something sooner, they could have saved that . . . that thing down there. They could have saved her mother—

Stop it. It didn't bear thinking about.

But she could think of little else as they climbed, the passage gradually growing wider around them. Lifting her light to the ceiling, she could see the roof bolts start up, set at six-foot intervals.

She breathed a sigh of relief.

The mountain pitched beneath her. Something snapped with a crack. Turning, Ben's arm slipping from her shoulder, she saw a great boulder, almost perfectly round, cut loose from the top and crash to the floor, shattering. Choking horror rose inside her. She knew what it was—the fossilized bole of an ancient tree—and she knew something else as well, the words miners used for such things, kettle bottoms—

—*widow makers*—

—because one of them had made a widow of her own mother. Emily had been nine then, and her memories of Boone Wood were scant indeed, a handful of washed-out photos, a few scattered recollections: his callused hands against her face, his stubble-roughened kisses. An abrasive tenderness. It was all she had of him.

"Wait—" Ben said, his hand closing about her shoulder.

But his grasp was weak, sick. She twisted free of him, running, calling Henry's name. Chunks of rock hammered down around the kettle bottom, blocking the way. She sank to her knees and started digging at the obstruction. Dust clogged her throat. Her fingers ached and bled.

"Emily."

She stared hopelessly at the collapsed roof. She had made no progress at all; there was nothing she could do.

"Help me," she whispered. "He'll die."

"We have to get out of here." Ben spoke slowly, the way you speak to a frightened child. "We have to get help."

An image of the abandoned coalfields possessed her, the endless vistas of snow, the darkened town below. And no hope to be had, no help as far as she could see.

"How, how—"

He seized her shoulders. The panic died away a little. "The sheriff's Blazer. There'll be a radio."

An absurd gratitude filled her. Some part of it must have shone through as she looked up into his bony face, for he did something unexpected. He leaned over and kissed her gently on the forehead. This is what a father does, she thought. This wisdom in a crisis, this momentary comfort.

But she didn't have a father.

She didn't have anyone at all.

Henry wedged the dented hard hat onto Perry's head and levered him to a sitting position.

"Okay," Henry said to himself. "Up we go."

He took a deep breath and lurched to his feet. Perry fell against him, dead weight, like a drunken man. Henry staggered. As they swung around, Perry's headlamp flashing, Henry caught a glimpse of the—

—*giant, angel*—

—the thing. The thing. Whatever it was. A flash of bedraggled wing and translucent flesh, a glittering pool of blood, black in the light. He sat down hard, Perry's weight crashing down on top of him.

He kept hearing voices in his head, disjointed snatches of conversation. The fallen ones, the healing ones. The Rephaim. He was twelve years old again, safe with his father in the rolling comfort of a funeral home limo. *God can go to hell for all I care.*

What did he believe?

"Fuck," he said. "Not now."

Clutching the flashlight with one hand, he pushed himself to his feet. Once again, Perry's full weight collapsed upon him, but this time, prepared, Henry managed to stay upright. He caught another glimpse of the bodies, Harold Crawford—

—*Grubb, he said his name was Grubb*—

—crushed and still beneath the thing's outstretched
arm. He ignored them.

"Okay, Perry. You ready to roll?"

Perry said nothing.

A vast convulsion shook the mountain. Cracks zagged
across the stone. Rock and dust pelted from the chill
blackness overhead. It took him a frenzied few moments
to negotiate the passage to the central heading. Perry's
feet caught a lip of rock. Stones the size of driveway
gravel pelted from the jagged crack overhead.

The mountain continued to shake. Something above
him tore loose with a shriek. "Shit," Henry cried. He
lunged forward, his muscles screaming, and then they
were out. The corridor collapsed at their heels, clamping
down in a cloud of dust like a slammed gate. He turned,
suddenly lost. The way out was gone, sealed behind an
avalanche of fallen slate.

A vein pulsed at his temple. "Wake up," he whispered, but Perry only moaned, his eyelids fluttering.

Lurching under his weight, Henry turned. Twenty feet
below, the corridor branched. Maybe he could skirt the
obstruction and circle back to the main shaft. It was
worth a shot anyway. He dragged in breath as the mountain settled.

"This isn't going to work, pal," he said. "I'm going to
have to drag you, okay?"

He lowered Perry gently to the floor, hunkered down,
and hooked his forearms through Perry's armpits. Still
clutching the flashlight, he started inching down the corridor toward the junction of tunnels.

The mountain rumbled threateningly, fell still.

Don't think about it, he told himself. Keep moving.

A black certainty was growing in him: He wouldn't
get out of here alive.

And again: Don't think about it.

But he couldn't help it. He couldn't put it out of his
mind.

He paused for breath at the junction. The main shaft
continued its descent. Narrow branches opened to either
side. He studied them for a moment, trying to determine

if either of them angled perceptibly toward the surface. The mountain uttered yet another of those premonitory rumbles, releasing another cloud of dust. He coughed, choking, into the stillness that followed. Maybe the worst of it was over.

"Okay," he said. "Okay."

Kneeling, he levered Perry up once more. Perry's head flopped back, his upturned face sallow, the color of a comic book zombie. His helmet clattered to the floor. Henry jammed it back on, fumbling to extinguish the headlamp, suddenly worried about batteries. Another phrase came swimming up out of the past—

—*I was afraid of the dark when I was a kid, did you know that*—

—and he thought abruptly about being lost down here in all this endless black. How long before you died of thirst? How long before the air went bad? Maybe it was bad already. What was the old expression? Canary in the coal mine. When the canary dies, you know it's time to head for the surface. He took a cautious breath, anxious to see if it was tainted with anything but dust. It tasted okay to him. But the gas—was it methane?—had no odor, no taste; thus the canary. They didn't use canaries anymore, of course. He supposed they must have some kind of meter, now, a gadget of some—

A wave of panic crested within him.

He dammed it away, took a breath.

Okay. He was okay. He just had to keep moving, he had to *get* moving.

He chose the tunnel branching off to the right. It arced away before him, curving almost imperceptibly. He tried to picture the mine in his head, to retrace the route they had taken down, to calculate the angles and turns that might bring him back to that central shaft.

Everything blurred together—his throbbing back, the sweat trickling into his eyes, the faint trails Perry's feet dug in the dust—a chaotic welter charged with glaring moments of clarity when the mountain shook beneath him and adrenaline jolted through his system. During the worst of the shocks, something unseen whizzed by his face, drawing a bright line of pain down his cheek. After that, the mountain grew still, an eerie calm broken only by occasional shiftings of sand, the faraway *plink* of water droplets into still, dark pools.

So he wouldn't die of thirst, after all.

Exhaustion maybe.

Occasionally, he turned into branching passages, always angling toward the surface. Two, three, four times he paused for rest, his back and shoulders screaming, only to stumble erect once again and hobble on. During the last such stop, he thought Perry had stopped breathing, thought he had been dragging a corpse. Mocking, ironic laughter welled through him. He cupped a hand before Perry's face. It was there, the faint whisper of respiration, like silk against his skin. He hooked his arms under Perry's shoulders and plodded on.

Faces hovered in the dark—Emily, Ben, his father—all talking, talking, but he couldn't make out the words. It was like overhearing a conversation from a distant room. And then even that was gone. There was only silence, stillness, the endless winding ascent. Sometime after that—he couldn't say how long—his flashlight died.

Henry sank to the floor in despair.

Stars.

As they emerged from the overhanging mouth of the mine, Ben stumbled away from Emily, sinking to his knees in the snow. Stars, he thought, staring up into the endless expanse of space, a black abyss sewn through with light. His lungs ached, and exhaustion rolled over him like a fog, blocking out everything beyond a radius of four or five feet, but somehow the stars got through, pouring down their radiance from a million years away. Pouring down their radiance like gods, he told himself, and the simile spurred another thought, an image really: that thing looming up and up, unfurling those mighty wings.

Like a fallen angel, like a god.

A big story, that was what he had told Henry that night in the kitchen. But that wasn't precisely what

Quincy Sleep had said. *A story that changes everything,* he had said, sounding like every crackpot conspiracy theorist Ben had ever met.

But maybe he was right.

"Come on," Emily was saying. "We have to get help."

She dragged him to his feet and they stumbled downhill toward the Blazer. He coughed and spat blood, bright arterial blood, black atop the snow, death planting a flag on the mountains of the moon. He knew he had to call for help, and he had a sudden sharp craving for a cigarette, and those gray banks of weariness kept rolling in, but Quincy Sleep's words cut through it all like the beacon of a lighthouse: *a story that changes everything*.

Should he write it?

Should anyone?

He could see before he realized he could see. He had been sitting against the cold stone, staring blindly at his hands, gathering the strength to go on. Anxious to preserve the battery, he had avoided turning Perry's cap light on while he rested. Now he leaned forward to do so, and he realized with a shock that he could *see* his hands, the dim outlines of his fingers. He'd been seeing them for some time now; he didn't know how long.

A hallucination, he thought.

But it was there. In the pale gray radiance, shadowy outcroppings of rock assumed shape and substance.

He looked up.

His father stood at the crest of the tunnel, framed in a faint grayish glow the color of a starlit January sky.

Henry stared up at him. He felt nothing.

He closed his eyes and opened them again. Quincy Sleep stood unmoving at the crest of the mining shaft, not twenty feet away. Henry's words to Asa Cade—

—*do you believe in ghosts*—

—came floating back to him. He lifted his fingers to his cheek, to the faded imprints of a dead man's hand, a dead man in a dream.

He lurched to his feet and knelt for Perry, leaving the

cap light off. He didn't want to drown out the faint
ghostly radiance from above. He staggered, cradling the
unconscious man like a bride, and started up the tunnel.
As Henry drew near, his father disappeared into a
steeply ascending branch.

Henry stumbled on behind him.

Perry moaned, and Henry glanced down into his face.

By the time he looked up again, they had emerged
into the central heading. The mouth of the mine lay not
fifty yards ahead, a scrap of star-sown sky, filled with
that gray January light.

His father had disappeared.

Henry staggered in a circle, looking down the tunnel
from which he had emerged. Nothing was there. No one.

He took another step and stumbled to his knees. Then
someone was kneeling beside him.

"Emily," he whispered.

Together, they lugged Perry Holland into the night.
Ten yards, twenty, the tipple looming up against the
dark.

"Ben?" Henry said. "Where's Ben?"

"I'm here."

He appeared out of the dark, clutched Henry's shoulder. "Help's on the way." He glanced at Perry, then
turned to Emily. "There'll be a first-aid kit in the
Blazer," he said.

"I'll get it."

Henry watched her for a moment, her figure diminishing as she sprinted down the hill. Then he slumped over,
exhausted. The snow was cold, his jeans soaked. It felt
wonderful.

"Henry, look at me."

There was something imperative in the voice. He
looked up. Ben's face was serious. "You did well."

"Thanks. Thank you." He caught his breath. "And
you, Ben, did you find your story?"

"Yes." He held Henry's gaze, his eyes intent. "But I
keep thinking about your father—this changes everything, he said. I don't know that I should write it."

"Why?"

"Do you want everything to change?"

Then Emily was back with the first-aid kit and Henry never got the chance to answer. He found himself tearing open a bandage instead, pressing it to Perry's face to stanch the trickle of blood at his temple.

"Smelling salts," Emily was saying. "There must be smelling salts in here somewhere—"

In the flurry of activity, neither of them noticed Ben as he stood up and walked away.

Now that Ben had made his decision, breathing seemed to come easier. The fear had retreated, too, though he didn't think the fear ever went away, not for anyone. It was fear of the unknown, after all, of borders you can only cross one way.

As quickly as he could manage, he strode up the hill to the mouth of the mine. At the summit, he turned back for a moment. Emily and Henry were hunched over the prone figure of Perry Holland, working easily together, a natural harmony they seemed wholly unaware of. They simply *fit*, as people sometimes do, and seeing them together dulled the edge of his own regret. He had never found that fit in his own life, but he had a good feeling about Henry and Emily.

He supposed it was the way a father might feel.

Turning on his flashlight, he stepped inside and began descending. He moved easily, with only the thick dust—

—with all this dust you could start a fire that might burn a decade—

—slowing him down, and as the mine enveloped him, his thoughts turned to the thing he had seen down there.

How long had it lain there, he wondered, shedding its beneficence on the valley below? How long had it been dying, each death throe releasing within the Run the natural passions and illnesses that were so much a part of life in other places?

He had no doubt at all that it was dying.

He had known that from the instant he stepped into the chamber and saw its wasted form curled upon that slab. He knew death too well. He had seen his own

failing body in that gaunt frame. Yet even then some
irrational fragment of his mind had continued to hope—
the same hope that must have led Perry Holland to re-
cruit Dr. Cade and Reverend Sleep, a desperate bid to
cure the affliction, physical or spiritual, that ailed the
thing. For Ben, the hope had been bound up in Sleep's
ruminations—

—*giant, spirit, healer*—

—about the nature of the creature.

For Ben, the hope had been personal.

His hope had died when Crawford plunged his knife
into that monstrous chest, and he felt its loss, a physical
ache, an added burden within his aching breast.

So what remained?

He coughed, a moist tearing in his lungs.

Decision, that was all.

He kept remembering the way the thing had lunged
forward at the end, aware perhaps that its own fading
powers rendered it vulnerable, welcoming the blade,
choosing it, maybe, over a more protracted and painful
death—a decision not unlike the one Ben himself had
reached up there beneath that canopy of stars.

A story that changes everything, Quincy Sleep had
said, and about that, as about so much else, he had been
right. Ben wondered what Quincy Sleep had envisioned
from such a story, what change he thought might come.
Had he thought of it—really *thought* of it—at all?

In these last fleeting moments, Ben had thought of
little else. It would be a comfort to believe, he thought,
if only to lift the burden of that long fall into dark. But
he had no love of organized faith, the way it twisted
moral principle into a rationale for hate. The world had
seen crusades enough. Let the evidence burn to ashes.
Some stories should remain untold.

He paused, feeling the pressure of time. It wouldn't
do if the others decided to come looking for him.

Was this deep enough?

It would have to be.

He switched off the flashlight and tossed it away. The
dark enfolded him as he fumbled loose a cigarette and

wedged it between his lips. Then he lifted the lighter, tracing with his fingers the words engraved there.

Yes indeed, he thought.

And then he struck a light.

The first sirens were audible by the time they realized Ben was gone. Emily had found the smelling salts, and Perry was stirring groggily when it hit Henry, Ben's words, that final question—

—*do you want everything to change*—

—suddenly leaping into his mind.

Henry scrambled to his feet. He barely had the strength to stand, but he staggered back toward the mouth of the coal mine.

He never made it.

The ground heaved under his feet. A vast roar shattered the stillness, and an enormous fireball pulsed at the mine's dark mouth. For an instant Henry wavered there, torn between this chill January night and a dusk weeks lost—

—*ages gone*—

—when he had parked in the scenic overlook high above Sauls Run, rocked by that momentary hallucination, each molecule of air erupting as the conflagration leaped down the ridges to envelop the Run itself. Then he felt the heat against his face. Shielding his eyes, he fell to his knees in the snow and waited for the sirens to arrive.

Coda
Sauls Run
Three Years Later

Henry Sleep stepped out of the offices of the *Observer*, lifted his collar against the cold, and gazed up into a January sky bluing off toward dusk. It was the same every winter: It all came clamoring back as the mountains turned cold for the season. This year, though, the memories had a renewed urgency. He thought of Emily, her belly already starting to swell, and he laughed in a kind of bemused wonder. Fatherhood. If that wasn't an act of faith, he didn't suppose he was capable of one. He only wished his own father had survived to see it.

Yet there were still so many questions.

He remembered a conversation with Arnold Mears, the heavyset deputy who had shown up at his house that first night, the night it all began. Not long after Crawford's death in the mines, Mears had been named sheriff—interim sheriff, anyway, until the election in the fall confirmed the appointment. He had been the one who investigated the case. He'd called Henry after answers about Crawford's past began to trickle in, and they'd walked down toward the Stone Bridge in a flush of March warmth.

"Your story about the sheriff," he had said. "The story about Delbert Grubb."

"Yeah?"

"Yeah." Mears gave him a sleepy glance. The laziness was an illusion. Henry had learned that in the weeks since the events in the mine. "Turns out Del Grubb was a beat cop in L.A. back in the early seventies."

The City of Angels, Henry thought, and a momentary chill touched his heart. They were standing on the bridge itself by then, watching as a train laden with bituminous from the deep mines up Copperhead crawled by below. They stood silently until the clanks and rattles died away, and the Run filled up once again with the drowsy hum of a warm spring afternoon. Henry looked at Mears.

"How did he end up here?"

"He killed a kid out there. Turned out the kid wasn't armed. The papers had a field day. Apparently Grubb didn't like his odds at trial. He lifted a birth certificate and a Social Security number, and headed for points east."

"So there's a real Harold Crawford."

"Hundreds of them, I reckon. It's a common enough name. The Harold Crawford in question, he died of leukemia in 1953. He was five years old."

"And that's it?"

"Not quite. Apparently, Grubb nearly killed some kid in school, too. Juvenile courts sealed the records."

"How'd you get them?"

"Right of privacy doesn't apply to dead men." Mears crossed his arms on the railing. "LAPD has pretty good reason to link Crawford to at least one rape-homicide out there—high school girl in 1971. There are a couple other possibles—FBI profile says there ought to be several—but that one's real solid. With Ray Ostrowski, the Cades, the fellow we dug up out at Crawford's farm, that brings the total to at least five. Six, if we add your dad." Mears gave him another of those sleepy glances. "We checked some other things, as well."

"For instance?"

"For instance, your father didn't buy the gun that murdered him. Crawford falsified information in the file."

"The ballistics report said Dad fired the weapon himself."

"There was no ballistics report." Mears stared at him,

measuring the effect of these words. "I don't suppose you'd reconsider your decision on the exhumation?"

"I think we know what we'd find."

"I could get a court order."

"Yeah."

Mears lifted his face to the sun. "Probably not worth the effort," he said. "I keep thinking, though. I knew Harold for years, worked with him, ate with him, rode with him. He was a gentle man. I thought he was a good man."

"Maybe he wanted to be," Henry said. "Maybe he wanted that more than anything in the world."

"Maybe so. It's a mystery—that's for sure."

Mears straightened, hitching his pants higher on his gut, and Henry thought the interview had come to an end. But Mears hadn't taken more than a couple of steps toward the courthouse, high atop the long hill, before he turned back.

"Perry Holland's story about exploratory work, re-opening the mines, it doesn't make any sense at all."

"I wouldn't know about that."

"Convenient how those old mines are burning. Had an EPA fellow in here last week—he said they might burn years yet."

Henry said nothing.

"I have a lot of questions, Mr. Sleep. I'd really like some answers."

Henry lifted his hands.

"So would I," he said.

So much had changed since then. It hadn't been more than a few weeks after that conversation—mid-April, it must have been—when Henry had barged into old Emerson MacCauley's office at the *Observer*.

MacCauley was in his nineties by then, a baggy old reprobate with three or four long wisps of hair orbiting an otherwise bald head.

"I don't suppose you came to give me an interview," he growled.

"Actually, I came for a job," Henry said.

"We like our people to report the news, not make it." MacCauley pushed papers around on his desk. "Can you write?"

"I've got two English degrees."

MacCauley made a face to show just what he thought of English degrees, but ultimately he relented. An English degree was bad, he opined, but at least it wasn't a degree in journalism. Last thing on earth he wanted was some fresh-faced college kid with visions of Woodward and Bernstein dancing in his eyes. Being a reporter in a place like the Run, he said, you spent most of your time covering garden club meetings and the like. At least Henry was a local boy and had no illusions of glory.

Henry didn't think he had any illusions left at all. But he found he liked the work, and now, three years later, he was still at it. He'd had more to cover than Mac-Cauley would have imagined, too. In the last three years, death had come to the Run. Emerson MacCauley himself had died not more than six months after hiring Henry. And the years since had seen the occasional small-town sensation—a barroom murder in the lower end of town, a stabbing in the courthouse jail.

"The normal balance reasserting itself," Emily said. "This is the way life *is*." Henry supposed she was right. She had been right about so much, after all.

So many changes, Henry thought, getting in his car and turning it toward Widow's Ridge. So many changes.

But the questions remained—private questions now, the kinds of questions you turn over in the small hours when sleep will not come, but questions all the same.

They had talked about it only once, he and Emily, behind locked doors in the Tipple, one evening a few months after he took the job at the *Observer*. It was one of Emily's last shifts, a steaming August night with the air conditioner running full blast and the ceiling fans churning the air inside the bar. She would be heading back to school in the fall. They'd just finished closing the place up, and now, with the pleasant blur of alcohol in his veins and some of Emily's music—Charles Mingus—on the house deck, Henry felt comfortable enough to turn some of those questions over in his mind.

Maybe Emily was thinking the same thing, for looking at him from behind the bar, she said, "You ever think about it?"

Pronoun reference he'd have said in his teaching days, but those days were over; he'd come to that by then, and besides, he knew well enough what she meant.

"All the time."

She was dipping glasses—twice in the soap, then to the rinse, then onto the rack to dry—and she didn't look at him as she spoke.

"Me, too," she said. "I keep thinking about that conversation we had at Ben's that night."

"The Rephaim," he said. "The healers."

"The very one." And now she did look at him, square in the face. "I think there was an element of truth to that, but I think it's more complicated somehow. I can see that thing in my mind at night before I go to sleep, and it doesn't make me feel safe or loved or anything like that. It didn't feel . . ."

"Christian?" he said.

"Yeah, it felt older somehow. I remember reading in Ben's books how Christianity transformed pagan myth, made it safe, harmless, domesticated it somehow. But a thing like that, it resists domestication."

"I remember the scars," he said. "Like it was a warrior or something."

"A war in heaven," she said. "A war between gods, or beings so like gods, they might as well be." She racked the final glass and stood in front of him, her eyes intent. "Do you think it was good?"

"That's a human term," he said. "Maybe . . . maybe it was just powerful, or had been once."

"And whatever effect it had on us, here, in the Run?"

"Purely incidental, I guess," he said.

They were quiet for a while. Henry listened to the jazz, following the music, complex, elusive. He could sense a pattern there, a meaning just beyond the surface, but every time he thought he had a hold of it, it slipped away somehow.

Emily said, "I guess it does comfort me. Just the fact that it existed at all. I guess that means there's something out there, and that helps a little, I suppose."

The music rolled on in the silence that followed.

"Henry," she said, "what do you believe?"

But he had no answer.

As he drove home from the *Observer*, the late-winter sky fading toward dark, he found himself pondering the question once again.

What do you believe?

After dinner, he sat late in the study. The three wrinkled sheets of notes were in the drawer where he had left them. He unfolded them carefully, and not for the first time traced with his fingers his father's words—as if he could absorb Quincy Sleep's thoughts, Quincy Sleep's faith. But faith escaped; it always did.

In his imagination, he saw the thing once again, rising up before him. The old words came back to him in a stir of wings—the fallen ones, the healing ones—but they seemed inadequate somehow, too cramped, too confining. No language could contain it.

Aquinas wound purring around his ankles, and as he bent to stroke the cat, he thought: I cannot believe, not in my father's god.

Yet he could no longer *not* believe, not anymore.

So he settled as always for half measures, Pascal's Wager, that sense of order running just under the surface of things—a dapple of tree-shot green on a sunny afternoon, the awful beauty of a rose. It was there. It was always there, just barely out of reach.

"Henry?"

He looked up, smiling.

Emily stood in the doorway. Through the nightgown, he detected the faint swelling of her belly, and once again that sense of mystery and awe possessed him. Faith and mystery. We live in it all the time, he thought. It surrounds us like the air, not answers but always more questions.

Maybe it was enough. He supposed it would have to be.

"It's late," Emily said. "Come to sleep."

He climbed the stairs behind her and undressed by the light of the bedside lamp.

"You missing your father?" she said.

"And Ben. I'd have liked to know him better."

"Me, too."

They were silent for a time, thinking of all the dead. Then she touched the bed. "Come here, you," she said.

So he turned out the light and laid himself beside her.

After a time, they slept. He did not dream.